AF424428

WAVES OF BURDEN

CURTIS IPPOLITO

Rock and a Hard Place Press

WAVES OF BURDEN: A Novel
by Curtis Ippolito
Copyright © and ™ 2026

Cover by Heather Garth

ISBN: 979-8-9938836-7-0 (Paperback)
ISBN: 979-8-9938836-8-7 (eBook)

10 9 8 7 6 5 4 3 2 1

Published by Rock and a Hard Place Press, an imprint of Rock and a Hard Place Press, LLC Woodbridge, NJ.
rockandahardplacemag.com
amazon.com/~/e/B08WPQG5YV

"A propulsive thriller about the bonds of brotherhood, Curtis Ippolito's **Waves of Burden** is a breakneck ride reminiscent of Don Winslow, and set against the backdrop of a sunny San Diego, populated by cold-blooded criminals and characters put to the brink to protect those they love. Read this now!"
—Lee Matthew Goldberg, acclaimed author of *The Mentor* and *The Great Gimmelmans*

DEDICATION

For Sharon, my favorite person in the world.

Chapter One

2022
San Diego, California

Wielding a six-inch tape knife, Drew Jones spread silky mud over the taped joint to smooth perfection. The tool was like an extension of his hand. His motions were automatic and precise—set to motor memory—yet pure artistry resulted nonetheless. He gave the knife a slight flick at the end of each run. The pure simplicity of his job made him happy.

He took a step back to examine the progress of his latest drywall install, and scraped what little mud clung to the knife's triangular tip against the inside edge of the mud pan.

"Clean as an infant's be-hind," said Mon Evans, Drew's general contractor on the job. A stout woman, she rocked a shaved head and full sleeves of intricate nature-themed tattoos on both arms. Though she carried herself with the vibe of a grizzled biker or no-nonsense bartender, she held the mantle as the most skilled GC Drew had worked for in his relatively short career.

Drew didn't acknowledge her comment right away. Normally, he wouldn't have heard her speak from behind him anyway since he generally wore ear buds, listening to 90s rock playlists—but today, he'd passed on music in favor of taking in the sounds of the job's natural surroundings. The crew he belonged to were working a total remodel on a white stucco home on Hillside Dr. in a cliff-topped neighborhood in La Jolla. The home was easily a fourth the size of the other multi-million-dollar mansions on the block, but what it lacked in size—and it still dwarfed Drew's one-bedroom rental—it made up for with a ridiculous view of the Pacific Ocean off the back of the property, and even though he couldn't hear the waves he saw crashing on the beach far below, it still relaxed him to pretend as though he could.

Turning around, he faced Mon. "Thanks for triggering me with that baby talk."

She patted him on the shoulder. "Stop it, dude. I keep saying it: You're going to be a great dad. When's Gaby due again?"

"Less than three months."

"Da-da-dum." The teasing came from the painter Mon had subbed. Drew couldn't recall his name, but he was there to go over color preferences ahead of Drew finishing the drywall.

"You're not lying." Drew turned around to gather his tools.

"So, hey," Mon said. "You prefer Zelle or Venmo?"

Drew spun back around, confused. "You know I'm not done yet, right? I still need to apply the two finish coats tomorrow after this one dries, then texture everything."

"Yeah, yeah, I know. But I'm out the next two days. Dentist appointments. Anyway, I know you'll get the job done. So, what'll it be?"

Drew smirked. "Have I told you lately how there's not a better GC in all of San Diego?"

"Stop telling me things I already know. And if you're flirting with me, my heart's already taken by the chubby pug waiting for me at home."

Drew held up his hands in surrender. "Okay. But your loss."

They both laughed.

"If you could Venmo me, that'd be cool," Drew said.

"Done. Make sure to email me your invoice."

"No problem."

"You taking off then?" Mon said.

"Yeah. I've got to get to Ocean Beach to place a bid on a gig. Twenty-four rental units."

Mon produced a low whistle. Rubbed her thumb and index and middle fingers together.

"No doubt. Wish me luck," Drew said.

Mon winked.

Drew's pocket buzzed. Phone call. Answering calls was one of the negatives about being his own boss. He hated them, same as about everyone his age. Prepared to let it go to voicemail, a bolt of panic shot through him that it might be Gaby calling. Retrieving the phone from his pocket, he held up a finger to Mon.

"No worries," she whispered, and backed off.

The number on the screen didn't look familiar, but it started with a local area code—619—so Drew answered.

"Hello?"

"Bro?" a male voice said. "Drew. It's Jake."

"Jake!" shouted Drew, then quickly flushed from embarrassment. He cupped his mouth and the phone and made his way out the back of the house through a pair of newly-installed French doors.

An ocean breeze blew across the sprawling back deck, cooling his skin. Even with nostrils coated in construction dust, he registered the ocean salt in the air and inhaled deep to appreciate it more. Once he reached the deck's railing, as far as he could get away from the construction, he spoke again. "What's up, man? How have you been? Are you okay?"

Jake laughed. "Slow down, bro. Everything's great. Calling 'cause I'm in town and want to see if you want to meet up."

"Man, that's great. I'm actually headed to Ocean Beach, so I can make some time for lunch if you're hungry. Where are you at?"

"It's kismet," said Jake. "I'm in OB, hanging down by the pier."

"Sweet. I can be there in fifteen. Hodad's sound good?"

Jake moaned his approval. "Fuck. Yes. I'll grab us a table."

***

Drew steered his 2011 Ford Transit Connect cargo van down the winding streets of the neighborhood and took a left onto La Jolla Blvd., headed south. He did his best to keep his speed under control since cops kept strict patrol of speeders through these rich parts of the city, but it was tough. He was so damn excited to see his foster brother that his entire body hummed. His palms went sticky, and arms shook with restless energy.

The last time Drew saw Jake was nine months before. July 2021. Jake had made a stop in San Diego after the Bay Area on his way to Phoenix. He'd hitched the whole way with a series of other vanlifers, nomads, and vagabond types. Drew didn't fully understand his brother's lifestyle, his desire to reject traditional forms of housing in favor of exploring the country living in tents and bumming rides and shelter in other people's vehicles, but part of him envied Jake's adventurous spirit all the same.

A Vons grocery store truck suddenly pulled out in front of his van, snapping Drew from the memory as he slammed on the brakes.

"C'mon," he groaned. Resisting the urge to honk the horn, he instead opted to take a deep breath and stare at the rustling tops of Mexican Fan palms lining the road. A deep yellow sun shone directly above the lush green treetops in the cloudless mid-April morning sky, creating a view worthy of an Instagram post. The Vons truck started to move, and Drew crept behind before it finally got up to speed, and Drew got on his way again.

Jake's last visit had been short. He didn't stay the night or even come over to Drew and Gaby's place. Instead, they'd met for dinner at a Mexican restaurant on the western edge of Balboa Park. The place had constructed an extended patio, complete with plexiglass partitions between tables that made Gaby feel more comfortable about avoiding COVID. She and Drew were vaccinated, but during that time, Gaby leaned toward extra vigilance thanks to seeing the worst of the pandemic at her job as an LVN at a private medical practice.

The meal and visit were great. The three shared street tacos and wonderful conversation. They caught up on the time elapsed since Jake's previous visit two years earlier in 2019—the longest stretch the brothers had gone without seeing each other. Drew didn't want the night to end. When it inevitably did, he squeezed Jake in an embrace so long and hard that Jake joked Drew had cracked a rib. Gaby called Jake a rideshare to take him back to his caravan because he refused to inconvenience them. That's the last time they'd seen him. Nine months wasn't a lifetime or anything, but with Jake being his only family, nine months could feel like nine years.

Especially sitting on big news.

Drew took a couple turns, taking him past Crown Point Park and over Mission Bay.

A lot had changed for Drew and Gaby since that dinner. The biggest development being they were now expecting a baby, and Drew hadn't yet been able to tell Jake. If he had one bone to pick with his older brother, it would be that Jake didn't believe in carrying a cell phone. Something about "living in the moment."

Drew sped past the SeaWorld exit and crossed over the San Diego River Estuary. He was now minutes away from their lunch meet-up spot. His stomach gurgled with a mix of emotions. Excitement. Nervousness. Happiness.

He couldn't wait to break one of his brother's ribs this time.

***

Hodad's was a San Diego institution. An iconic burger destination located on Newport Ave., a block from the beach—so close sand covered the sidewalk out front and seagulls scavenged for food remnants in the Dumpsters out back. Inside, Hodad's menu provided juicy offerings for meat eaters and vegetarians alike. On the weekends, the line to get a table wrapped around the building, so locals took advantage of the slower weekdays. Slower at least until summer hit and the hoard of tourists flocked into town.

Walking in, Drew spotted Jake right away. He sat at a two-top on the left side of the place, his back turned from the rest of the dining area. It was him though. No doubt. His greasy brown hair—now neck-length—tucked under a brown ballcap. He wore a thin, faded yellow T-shirt with a frayed neckline, and his trademark Army green backpack smothered with iron-on patches from his many travels laid flopped against the leg of his chair.

Drew sneaked up on him and launched himself. Grabbed his brother in a headlock, locking the crook of his elbow around Jake's chin.

Jake thrashed. "What the hell—"

Drew released him. Jake spun around. Their eyes met, and Jake jumped out of his chair. "Dude!" The two bear-hugged. Jake's ballcap got knocked off his head. As Drew squeezed Jake, he was reminded of a small, stray Terrier he saw at a job the previous week, its ribs sticking out of it scruffy coat. Drew let up on his hug a bit.

"Where have you been?" Drew pulled away and looked Jake in the eyes again. "Never mind. We'll get to that. It's so fucking good to see you, man."

"Bro, I know. I've missed you like hell." He smacked Drew on the shoulder and gestured for him to take a seat. Drew did, and Jake sat as well. "It's been too long. My bad."

"Don't sweat it." The energy surging through Drew's body made it difficult for him to settle in his seat. "I'm just stoked you're here."

Jake hopped off his chair and scooped up his ballcap. Tucked his hair behind his ears and plopped the hat back on his head.

"Hey! Go, Pads," Drew said, noticing the interlocked gold SD on the hat, the logo for the San Diego Padres.

"It's the one you and Gaby gave me last time I was here."

"I thought I recognized it from behind. Looks well-worn for only nine months."

"Shit ya," Jake said. "It's not a vacation roaming around out there, even if it feels like it most of the time."

"That's so cool."

"You need to go with me on a road trip again soon."

"Man, I'd love to, but—"

"Remember that time I grabbed you out of school your senior year and we drove to the Grand Canyon?"

Drew beamed. Of course, he remembered. He had to call his foster parents from the road to let them know he was okay and would be back in a few days. He held the trip firm as a cherished memory. "That was a blast," Drew said. "Even though I almost flunked History by missing the final."

Jake laughed, throwing his head back; lost in the memory. "I've never seen anyone eat so many Twizzlers as you did on that trip."

"Shit," Drew said, drawing out the word. "I ruined Twizzlers for myself that trip."

A blonde, college-aged waitress approached and handed them each a menu. "I'm Kimmy. Can I get you two started with anything to drink?"

"Iced tea for me, please," Drew said.

Jake shot him a look that he immediately understood as "You buying?" Drew nodded, flicked two fingers at him.

"Uh, I'll take the Surf Punk Lager and a glass of water with lemon."

"Sure thing," Kimmy said. "Be right back with those drinks and to take your order."

She left. Jake thanked Drew, who told him it was no big deal.

"And look at you," Jake said. "Dressed like the Michelin Man, but with none of his rolls. Look at those guns." Jake reached over and squeezed Drew's bicep. "You're jacked."

Dropping his head, Drew said, "Perk of the job." Changing the subject, he asked, "So, how long *are* you in town for?"

Jake shrugged. "Not sure. Depends. A few days? Maybe a week?"

"You have to stay with us. I won't take no for an answer."

Rubbing his chin, Jake gave the appearance he was thinking about. Then, he broke. "How could I say no? Thanks for not making me beg."

Drew laughed and the two fist-bumped.

"This will be sweet. We can hang, watch Padres games, go to the beach . . . Hold up," Drew said, pulling out his phone. He jumped out of his chair, grabbed Jake around the shoulder and took a selfie of the two.

Jake laughed. "Thanks for the warning. So, what's new with you?"

Drew sat back down, straightened up tall.

"Uh-oh," Jake said.

"What?"

"You're getting serious on me . . ."

"Whatever."

"Only messing around, bro. Spill it."

Drew paused. His brother's face was scraggily with weeks-old stubble and his skin looked dry and red from getting too much sun. Despite his lack of grooming, he still possessed the brightest blue eyes, and his smile was as magnetizing as ever.

"Gaby's pregnant . . . I'm, I'm gonna be a dad."

Drew could hardly get the words out before Jake rushed Drew, pulling him into a tight neck hug.

"Bro! I'm so happy for you."

Drew recoiled from his brother's booming voice right in his ear. "Thanks," he managed, still locked in Jake's tight grasp. Jake let up, grabbed Drew by both shoulders and shook him.

"You're going to be a dad."

"I know."

"You. My little brother. I can't believe it."

"Yeah, sometimes I can't either." Drew's voice trailed off.

Jake retreated to his seat. "Okay, so what's that about?"

Drew's eyes wandered the restaurant. The walls were plastered with dented license plates from all over the country, old skateboards, and every kind of sticker imaginable.

"I don't know," he said. "We didn't really plan for it, you know? One of those pandemic babies, I guess."

Kimmy dropped off their drinks then, and Jake grabbed his beer and took a big gulp.

"We ready to order?" asked the waitress.

Jake gasped his satisfaction of the lager. "Think we need another minute." He winked at her, but she didn't act like she saw and left.

"What are you doing?" Drew asked.

"What? I'm being friendly. Back to you becoming a dad. What's the hesitation about?"

Anyone else playing burger stool therapist, and Drew would have shut down. But this was his big brother, his only family. If he couldn't open up to him, who could he? Drew took a drink of his tea, wiped his lip with a napkin. "I don't know. Guess I'm worried I'll fuck him up."

Jake, after taking another drink of his beer, asked, "How so?"

"I don't know. I mean, what do I know about being a parent? Not like I had the most stable home life. Either of us."

Jake snorted. "Seems to me you earned a freaking PhD in parenting with all the foster homes you went through."

Drew laughed.

"I'm kidding. Mostly. Seriously, though. Think about it. You said it yourself. You had so many 'parents'—he wrapped the word in air quotes—that you know what makes a good one and what makes a bad one."

Drew hummed a long note, processing his brother's logic. "So don't smuggle migrants or drugs," he said. "Check."

"Ha," Jake said, shaking his head. "The Millers. That shocked me."

"You and all of San Diego."

"But, hey, you had good homes after that."

Drew dragged a hand across his face. "Yeah, true. It's just, they kind of messed my head up, you know? They were so nice, so good, and then my whole world got flipped upside down when they got raided and everything came out."

"I mean, I get that," Jake said. "But listen. You're not going anywhere, right? You and Gaby are great together, and that kid is both of yours. That right there means they'll have it two-hundred times better than we did."

"That's true."

The waitress came by again. They each ordered a bacon cheeseburger with a side of onion rings.

"Can I get a ranch with that, too?" Jake asked.

"You bet," Kimmy said, and winked at him.

After she walked away, Drew said, "I'll be goddamned."

Jake grinned and shrugged. "She must dig the beach bum vibe I'm giving off."

"More like desert bum vibes," Drew quipped.

Jake laughed, choking mid-drink of his beer.

Their order came out fast and aside from regular moans, they suspended the conversation in favor of devouring their food. Hodad's burgers were notoriously juicy, requiring vigilance to make sure the juices didn't drizzle down your arm while eating one.

After cleaning themselves up, Jake cleared his throat.

"Gaby okay with my staying with you guys?"

"Yeah, of course," Drew said, his voice going high. "I texted her on the way over." He had—before he got in his van to leave the jobsite. She just hadn't responded yet. "You know she loves you too."

"She better," Jake said, swatting Drew with his ballcap.

Drew paid up, and they walked out.

On the sidewalk, Jake slung his backpack on his back and stretched. "I'm full as hell."

"Me, too," Drew said. "So, hey. I've got some work to do—nothing too involved. I have to put in a bid on a job. You're welcome to tag along, or . . ." Drew trailed off, unsure of Jake's interest level.

But Jake said right away that he'd love to go with.

"Cool," Drew said. "After, we'll grab a few things for dinner and head to the casa."

"Sounds like a plan," Jake said.

Chapter Two

Jake slept in the Transit Connect while Drew walked the grounds of the twenty-four rental units with its property manager, an attractive woman named Lydia.

The units were blocky one-story apartments, situated tightly on a rectangular parcel of premium real estate off Niagara Ave., adjacent to the Ocean Beach Pier. The most western units overlooked the Pacific Ocean, with only a scraggly hedge separating them from the sandstone cliff and the forty-foot drop to the water below.

New ownership of the Surfview Cottages wanted a complete facelift of the units, inside and out. Drew recognized right away that the wooden units were in desperate need of a fresh coat of paint. Not that exteriors or paint were his areas of expertise, but even he could tell they were as dated as they were run down. Every unit bore a dingy off-white base with faded emerald green trim. Paint chips littered the ground around the perimeter of the cottage they walked up to, and whole sections of bare wood were exposed underneath. It appeared years of maintenance had been neglected, and the salty air had done its corroding and eroding best.

"Looks like you've got your work cut out for you," Drew said.

Lydia inhaled deeply through her nose. "You're not kidding. Here, let me show you inside." Unlocking and opening the front door, she moved to the side to allow Drew to enter.

The space reeked of mildew. There was no furniture. The carpet was ragged, dirty, and worn, showing where said furniture once lived, where people had once lived. Now it was an empty, dark space thanks to no overhead light fixture, so common in older structures throughout the city.

"Are all the units the exact same footprint?" he asked after she joined him.

"Yes. As cookie-cutter as it gets."

Drew nodded, bouncing a tape measure in his hand and inspecting the grayed, pockmarked walls. The unit had most recently housed a smoker with a temper, judging by the multiple holes in the sheetrock and bashed-in walls ends. "And I assume you're having everything taken down to the studs?"

"Correct. A demo crew is scheduled to start tomorrow. Should be done by week's end."

After confirming with her the property's preferences on things like texture, popcorn ceiling or not, and so forth, Drew was set. "Okay. Let me take some measurements, do the math, and I'll work up my estimate."

"Great," Lydia said.

"Is it all right if I open the windows? Let that ocean breeze in?"

She smiled. "That's fine, as long as you close them when you're done."

He agreed, and she left the cottage to allow him to work.

It didn't take long to grab measurements of the diminutive living room and dining area. On his way to the bedroom, his phone buzzed in his pocket. A text from Gaby.

It read, "I see you bought your brother lunch."

"Hey, babe," he texted back. "Hope that's ok."

She didn't reply as quickly as she normally did. Drew stared at the screen, waiting. Then, the phone rang.

"Hey, baby," he said, answering.

"Forty-two dollars for lunch? Where did you two eat?"

"Oh, yeah. We went to Hodad's, and with the tip and—"

"Okay, well . . . Keep in mind that we're still saving to buy a house . . . eventually."

Drew squeezed his eyes shut. "I know, I know. But forty bucks isn't going to be the reason why we can't afford a three-quarter of a million-dollar house or not."

"You still there?"

"Yes, I'm here." She took a shallow breath. "I'm going to let you have this one cause it's your brother, and I know how you get when he's around." There wasn't any disdain in her voice, only slight resignation and definitely some tiredness. "Just don't let your regular lunch go to waste, please."

"It's still in my lunch cooler. It'll stay good till I get home."

The two fell silent for a long moment. Drew broke first, asking her about work, and how she felt. Gaby blew exasperated air into the receiver. "Fine, I guess."

"I want to hear about it tonight, all right?"

"Yeah."

"Hey, I'm going to pick up some beer for the game."

"Okay."

"And grilled chicken and squash still sound good?"

"Sure," she said, unconvincingly.

"All right. Gotta go and finish this bid."

"Okay, good luck. I love you."

"Love you too, babe."

After getting off the phone, Drew completed his measurements, and closed up the cottage's windows. The ocean breeze had aired out some of the mildewy odor. Drew looked around and recognized the potential these small units held. Perfect location, good bones—but the small size was still prohibitive. The cottages were likely only ideal for single retirees or for use as vacation rentals. Still, if he won the bid, installing floor-to-ceiling drywall in twenty-four units could net him a pretty penny, most of which could go toward a down payment on a house.

Drew went back to his van and worked up the math in the cab while his brother slept next to him in the passenger seat.

Eventually, a groggy Jake stirred. Moans and groans, and stretching, like he wanted Drew to know he'd awoken. Drew was so caught up with filling out the proposal form that he didn't pay him any attention—at least not until his brother let loose, filling the van cab with acrid hell.

"Dude." Drew tented his nose with his shirt collar. "Not cool."

Jake chuckled until it turned into a full-on laughing fit.

Drew rolled down the windows and fanned the cab with his clipboard.

"Seriously. I can taste your onion rings."

Unable to catch his breath, Jake turned red. Which made Drew start laughing uncontrollably as well.

When they both finally caught their breath and collected themselves, Jake slapped Drew's back. "Missed you, bro."

"Yeah," Drew said. "Missed you, too."

Chapter Three

Leaving the Surfview Cottages, Drew drove a circuitous route, first heading south through Point Loma, past Liberty Station with commercial planes roaring above them, and eventually onto Harbor Drive, which traversed along the San Diego Bay. At the Laurel Street light, Downtown San Diego sparkled in the near distance like a postcard. The glistening Bay with a full marina of sailboats to their right. Once the light turned green, Drew drove them to Balboa Park.

"You forget I grew up here too?" Jake said, the corner of his mouth turned up in a smirk. "Taking me to the zoo next?"

Drew rolled his eyes. "Ha-ha. I thought this would be a nicer drive than the highway and, we could keep the windows down. Besides, I want to hit up this liquor store on the way home."

Drew turned right onto University Ave. and the late-afternoon traffic crawled past colorful restaurants, bars, and small businesses comprising the heart of Hillcrest—the wonderfully vibrant LGBTQ hub of San Diego. It took ten minutes to reach the Georgia Street Bridge, which served as the unofficial entry point into the neighborhood of North Park. Drew noticed Jake looking side-to-side all of the sudden, as if he was discovering the area for the first time, not like they'd entered the very neighborhood where they had lived with Joseph and Rose Miller, the one and only foster home the brothers shared, and where they bonded. Maybe Jake hadn't seen it since back then?

The North Park neighborhood bordered Normal Heights, where Drew and Gaby lived, and though North Park held complicated childhood memories for Drew, it was near impossible to avoid if you lived in the central part of the city.

A couple minutes later, they arrived at the liquor store. Drew pulled into the rear parking lot to save the hassle of finding street parking. After exiting the van, Jake stretched, baring his skinny core.

"Hoppy Time Liquor," he said, reading the red neon sign above a rusted metal door propped open with a brick.

"Pretty dorky, huh?"

Jake swung on his backpack, and closed the passenger's side door. "I don't know. It's not so horrible as far as puns go."

The two walked into the store and Ahmed, the clerk, greeted them. They said "hey" back, and separated. Drew headed for the drinks at the back of the store, taking note of preparations for future construction. Half the coolers were covered with black plastic, and two aisles were taped-off. Meanwhile, Jake perused the snack aisles.

"How's Stone sound?" Drew called over to Jake.

"Sounds pretty great, little bro."

Drew grabbed two six-packs, then went to find Jake. He found him eyeing a glass case on one of the end caps filled with donuts, pastries, and . . .

"Julian Pie . . ." Jake said, his tone one of astonishment. "They've got slices."

A greater San Diego purveyor of homemade pies, the Julian Pie Company was located roughly 60 miles east of the city, in the little mountain town of Julian. Its pies were a staple at holidays and celebrations, and given as gifts by generations of San Diegans. Jake's eyes were huge.

"Get a slice," Drew said. "It's on me."

With no further hesitation, Jake palmed a piece of sanitary tissue paper, opened the glass case, and retrieved a golden-brown slice of apple pie.

"If you want to warm it up, sir," said Ahmed, "there is a microwave over there." He pointed toward the back, left corner of the store.

Jake thanked him and practically skipped there.

Drew set his beer on the counter.

"Hey, Ahmed. How's the family?"

"They're good, thanks. How about yours?" Ahmed smiled, rang up Drew's items.

"We're hanging in there. So, looks like you're doing some upgrades back there?" Drew thumbed behind him. "Saw the black plastic sheets. You expanding?"

Ahmed didn't look up as he totaled Drew's sale. "Yes, we're punching through the wall next door, expanding our footprint and upgrading the chillers. Doing some other upgrades as well. Sorry for the mess."

"It's no bother," Drew said. "Business must be really good to invest that kind of money."

Ahmed didn't respond.

The microwave rang. Drew looked over his shoulder for Jake, but the snack aisles in the middle of the store obscured his view and he didn't see him. Ahmed placed the beer in a black plastic bag, and Drew thanked him.

As he rounded the corner to the back where he expected to find Jake at the microwave, he wasn't there.

"Jake?"

Before Drew could call again, he heard a gruff male voice shout, "This area's off-limits. Out." and next saw Jake cower out of the back room, hands held up in surrender.

"Sorry," he said. "Was only looking for a restroom."

The owner of the gruff voice appeared after him in the doorway. Slim, wearing jeans, a black sleeveless shirt, and tan work boots. He looked close to Jake's age. "No public restrooms."

"Got it."

"We're close to home if you can wait," Drew offered.

"Yeah, no sweat. Let's go."

"Don't forget your pie."

Jake grabbed the slice out of the microwave. They exited the store with the skinny store manager, or whoever he was, still guarding the back room.

Once inside the van, Jake dove into his snack, with no mention of the awkward encounter inside. The smell of warm apple pie filled the van's cab. Drew exited the parking lot, and eased the van to a stop at University Ave., where he waited on traffic to clear to take a right.

Jake sat, sucking apple filling and sugar off his fingers. Then, something across the road caught his eye. "Hey!" He jutted his head. "That's where the Millers used to live. Right there."

Drew didn't respond.

Jake swatted him. "Drew. The house on the corner. That's the one, right?"

Flashing on a memory, his old bedroom door flew open. A large, bald guy wearing a navy-blue windbreaker with FBI in yellow lettering on his left chest barged in and grabbed Drew by the wrist. The man dragged him through the house while cops from three government agencies turned the Miller's home inside out. Drew heard the cries of Joseph and Rose; was blinded again by the swirling blue and red lights.

"Aren't you going to say anything, Drew?"

"What do you want me to say?" snapped Drew. What he wanted to say was how it still bugged the shit out of him that Jake left town two months before everything went down. How he'd lost his best friend when Jake flipped the Millers the bird and took off to explore the world. He cranked the steering wheel, gunned it onto University. "Yeah, that's our old house," Drew said.

Jake swiveled in his seat. Looked back intently at the Tudor. A few seconds later he plopped down and cast a theatrical look at Drew, but said nothing.

"It's only a house," Drew said.

"Uh-huh. If you say so. You think you're holding on to some shit it's time to let go of?"

He and Jake had never talked about what happened that night when Drew was fourteen. The night he fell asleep thinking about seeing Jenn Fletcher at work the next day, and how he was startled awake at 2:30 in the morning by the sounds of the FBI and IRS splintering open the Millers' front door. A frustration he rarely felt with his brother bubbled up. A dull ache suddenly pulsed from behind his eyes. Jake had never asked Drew about the night of the raid. And Drew had never told him specifics, either.

Like how he'd been sat on the cold concrete curb in the middle of the night and had to watch Federal agents and San Diego cops rush all about, the emergency lights from their vehicles lighting up the yard like a rabid Fourth of July laser light show. Or how he felt helpless when he spotted Joseph and Rose, two pillars of the community and the nicest, most generous adults Drew had known, sitting in the back seats of two different SUVs, separated from each other, each wailing. How they'd been handcuffed behind their backs, squirming and fighting like they had hope of freeing themselves, Rose still with rollers in her hair, tears streaming down her face.

Drew felt an urge like never before to confront Jake, about how his brother always ran away from his problems, always left others to deal with the fallout, alone and scared. Instead, he swallowed the painful memories and under his breath said, "Probably."

Chapter Four

J ake changed the subject quickly, making the rest of the drive home pleasant.

He talked all about his stops after he'd last seen Drew and Gaby. Phoenix was a bust, but he grabbed a ride up to the Pacific Northwest. Highlighting that trip was a four-month stay in Vancouver. Snow-capped mountains and surrounding blue ocean. A vibrant art scene. The air so clean and refreshing.

Sounded to Drew like San Diego on steroids.

"Here we are." Drew steered the Transit Connect out of the alley and wedged it into its parking spot between the beefy trunk of a fifty-foot-tall Canary Island date palm and the back of his and Gaby's rental home.

Jake's face whipped to the right as they pulled in. "Whoa, whoa, whoa." He wiggled in his seat, impatient for Drew to come to a stop. "You held out on me, little bro."

Drew killed the engine and Jake jumped out. Drew followed quickly after. He rushed past an excited Jake to the chain link gate that led to the house's side driveway and small yard. Unlocking the padlock, he swung the gate open.

"A Chinook?" Jake's voice was high-pitched, coated with disbelief. "You bought a motherfucking Chinook and didn't tell me?"

"Yeah, wanted to surprise you."

"What year is it?"

"Ninety-four."

"Same year *Vitalogy* came out."

Drew smiled. He and Jake still shared a love of Pearl Jam and everything Grunge and 90s rock. Soundgarden, Nirvana, Rage, STP, Alice in Chains, the Pumpkins . . . Even though both experienced music consciousness in the aughts, several of those giant 90s bands were still making music when the brothers were teenagers. The first week Drew came to live with the Millers, Jake shared with him his love of the hard-driving, dirty sound. Drew devoured it, particularly drawn to the angry, and in some cases, nihilistic lyrics. Words that felt like they described every feeling he kept locked in his chest. He also took pride in favoring music from a half-generation before them over what was popular at the time. His small act of rebellion.

Jake ran his hand down the side of the RV, pausing on the white lettering spelling out "Chinook" located above the rear tire. "Look how fresh the stripes still are."

"You've got to check out the inside. Let me grab the keys. Stay here." Drew hurried up the driveway, leaving Jake gawking at the RV. Before Drew could round the corner of the house, a voice called out from behind the neighbor's white vinyl fence.

"Drew? Is that you?" It was Bernie. Their friendly, fifties-something landlord.

"Yeah, it's me, Bern." Drew climbed the porch steps and paused before unlocking the front door.

The fence gate creaked open and Bernie poked his head through, trying to be unobtrusive. "Only checking if that lovely wife of yours is around."

"Nope, but she should be home soon."

"Tell her to come over when she's able to, mmk?"

"Sure thing." Drew waved goodbye, turned around and unlocked the door. He didn't even need to step inside the house. Reaching into the turquoise glass bowl on the built-in directly inside the door they used for random junk, Drew fished out the Chinook's keys.

Rejoining his brother, he said, "Let me open her up."

"Sweet."

The brothers walked to the rear of the RV and Drew unlocked the door. Jake vaulted himself up the one step and inside. Drew followed.

"This baby's cherry. Fold-out is clean, no holes or stains . . ." Jake doubled back to the rear of the RV and flipped a switch. The generator kicked on. "Generator fires right up and sounds great . . ." Flipping it off, he ducked into the tight bathroom. "It's nicer in here than ninety-five percent of the rest stops across the United States. Trust me."

Drew waited outside the restroom, smiling. Jake popped out, clapped Drew's shoulder.

"You must have dropped some serious bank on this baby."

"You might be surprised," Drew said. "A guy a couple streets over sold it to us for a hell of a good deal. He bought it for retirement, but his wife stepped out on him. Said he wanted to see someone get some use out of it. Gaby and I were forced to use most of our savings for a house to stay afloat when the pandemic shut down things and fucked up my work, so I figured why not use what we had left and buy this? Not like what we had would be enough for a down payment on a closet, much less a house in this market. This way, we can get out and see the world like you if we can't buy a place of our own."

"How much?"

"Twelve grand."

Without missing a beat, Jake said, "That's a hell of a deal. So, where've you taken her?"

Drew squeezed the back of his neck. "Nowhere yet. We've both been working so much to play catch-up. Maybe we'll camp at some beaches this summer. Depends how Gaby feels."

Jake raised an eyebrow. Then smiled. "Well, I love it."

"I'm glad to hear you say that, cause inside the house is pretty tight right now—"

"And you want me to stay out here?"

"That cool?"

"You kidding me? I had a Concourse like this one back in the day. Remember?"

Drew nodded. Jake had driven them to the Grand Canyon more than a decade ago in a Chinook. Probably the reason the model always stuck with Drew. Sadly, Jake lost his Chinook not long after that trip, telling Drew he needed to pay off bills. That never connected for Drew. Having fewer bills was supposed to be one of the points of van life, right? Whatever the case, losing the Chinook thrust Jake into his current existence as a ride-hitcher in the nomad world.

"This is perfect," Jake said. "Thanks, little bro."

"Oh. Almost forgot. Don't think you'll need it since it's so nice out right now, but the A/C isn't working. I need to get the condenser replaced."

"No worries. Natural air is the way to go anyway."

Drew tossed the RV keys and Jake caught them. "Keep it locked up when you're not inside, por favor."

"You got it," Jake said.

"Let's grab the beer out of the van and I'll get dinner going. Gaby'll be home soon."

"Right on."

***

Drew was walking a platter of seasoned chicken thighs to the grill when he heard Gaby's old Kia Rio come to a squealing stop out front of their landlord's, where she always street-parked. He prayed the shrill sound was only the brake pads, but he'd been wishing that for months, and now feared the metal-on-metal sound could be shot rotors, a pricier repair. Of equal concern, the engine had started leaking oil. Gaby needed a newer vehicle before the baby came. They both knew it, but didn't speak of it. If they were to, the conversation would inevitably return to what an ill-advised decision it had been for Drew to buy the Chinook.

"Jake." Drew called over his shoulder to the house. His brother was inside wrapping up a shower and change of clothes.

Jake came out. "What's up?"

"Mind grabbing the gate for Gaby?"

"On it." Jake hustled down the porch.

"Jake," said Gaby when he opened the gate. "Thank you. I'd hug you, but—"

"Here, let me help you with that stuff."

Drew watched his brother unload Gaby's hands of her lunch bag and purse. The two of them made their way into the yard, splitting apart with Jake heading to the house, and Gaby approaching Drew.

"Hey, babe." Drew waved to her with the barbecue tongs.

She headed his way. The sun made the natural highlights in her auburn hair glow. She had it parted in the middle and tucked behind her ears, like most days.

"Rough day?" Drew asked.

She wrinkled her nose at him. Pouting her lips, she extended her arms. Drew set the tongs down and pulled her into an embrace. She smelled like work: baby powder and latex gloves. "My feet are fat," she whimpered into his ear.

"What? No . . ."

"They've been swollen all day. They're fat and ugly." The crack in her voice, the vulnerability it held, weakened Drew, made something hitch in his chest.

"Aw, baby . . ." This minor consolation was about all he felt qualified to offer. When her feet swelled up the first time, he'd been taken off-guard. Wanting to help, he asked if she could sit more at work. She laughed. Asked how that would work at a job where she had to be on her feet all day. So now, a gentle touch and kindness were his go-tos, and he hoped it would be enough to carry them over the finish line.

"I'll massage your pretty feet after dinner. Sound good?"

Gaby blinked her amber eyes at him. "Okay."

"Go inside and rest. Dinner will be ready in twenty or so."

She turned to go, but stopped. Turned back. "Jake's going to ask for money, you know."

Drew scoffed agreeably. "Yeah, probably."

"We should ask him to earn it this time."

"How do you mean?"

"What if he goes to work with you for however long he's in town?"

Drew arched an eyebrow. "That could work."

Gaby smiled, kissed him. "He's staying here, right?"

Drew nodded. She patted his forearm. Then headed to the porch. Halfway up the stairs, Drew remembered something.

"Oh. Bernie's looking for you."

"Okay," she said walking into the house.

***

Jake set the little four-seat Bistro table on the patio, and brought out a couple Stone beers for he and Drew and a glass of ice water for Gaby.

It was early evening, around 6 p.m. A gentle, cool breeze blew through the yard. The strong fragrance of citrus blooms hung in the air.

"This is nice," said Drew, setting down the platters of food in the middle of the table.

Jake drinking, grinned. Gaby, holding her stomach with one arm, smiled as well.

"Thanks for letting me crash with you two," Jake said.

Gaby patted his arm. "You're always welcome. You know that." She meant it, too, and Drew loved her for it.

"Thanks, Gaby." Jake took a pull of his beer. "Now feed my belly with that chicken."

Dinner didn't last long.

Jake killed his plate like it was his last meal, and Gaby cleaned hers nearly as quickly, blaming it on eating for two. Drew, however, finished before either one of them, anxious to get inside the house for first pitch of the Padres game.

All told, they licked their plates clean, cleared the table, and brought everything inside with ten minutes to spare before Yu Darvish climbed the mound for his second start of the season.

"Sit, both of you," Drew said, gesturing to the couch while bodying them out of the kitchen. He'd already turned on the game while shuttling things in from outside. "I'll handle the dishes and get some popcorn going for us."

Jake made a mocking face and Gaby giggled, but both followed Drew's orders, plopping on the couch.

"Hey, can you see the TV from way over there, bro?" Sarcasm clung to Jake's tone, but Drew didn't pick up on it until too late.

"Yeah, it's right there." Drew pointed straight ahead through the open area between the kitchen and the living area to the flatscreen mounted on the wall.

Gaby giggled again. Jake snorted, covering his mouth.

"Ha, ha. So funny." Drew waved a dismissive hand at them.

On screen, the broadcast began. Graphics flashed, followed by the lineups for each team. Drew loaded the dishes into the dishwasher, keeping an eye on the TV. Jake wasn't paying attention though.

"Drew, what's this popcorn sitch?"

Gaby cut in before Drew could reply. "Oh, you're in for a treat. Drew goes all out. Tell him, baby."

"Yeah, sure. So . . ." Drew was tearing open packages of microwave popcorn from their plastic sleeves. He tossed one package in the microwave, closed the microwave door, hit start, and spoke up to be heard over the whir of the appliance. "You can go with classic butter and salt—"

"Basic, in other words," interrupted Gaby.

"What else, Drew?" Jake asked.

"Yeah, so . . . looking at what we have in the pantry . . . I can make my Reese's Delight—Reese's Pieces for toppings. Or Fluff and Stuff—mini marshmallows—or Gaby's favorite: Chile Classico—popcorn coated with butter and Tajín Clásico Chile Lime seasoning.

"Damn, tough choice." Jake pantomimed elbowing Gaby, who sat at the other end of the couch, feet resting on the ottoman. "You going with your favorite?"

Holding her belly, she nodded.

"Two Chile Classicos, Popcorn King."

"Coming right up," Drew said. "Hey, could you turn up the TV a bit?"

Jake scanned the area for the remote, but Gaby grabbed it and increased the volume.

"What's the Padres record anyway?" Jake asked.

Over the sound of popcorn popping, Drew said, "Four and one. They dropped the first game to the Giants yesterday, so they need to win tonight to even the series. Should be doable with Darvish pitching. Dude threw six scoreless on Opening Day."

"So much information," muttered Jake, winking at Gaby.

"I heard that."

"I wasn't trying to keep it from you, bro."

Drew kept his head down. Smiling. Working three bowls of popcorn, tossing each with butter and Tajín.

When he finished, he took the bowls to the living room, handed them off, and plopped on the couch between Jake and Gaby.

They all settled in and began snacking. Gaby patted Drew's leg. He smiled. A Giants hitter reached base. "It's okay," Drew said. His optimism proved short-lived, however. Brandon fucking Belt smacked an opposite-field homer to left, putting the Giants up 0-2.

"Goddam it!" Drew swatted the couch. In his periphery, Jake and Gaby shrunk, but smirked at each other.

"Number one fan over here." Jake hooked a thumb at Drew.

"Shut it," Drew said.

The rest of the inning went downhill from there. Darvish gave up six runs before getting out of the 1st. Typical Padres.

Drew's dismay dissipated slightly when in the top of the second the Padres put a run on the board to cut the deficit to 1-6.

Then the Giants poured it on in the bottom of the 2nd, tacking on four more runs.

"Shit," Drew said. "Ten to one? This game's over."

Gaby and Jake sat mum, but Drew could feel their eyes on him. Sitting with an empty bowl of popcorn, Gaby changed the subject. "Jake, did Drew tell you what we're having?"

"A baby?" he answered dryly.

Drew, still miffed with the game, snorted.

"Pssh. No, dork," Gaby said. "I mean did he tell you the baby's—"

"Kidding. I know," Jake said. "And you know what? He didn't tell me."

Drew gave Gaby his best look of contrition. "Sorry, babe. I guess I forgot."

She let out a little huff. "We're having a boy."

Jake stared at the TV, pretending not to care. "That right?" he mumbled. Then, he pounced and sat on Drew. Grabbed him into a headlock. "You're going to have a boy and forgot to tell me?"

Drew laughed, and tried to push Jake off. After a brief struggle, he succeeded. "Sorry, sorry. Yes, we're having a boy. Geez. To be fair, you didn't ask what we are having."

"I figured you didn't know yet."

"Come on, Jake," Gaby said. "I'm more than six months along."

"Hey, I don't know shit about these things."

"You men . . ." She began to get up. Drew quickly realized and gave her a hand.

"You two have a name picked out?"

"I like Lucas, but Drew's not sold on it."

"Lucas is cool," Jake said. "You're going to teach him Spanish, right?"

Gaby shook her head slightly. Drew gave her the same look he always did when she brushed him off about the subject.

"I want us to," Drew said. "But Gaby doesn't think her Spanish is good enough."

"I can understand it, but I've never felt confident speaking it," she said.

"But you and Ester talk to each other in Spanish all the time."

"Somewhat." Gaby leaned into Drew and whispered that she was going to take a shower. He said okay and went to follow her.

"Stay. Watch the game with your brother."

He kissed her on the cheek and sat back down.

While she showered, the Padres managed to squeeze out another run in the 5th. Drew slouched across Gaby's seat, resting his hands behind his head. Jake was picking at a few kernels of popcorn in his bowl and finishing off his beer.

After a while, he gathered up the bowls and bottles and took them to the kitchen. Drew thought he heard Jake make a sound like he was going to say something.

"What's that?" Drew asked.

"Uh. Nothing. I mean . . ."

"Spill it."

Jake came back into the living room with his hands stuffed into his pockets and a sheepish look plastered on his face. "I hate to ask because you two are already letting me stay here, and feeding me, but . . ."

Drew said, "How much do you need?"

"Bro, you know I don't like to bum off you. But I need a couple hundred to cover my share of gas for the next road trip the crew's taking."

"Where's that?"

"Yellowstone. It's dope in the spring and we want to get there before all the tourists do." Jake cleared his throat. "I don't need it until early next week. That's when we plan to head out."

"What I'm hearing is I'm feeding you for the rest of the week."

"Ah, man. It's not like that—"

"Now *I'm* messing with you." Drew chuckled. "We're happy you're here, man. Really."

A look of relief washed over Jake. "I'm happy we get to spend some time together."

Drew stood up. Playfully shoved Jake. "Okay, money's yours . . . with one catch."

"Yeah? What's that?"

"You've got to work for it."

Jake looked puzzled. "How?"

"You come work with me."

Jake's forehead wrinkled and his lip curled. Then, he broke. "Shit ya. That sounds great."

Drew couldn't help but smile. Gaby was right. It worked, and he would get to spend more time with his brother as a bonus.

"Drew? Can you come here?" Gaby, calling from their bedroom.

Jake waved for him to go.

Drew patted his brother on the shoulder and hustled to see what Gaby needed.

When he walked into the bedroom, she laid on the bed in her pink bathrobe, her hair wet.

"What's up, baby?" He closed the door and sat down on the bed next to her. Kissed her softly on the lips.

Her eyes were pleading. "Can I get that foot rub now?"

"Aw. Of course." Drew scooched down the bed to her feet. He propped both on his lap and began massaging the sole of her left foot first.

Gaby's eyes rolled to the back of her head. She immediately produced soft moans.

"Feel good?"

"Mm hmm."

"Hey. I wanted to apologize for spending so much on lunch without giving you a heads-up. Mon paid me early and I felt flush. And with Jake in town, I wanted to treat him, is all."

Gaby opened her eyes. Kindness on her face. "I get that. And I'm not upset. But you don't have to buy his love. He already adores you."

Drew switched to massaging her other foot. "Yeah."

"That said, I don't have to remind you that we agreed to tighten our belts: packed lunches, no entertainment or shopping for anything but the basics."

"Right, I know. And I'm working my ass off to earn back the money we lost."

"I know you are, and I'm working my ass off too, you know."

"Sorry. That's not what I meant. I know you are."

"And we didn't lose that money, Drew. We used it to keep our heads above water. It wasn't something that could be helped. It wasn't our fault."

"Yeah," Drew said.

"I still want a place of own. I really wanted to decorate a baby room, but that's obviously not going to happen. So maybe if we keep things tight, in a couple of more years we could be decorating our little toddler's room with Padres gear." Gaby winked.

Shoulders slumped, Drew stopped massaging her feet. "In a couple more years houses will cost a million and a half, or we'll have to buy a shack in bumfuck East County." He'd aimed for hyperbolic, but truth was, he hadn't exaggerated much. Current values meant there was no way they could afford to buy in Normal Heights—where they rented—with houses going for well over $1 million. And with no savings, they were severely behind the eight ball when it came to buying anything in San Diego County, where the average modest three-bedroom sold for more than $900,000. Only four years earlier, when they had started saving, the same sized houses sold for $570,000. They thought they'd experienced sticker shock then.

Gaby set a hand on Drew's knee.

"I want all that too," Drew said. "It just seems so unlikely."

"Come here," she said. He did, and the two hugged. "We'll figure it out. Maybe the market will crash at the same time we get our savings rebounded."

"Yeah? And maybe I'll find out I have a long-lost rich relative who left me everything when they died."

Gaby snickered, and quickly covered her mouth. "Stop that. Feeling sorry for yourself won't fix anything. Now get back out there and finish watching your game."

Drew sighed. "Oh, it's over. Same old Padres." He kissed her. "Love you."

"Love you, too."

As Drew softly closed the door behind him, he caught in his periphery Jake rush back to his seat. Then the sound of groaning couch springs. In the living room, Jake sat a little too fixated on the game. Reminded Drew of when they were kids and Jake would eavesdrop at Joseph and Rose's closed bedroom door, then dart back to his bed when he heard them coming. Neither of their foster parents busted him on it, but they had to know he was snooping by the way he would cartoonishly fake being asleep with clenched eyes and over-the-top snoring.

"Everything all right?" Jake asked

"Yeah," Drew said. "Massaging Gaby's feet, is all. You know. Living the dream."

Jake blew air through his nose. "Padres are down 13-2. Rally cap time?"

"Nah. It's over. We'll get 'em tomorrow." Drew got comfortable. Taking a shallow breath, he shook off the house talk. He looked over at Jake and smiled. It felt great to have his brother home.

Chapter Five

It was technically twilight when Drew and Jake set out for work the next morning. The atmosphere was fully illuminated—pale pink clouds drifting across a tangerine sky—even though the sun hadn't yet peaked the mountains to the east.

A few vehicles were starting up, their owners getting an early start to the day as well. The neighborhood reeked of skunk, as it often did. Too many skunks roaming around with too many dogs left out at night to agitate them.

Gaby still slept as Drew snuck out of the house and made his way to the Chinook. To his surprise, Jake answered the back door fully dressed in the extra set of contractor whites Drew lent him the night before.

"You're ready." Drew said it like a question.

"You said early, so I figured that meant 5 a.m. or something."

Drew handed him a mug of coffee.

"Bless you," Jake said.

"Sorry, I should have been more specific. County doesn't allow us to start before seven."

Slurping his coffee, Jake reached back into the RV for his backpack and shouldered it. "I got in some meditation time, so no worries."

After getting settled inside the work van, Drew tossed Jake one of two breakfast bars he'd pulled out of his lunch cooler.

"Coffee *and* breakfast? Thanks, bro."

"Hey, can't have you working on an empty stomach. I packed us turkey sandwiches and chips for lunch, too. This house has a killer view, so I figured we can eat and watch the ocean."

Jake flashed the shaka. "Right on."

They rolled up to the La Jolla house a minute before seven. Traffic on the 5 had been backed up the entire way, making Drew sweat arriving late. Mon preferred her subs to be timely. Thankfully, he remembered she wouldn't be there today, and anyway, they were on time.

The tile subs were on site; one skinny Mexican kid that looked no older than fifteen setting up a wet saw on the driveway, and a heavyset Mexican man unloading boxes of tiles from the bed of a beat-to-hell Toyota Tacoma.

A three-guy solar crew were also unloading gear and getting a move on. Drew held dreams of buying a house with solar to knock down the ridiculous electricity prices they paid. Even with their one-bedroom, the monthly bill fluctuated between $100 and $150, and they barely ran much more than the TV and microwave. When they used the window A/C unit in the summer on rare hot days, the bill jumped another fifty to seventy-five bucks.

While the brothers carried in tools and supplies, Drew explained what he needed Jake's help with today: mixing mud, moving the gear and tools from room-to-room. Mostly, Jake would be his gofer.

Jake tugged the bill of his ballcap and saluted. "Roger that, boss."

Drew shook his head, smirking. "Knock it off, fool."

A full day of work lay ahead of them. An estimated two hours to spread the finish coats on the walls in the living and dining rooms and the downstairs study, and another three to four hours to texture the dried walls throughout the rest of the house after sanding any areas that required such. Drew took pride in ensuring his joints needed minimal sanding, saving him time and clean-up. In an effort to get to it, Drew mixed up the first batch of finish mud, showing Jake the thickness and consistency that he preferred and how to achieve his standard. Jake took over after, allowing Drew to get to work.

Before doing so, Drew opened a playlist on his phone, skipping through it until the first song he let play was "Corduroy" by Pearl Jam. A spark of recognition flickered on his brother's face as the guitar intro built. The drums kicked in, first slowly, then leading all instruments into a crescendo that only a bolt of lightning could rival in power. Jake looked up and flashed devil horns. Drew reciprocated.

He turned around and began working on the finish coats. Dragging his knife back and forth; wrist flicking, mud spreading smooth and even, his mind switched to the static realm of automatic—the place where no fears or worries could touch him.

***

At lunch time the brothers relaxed on a built-in teak bench on the back deck, watching the white caps way down below while they ate.

"On a really clear day, bet you can see straight up the coast to Santa Barbara," Jake said.

The claim sounded dubious to Drew, but he didn't call his brother on it. "Never been."

Jolting like he'd been shot, Jake let out an exaggerated gasp. "What? But you're so close. It's only a four-hour drive away."

Drew shrugged. Chewed and swallowed a bite of sandwich. "Never had the time or money. I'd love to take Gaby one day. Just hasn't worked out."

"Pssh. Go before the baby comes. Drive the Chinook up there and park it at the beach."

Drew considered the idea until an authoritative voice behind them shook him out of the brief daydream.

"Who's this, Jones? You finally hire a crew?"

"Mon," Drew said. He hooked a thumb at Jake. "This is my brother Jake. Jake, this is the best general contractor in all of SD, Mon Evans."

Jake jumped up, darted over to her, and thrust out his hand. "Jake Dwyer. Nice to meet you, boss lady."

She shook his hand. "Mon is good."

"Right on."

"So, your last name is Dwyer . . ." She looked confused.

Drew walked over to them. "Yeah, we're not biological brothers—"

"We might as well be," said Jake, pulling Drew into a one-arm hug.

Mon's face brightened. "That's nice. Hey, Drew. Thanks for sending your invoice over so promptly. Wish my other subs were half as responsible as you."

"No worries. Hey, I thought you were off today."

"Dentist appointment got bumped. Fine by me. You don't want to be around me when I'm doped out of my gourd."

"We'll take your word for it."

"Hey, did you land that twenty-four-unit gig?" she asked.

"Too early to know," Drew said. "Think they're taking the rest of the week to decide."

"Well, fingers crossed for ya." Mon extended a fist. Drew bumped it.

Drew nudged Jake with an elbow. "What do you say? Let's get back to it. I'll show you how to texture two-thousand-square-feet of walls in less than two hours."

Making a goofy face at Mon, Jake said, "I've waited my whole life."

Mon snickered.

"C'mon," Drew said.

***

They finished everything by a little after 3 p.m. Jake proved himself to be a hard worker, doing everything Drew asked promptly and correctly. Drew would have sworn his brother had picked up work as a construction site gofer some time before, maybe as a side hustle to keep some money in his pockets, but Jake denied it. He told Drew he usually opted instead for seasonal retail jobs that lasted a few weeks, in addition to regular donations of plasma and collecting recyclables when in states that paid reimbursements.

Loading up the Transit Connect, Jake seemed to be lost in his thoughts and whacked his shin on the van's running board. He grimaced, sucked his teeth.

"You okay?" Drew asked.

"Yeah. I'll live." Jake plopped down, rubbed his bruised leg.

Drew left him to grab the last of their gear. When he returned, Jake was still sitting, but didn't look to be in much pain now. Drew set his toolbox in the van, pushed it against the other gear. Jake looked up, said, "Hey, think we could swing by that liquor store near the Millers' old house on the way home again?"

"We've still got plenty of beer at the house . . ."

"Nah, man . . . I want to grab another slice of Julian pie."

Drew smiled. "How can I say no after the solid day of work you put in? My treat."

Jake pumped a fist. "Hell yeah!"

Chapter Six

"Street-park it," Jake said, pointing to a row of open meters along the front of Hoppy Time Liquor. "I'll run in. Want anything?"

Drew pulled the van to the farthest meter, shoved the shifter into park. "Yeah, get me a slice of apple, too." He dug into one of the cargo pockets of his pants, pulled out his wallet, and handed his debit card to his brother.

Jake lifted his backpack from between his feet, rested it in his lap. He took the card. "Thanks, bro. Be right out."

"No rush." Drew watched Jake hop out, shoulder that well-worn green backpack of his, and disappear in the van's blind spot.

After stretching, he let his arm hang out the window. The Tudor house across the street—the Millers' old home—grabbed his attention. The front porch overhang sagged and the wood siding needed a fresh coat of paint. Staring at the window of his old bedroom, Jake's comment from a day earlier echoed in Drew's head.

Think you're holding on to some shit it's time to let go of?

Drew rubbed his forehead.

He'd never really tried to "let go" of any of it. How would that even work? He realized then there must be a reason he was a regular of a liquor store right across from his childhood house, yet he always tried to ignore it. But what reason? It wasn't like he never thought about that night. The night of the raid. About Joe and Rose. Far from it. They were always somewhere in his mind. How they'd twisted his perception of what good parents were.

Drew could still feel the cool breeze that drifted into his room that night, carrying with it the sounds of the North Park neighborhood after midnight. Clinking glass bottles. Someone digging recyclables out of trash cans along University Ave. The neighbors' sprinklers. A red-eye flight on final descent into San Diego International Airport. The plane had made him think about Jake taking off two months earlier. He'd lost his someone. Someone to play catch with. Someone to listen to music with. Someone to give him girl advice, even if he was too chicken shit to follow through on it.

Lying there, Drew had read his brother's farewell note—the one Jake had rubber-banded to a rock and stuck in Drew's underwear drawer—for seemingly the hundredth time.

Hey little bro. Guess by now you know I bounced!
Wanted you to know you didn't do anything wrong.
Joe and Rose are good fosters . . . I just need to explore
this big world. Find my own way is all. Keep working
on your fastball and I'll come back and see you soon.
Real brothers forever. Don't you fucking forget it.
P.S. Pearl Jam rules!
-Jake

Even though Jake had said their foster parents were good, they were the reason he left.

Joseph and Rose Miller were the nicest, most generous adults Drew had known. They welcomed him to their home two days before his twelfth birthday. Treated him like he was their actual son. Bought him new clothes. Cooked his favorite foods. Best of all, they promised he would always have a home. The two years living with them proved his longest stretch at any one foster home. On top of that, the Millers were community celebrities. They owned a chain of non-profit thrift stores named Joseph's Home with locations all over San Diego County. Proceeds from the stores funded programs that fed, clothed, and sheltered the city's homeless population. And at the end of each month, Joseph's Home loaded up a semi-truck full of necessities for all ages, including clothes, new socks and underwear, baby formula, toiletries, gently-used eyeglasses, and whatever else was needed most at the time, and had it driven to Mexico where the homeless and poorest families and their children benefitted from the Miller's generosity.

All that was superfluous to young Drew, though. Belonging to a family—a real family—and knowing the Millers wouldn't give up on him like all his previous fifteen foster homes, made him feel safe for the first time in his life. Then in stormed the Feds and the cops and destroyed everything—ripped apart the stability he'd been given, stole security and love from a young man finally learning to trust people.

Drew smeared a hand down his face, the memories still so vivid, painful.

Once the Millers had been driven away that night, and Drew left to wait for Social Services to arrive, he'd asked the FBI agent who stormed his room why all this was happening. None of it made sense.

"Your goodie-goodie foster parents aren't heroes, kid," the agent had said. "They've been smuggling in drugs and migrants up from Mexico. They're nothing but greedy fucking criminals."

Drew screamed at him. Told him he was wrong. The Millers were good people. In the end, though, the agent was right. The Millers were prosecuted on dozens of immigration and drug smuggling charges.

It probably didn't help Drew to move on that he followed his foster parents' trials in the newspaper. Or that he could take you to Joe's burial site—he died in prison five years into his twenty-year term—or to the halfway house at which Rose now resided. Certainly, he wasn't helping himself move on by driving by their house on a semi-regular basis. What could he possibly gain by doing so? Like he'd finally find the ghost haunting his psyche hanging out on the porch so he could grab it, strangle it once and for all? He groaned. He'd considered counseling before, but never acted on it. After the raid, Social Services provided therapists to speak to, but he couldn't untangle his feelings enough to spit out anything coherent, so he never shared. Thankfully, with time came some clarity, to the point where Drew realized in recent years the Millers were simply like every other human: neither all saint, nor all villain. So what good would it do to have his lingering feelings about the Millers or that night analyzed to death? He didn't need a $300-an-hour shrink to tell him what he already knew.

The odds were stacked against him.

Nothing in his unstable childhood prepared him to become a good father.

Messing up his child was a more likely outcome than not.

Drew tried to take a deep breath, but it came up shallow. He closed his eyes and tried another. This one filled his chest, exhaled smooth. The way he saw it, he still had three months to accept becoming a father. Try his best to be a good father once the baby came. He'd play those odds because he loved Gaby with everything in his being. He only hoped she hadn't picked up on his apprehension.

Farther up on University, a squawking flock of wild Monk parrots flew overhead, then landed in a palm tree. Their flapping wings were a sea of green feathers dancing among the fronds.

As he stared at them, a loud popping noise startled him. He shifted in his seat. Looked all around, unsure of what he'd heard. Until it happened again a second later.

POP.

Gunshots.

Drew froze.

Panic flooded his body. Who was shooting? A bead of sweat rolled down his back. Where did the shots come from? His vision tunneled, as all he could think about was the FBI storming into his bedroom so many years ago.

But he wasn't fourteen anymore. He was a grown man. Do something, he told himself. Anything. Duck for cover. Call the cops. Drive away.

But Jake. Where was Jake?

As if on cue, shoes pounded on concrete. Then Jake slammed his hands on the passenger's windowsill.

"Jake! Did you hear those gunshots?"

Jake swung open the door, jumped in, closed the door, and hugged his backpack to his chest seemingly in one lightning-fast moment. "Drive."

There were red dots speckling Jake's face, arms, and his contractor whites. Drew's head swam. "What?"

"Drive, Drew."

"Is that blood? Were you . . . shot?"

"No." Jake continued looking forward, hugging his backpack. "Just get us out of here."

Drew started the van, put it in drive. He stepped on the gas, but then let off.

"What are you doing?" Jake said.

"What happened in there?"

Exasperated, Jake swatted his knee. "Someone tried to rob the place. The clerk shot him. Can we *please* get the fuck out of here now?"

"Is Ahmed okay?"

"Yes. Just DRIVE. I'll tell you everything."

"Shouldn't we call the police? I mean, if you're a witness . . ."

Jake turned to him. His eyes were wide, unsettled. They held an emotion that went far beyond fear. Desperation, maybe. Sweat trickled down his temples in rivulets, licking up drops of blood before falling onto his white shirt. "Do not call the cops. I . . . I have warrants out on me, Drew. Please take us home. There's nothing we can do."

Drew had never seen Jake so shaken, so unstable. It tugged at everything in his chest.

Through a heavy breath, Drew said, "Okay."

Chapter Seven

Jake stood slack-jawed; arms flopped at his side. His eyes glazed over on the wall like he saw something no one else could. He hadn't offered a word since they fled the liquor store. The drive home was quiet and tense. Standing in the bathroom now, Drew helped Jake shed his contractor whites with the intent of getting him into the running shower.

"Lift your arms." Drew pulled up Jake's shirt from the bottom. Jake grunted, then raised his arms. "Good. Now how about the pants?"

Jake twitched, blinked to life. "Sorry. I got it." He brushed away Drew's hands. Fumbled with his pants button, failing twice to get it loose. Finally, he succeeded. The jeans dropped to the floor. An awkward moment occurred when Jake tried to step out of the jeans, but they caught around his ankles and he tripped and began to fall. Drew caught him, held him upright by Jake's shoulders.

"Thanks."

"Sure." Drew gathered up the jeans and balled them up with Jake's bloody shirt.

"I'm good. I got it." Jake dropped his underwear and stepped into the shower.

Drew retreated from the bathroom and closed the door, leaving it cracked an inch.

He rushed to the kitchen where he tossed the clothes into the sink and inserted the metal stopper. Next, he turned on the cold water. While it ran, he scrounged around in the cabinet underneath the sink until he came up with a bottle of bleach. He glugged way more of it into the sink than he thought he needed. Choked on the fumes, snorting and coughing.

After the clothes were fully submerged and soaking, Drew turned off the water and fell back against the sink.

What the fuck happened back at the liquor store?

He pulled out his phone to look at the time. It was 4:25. Gaby wouldn't be off for another thirty minutes, meaning she wouldn't be home for another hour or more, depending on rush hour traffic. Opening their text thread, he typed, "Something happened. We're ok, but Jake was in a shooting and we left and came home. Not sure what to do now. Freaking out a bit."

He hovered his thumb over the send arrow. Then backed out the message. Tapped a new message reading, "Will you be home normal time?" Hit send.

The inside of the house felt stuffy, so Drew opened the living room windows and turned on the tower fan.

His phone buzzed. Gaby. "You ok?"

"Hope so. Need your smarts."

"Ok baby. Leaving now. I'll be home soon."

Drew breathed a momentary sigh of relief. A second later, the water in the bathroom cut off. A towel yanked off the towel bar.

Drew grimaced. The knot in his stomach tightened. Jake needed to tell him everything that happened in that liquor store. Only then would he know if it had been the right decision to drive away. Only problem, Drew wasn't sure he wanted to hear the truth if it differed at all from what Jake already told him. He could live with Ahmed protecting himself, but Drew had no idea if Ahmed kept a gun hidden behind the counter. Didn't seem like the type to be packing, but what did he know?

The thing nagging Drew most about Jake's short account was him being covered in blood. How did that happen? Had he been standing right next to the robber when he got shot?

Drew stopped pacing when Jake cleared his throat. He appeared in the entry to the living room, a bath towel wrapped around his waist. Hair wet, slicked back.

"Think you could run out to the Chinook and grab a change of clothes for me?"

Drew flicked his chin. "Course."

"Thanks. Everything's on the table."

Drew hustled outside, and climbed into the RV.

The clothes—the same pair of shorts Jake wore the day before, a black T-shirt faded so bad it looked purple, and boxers—were folded, stacked right where Jake said.

On the way back to the house, Bernie was standing with the gate wide open between their properties, giving Drew the stink eye. *Shit.* Had he seen them rush into the house earlier? Or worse, seen Jake covered in blood?

"Drew," he said, tapping his flip-flopped foot. "I've got a bone to pick with you."

Oh shit. "Hey, Bern. What's up?" Drew kept his tone light, upbeat. Walked over and shifted the clothes under one arm and extended a fist. Instead of giving Drew knuckles, Bernie awkwardly smothered his palm over Drew's fist.

"Mr. Jones. Did you forget to tell your beautiful wife I wanted to talk to her?"

Drew let out a breathy "ha," relieved that's all it was. "I did tell her. But she got sidetracked last night is all. My brother's in town."

"Ohhh, so that's who that rambler-looking stud is." Bernie propped his hands on his hips. "I wondered why you haven't introduced me."

Drew smiled. "Trust me. If he was gay, I'd run him right over."

"Well . . ."

"But that brings up a question. Have you been spying on us?"

Bernie shoved Drew playfully. "No, course not. I caught a glimpse here and there, is all."

Drew gave him a side-eye. "Okay. And I'll tell Gaby again that you're looking for her."

"Thanks. It's nothing urgent. I wanted to see how Mommy and baby are doing is all."

"Cool." They exchanged good-byes, and Drew returned to the house. Once inside, he handed Jake his clothes.

"Thanks. What did your neighbor want?"

"Oh, that's Bernie, our landlord. He's a great guy. And he thinks you're a total snack."

Jake snorted. "That right? Good to know I've still got it."

While Jake dressed, Drew decided to wait until Gaby got home to try to get answers out of his brother. Jake would only have to repeat himself, and maybe giving him more time to process things would help him calm down and want to open up to the both of them.

"How about a beer?" Drew asked.

"Shit. Thought you'd never ask."

***

The brothers had finished two beers each and were on their third when Gaby arrived home. Drew jumped up, ran outside, and helped her inside the gate. Kissed her.

Looking him in the eyes, she said, "What's wrong?"

He gestured to the house. "C'mon. Get settled, and we'll get into it."

Gaby's eyebrows raised. "Yikes." She turned and headed to the house. Once on the porch, Drew waved for Jake to join them inside. He did.

"Why's it smell like bleach so strong in here?" Gaby asked.

Drew and Jake exchanged a look. "Jake's clothes are soaking in the sink." Seeing the perplexed look she gave him, Drew guided her to the couch, where she sat down. "We . . . Um, Jake was involved in something—"

"I wasn't *involved*," Jake said. "More like present."

"Okay . . . Jake was *present* for something bad this afternoon on our way home."

"Want me to tell her?"

Drew waved his hands. "Go ahead. While you're at it, tell us everything, 'cause I'm confused about what actually went down."

"You two are worrying me," Gaby said.

Drew sat down next to her, leaving Jake standing in front of them.

"So, this is what happened," Jake started. "I ran into the liquor store to get us some pies. While I was selecting the slices, a dude about our age flies into the store from the back, yelling. Told the clerk to empty the register. It happened so fast. When he yelled, it startled me. I turned around and he stood two or three steps away from me, back turned to me like he hadn't even seen me when he came in. Anyway. The dude is pointing a gun, a pistol, at the clerk—"

"Ahmed," Drew said.

"Yeah. Well, Ahmed has his hands raised. Slowly, intentionally, he starts lowering one arm with his index finger pointed down—clearly telling the dude he's gonna open the register. I don't know what came over me, or what I was thinking, but as soon as Ahmed hit the key and the register chimed, I chopped the dude's arms down from behind, pulled him in a bear hug. I expected him to drop his gun, but he didn't, and we started grappling with each other."

Gaby gasped.

"Next thing I know, a shot goes off and I think I've have been shot 'cause I don't know where the dude's gun is, and my face is wet all the sudden. Then my ears start ringing. I panic. Then another shot goes off and the dude goes limp in my arms and falls to the ground."

"Fuck," Drew said under his breath.

"Yeah, so I look around and the clerk's standing there behind the register, holding a smoking pistol of his own. I didn't know what to do. I didn't know if the robber died or what. I bugged the fuck out of there." Jake palmed sweat off his forehead. Sucked a deep breath.

"But why'd you run if you helped Ahmed and he saved your life?" Drew asked.

"Well, for starters, I'm not used to being around guns, much less people firing them in my direction and getting sprayed with blood. So, there's that."

Gaby groaned as she got up. "Let me see you." She pulled Jake's face into her hands, turned his head side to side, inspecting him.

"I'm good, Gaby. I took a shower when we got home. Didn't find so much as a scratch."

"Well, that's good." She turned around to Drew. "What about you? Where were you while this was going on?"

"Waiting out in the van."

Jake said, "Good thing, so we could book it out of there."

"So, wait," Gaby said. "You fled the scene? Why? Jake, I understand, being freaked out. But why didn't you call the police, Drew? Wait to see if they needed to talk to him?"

Jake cut in before Drew could respond. "Gab. I begged him to drive away. I have warrants out on me and I didn't want to risk getting rung up. I know it was selfish."

"So let me see if I've got this straight," Gaby said. "You played hero, then ran, and you—pointing at Drew—played savior to your brother. I've got that right?"

Jake nodded. Drew looked away.

"Either of you look up if the news has reported on this yet?"

Drew pulled out his cell phone. "On it." He typed in "shooting North Park," clicked the news tab, and followed a link to a local NBC story. "Uh, here's something . . ." He read the report. "A shooting occurred at a North Park liquor store in the 2500 block of University Ave. at approximately 3:57 p.m., according to a San Diego Police Department spokesperson. An unidentified man was shot twice. He was transported to Scripps Mercy Hospital where his condition is unknown at this time."

The three of them stood speechless for a few seconds, each looking unsure as to what to say or do. Then Jake offered a thought.

"I think we're good, right? I mean, it doesn't say police are looking for anyone, and I'm sure the clerk told them everything already."

Gaby didn't look so sure.

"What is it, babe?"

She sucked her cheek. "I don't know. Maybe you're right, Jake. Feels wrong somehow, though. I mean, your bloody clothes are soaking in my sink for god's sake."

"Would you really get arrested for your warrants if you checked to see if they need your account?" Drew asked.

Jake shrugged. "Hell if I know. But I'm not lookin' to find out."

"What are your warrants for anyway?"

"Ah, man." Jake looked away, avoided Drew and Gaby's eyes. "Stupid shit. Mainly for stealing some food and essentials from a Walmart in Phoenix."

Gaby squeezed her eyes, pinched the bridge of her nose. "What happens if the police find you anyway, and what about Drew's role?"

"Wait, what do you mean?" Drew asked.

"You two fled the scene of a crime. You were driving. That can't be legal, right?"

Jake threw up his hands. "Shit. I'm starving. Can we get some food if we're going to keep analyzing this?"

Drew looked at Gaby. She rolled her eyes, but her body language let on that she could use some food too.

"How's pizza sound?" he asked. Jake and Gaby nodded.

Drew got on the website for Zia's, a few blocks over on Adam's Ave. "Pesto Pepperoni?"

"Sounds good," Jake said.

"Yeah," Gaby said.

While Drew put in the order, the three of them disbanded. Gaby went to take a shower and change, while Jake plopped down on the couch and turned on the TV. Drew needed fresh air, so he finished the order on the front porch, where he stayed to wait for the delivery person.

Outside, the light faded fast and the temperature held a snap to it. The cool air felt good. Still, Drew found it hard to relax, his nerves fried. He tried taking a few deep breaths, but had difficulty. He could breathe in just fine, but he couldn't exhale without several body-jerking attempts. It felt as if he'd been punched in the stomach. The next few attempts weren't any better. Soon, he couldn't inhale smoothly either. Attempts to simply breath normally turned to sharp, ragged attempts to suck air.

Disoriented and confused, he bounded off the porch and ran to the little grass yard. Found a spot where he didn't think he could be seen by neighbors or his family. He doubled over, clutching his knees. His chest burned and a solid mass tied his stomach in knots, the combination feeling as though he might throw up and could be having a heart attack at the same time. He tried to call to Gaby for help, but nothing came out. He dropped to his knees and pulled his shirt over his nose and mouth. Blood pounded in his ears, turning them hot and mixing the surrounding noises into a static soup. Somehow, through it all, he heard the house's storm door fly open and slam closed. He felt the earth around him tremble as heavy footsteps approached. The fresh-showered smell of his brother reached him before Jake's words. "Drew. Are you okay?" Jake grabbed him up, wrapped his arms around him. It took forever for Drew to catch his breath enough to speak. When finally able, he blurted out through tears, "I'm so glad you're alive, Jake."

Chapter Eight

Drew couldn't focus on anything except how his brother could have been shot yesterday.

The worry had coiled itself in his brain. His eyesight glazed over. Through a thick fog he heard a voice outside his head speaking, but it might as well have been white noise.

Gaby smacked his arm.

"Drew."

He removed his cloth mask. "What? Oh, I—"

"Did you hear what I said?

"No, sorry."

Gaby pulled down her surgical mask to her chin. "When the doctor comes in, don't forget to ask her *your* question." She winked.

For the life of him, he didn't know what she was talking about. He'd promised himself he would be more present at this prenatal visit than he'd been at the last one, and here he was spacing the fuck off. She deserved better. For starters, his full attention.

"What was my question again?"

The paper on the exam table crinkled as Gaby shifted her weight. "About sushi, remember?"

Drew smirked. "Oh, right . . . Can my wife really not eat sushi? I forgot all about that very important question of mine that I came up with all on my own."

"Smart ass. Just ask her for me, okay? I don't want her thinking I'm not taking this seriously." She tucked her chin and pouted.

Drew leaned over and kissed her forehead. "Sure, no problem."

Gaby smiled. "Thank you, baby." She bit her lower lip and paused before speaking again. "So, hey. You're still thinking about yesterday, huh? That's why you've been so quiet?"

"Yeah, I'm sorry. I'll try to focus more."

Gaby rubbed his arm. "I get it, really. You know how relieved I am that you stayed in the van? What happened to Jake was awful, but he is okay."

"You're right."

A knuckle rapped on the exam room door and Gaby and Drew put their masks back on.

***

The baby check-up portion of the appointment went well. Unfortunately for Gaby, however, her OB/GYN dashed her sushi hopes and dreams. Drew couldn't keep up with the multitude of small procedures the doctor performed beyond the ultrasound, the main event. They saw their baby again, now the size of a rutabaga. Drew also witnessed him kick, and felt it occur for only the second time. He'd been kicking in recent weeks, but the milestone hadn't excited Drew in the same way it did Gaby. If anything, it booted his fears up to another level.

Pulling out of the medical center's parking lot, Drew tried not to floor it to get home to see Jake and reconvene things from the night before.

Over pizza and beer, the three of them had talked through what to do. Gaby said the brothers should provide the police with their accounts. She contended the odds of Jake being arrested for out-of-state warrants when he helped prevent a crime seemed low. Jake, did not agree. Drew had his doubts as well.

The only thing they could all agree on: to get some sleep and decide what to do after Gaby and Drew returned home from their appointment. Gaby had taken the day off, so Drew took it off as well, clearing with Mon to finish the little bit of texture work at the La Jolla house on Friday. They had the rest of the day to come up with what to do using clear heads.

"What if you call the police anonymously and feel them out?" Gaby asked Drew as he merged into traffic on the 163. "You could pose hypothetical questions about if two witnesses would be in trouble for leaving a crime scene."

Drew thought about it. "Maybe. Let's run it past Jake when we get home."

***

The brakes on Gaby's car squealed when Drew brought the Kia to a stop in front of a house one over from their landlord's.

"It's getting worse," Gaby offered, reacting to Drew's grimace.

"Yeah . . . If I win the Surfview bid we'll get it fixed." Seeing her struggle for a second with the passenger door, Drew jumped out and ran around the car to help her get out.

"I'm six months pregnant, not nine," she said with an edge to her voice, ignoring his outstretched hand.

"Doesn't mean you should have to struggle if I'm here to help."

She blew air from her bottom lip, took his hand. He helped her out of the car. "Thanks. Since you're being so helpful, could you grab my purse?"

"Of course."

After gathering everything, they walked up the sidewalk holding hands, fingers interlaced. It was another beautiful day in America's Finest City. Barely sixty-five degrees. Clear with a breeze filled with the scent of flowers. All around them birds stoked on spring chirped.

Making their way past Bernie's house to their gate entrance, Drew caught a glimpse of their landlord through the window over his kitchen sink. Bernie saw them too and waved, then held up a finger.

"Bernie. Incoming," Drew said.

Gaby gave him a playful shove. "Stop."

"Kids." Bernie walked through the gate on his side of the property. "Gaby. Did Drew tell you I've been looking for you?"

"Hey, Bern." The two hugged and Bernie pecked her on the cheek.

"Wanted to see how you and . . ." he stretched out the "and," probably hoping they'd divulge the baby's name, which they hadn't decided on yet. ". . . the baby are doing."

"We were just at the doctor and everything looks good. He's the size of a rutabaga now." Gaby pulled from her purse the sonogram picture they'd received and showed it to Bernie.

Bernie awed. "How wonderful! And how are you feeling, hon?"

"Better. No more morning sickness, thank god. But my feet keep swelling up lately."

"And our man Drew's been massaging them for you, I'm sure?" He gave Drew a sarcastic skeptical look.

"I have been."

"He has. He's doing a great job taking care of me."

"Well, good. That's what I want to hear. Changing the subject: How long is your brother in town for, Drew?"

"Oh, I think he said he's leaving early next week."

"That's good," Bernie said. "Any longer and I'd have to raise your rent."

Gaby groaned. Loud. Drew said, "Oof."

Bernie made a cringe face. Threw his hand onto Gaby's arm "Oh, gosh, kids. I was only kidding. What a bad joke. I'm so sorry."

Drew felt bad for him, tried to let him off the hook by waving a hand.

They had no right to give Bernie grief. He was giving them a sweetheart deal on their rent as it was. All other mother-in-law units like theirs in the neighborhood rented out for hundreds more than theirs, and increased sharply over the last two years. Not Bernie. He'd kept their rent the same as when they moved in, for what reason, Drew didn't know. Maybe simply because he loved them that much.

"Please don't be upset," Bernie said. "I'm an old man not reading the room. I know money's a tough subject with, well, everyone these days. Gas prices alone, right?"

"Don't get Drew started on gas prices," Gaby said, play rolling her eyes. "You're fine, Bern. Don't worry. But I've got to get inside and off my feet. So, catch up with you later?"

"Okay, dear."

They waved, then went their separate ways.

Drew opened the gate and held it to allow Gaby to enter first. The chopped gravel pathway leading from the gate to the brick patio crunched under their steps. Ahead, the California Lilac bush screening the driveway from the pathway was bursting with purple blooms.

Rounding the corner, something felt off.

"Uh, where is the RV?" Gaby said.

Drew whipped his head toward the driveway. "The fuck?" He ran over to where it should have been and threw out his arms in disbelief.

"Jake?" Gaby called at the house. "Jake, are you inside?" No answer. She slowly made her way to join Drew on the side of the house. "Did Jake really just steal our RV?"

Drew was too stunned to know what to say. He swung his head side-to-side, as if the Chinook would magically reappear.

Gaby dug through her purse. After a couple seconds, she came out with her phone. When Drew noticed her open the phone and tap 9-1-, he grabbed for it.

"Hey!" She pulled away from his reach. "What are you doing?"

"What are *you* doing? You can't call the cops."

"Drew, he stole our RV."

"You don't know that for sure. Just . . . give me a minute to think."

Her eyebrows were knitted together. She stared him down, unflinching. She took a shallow breath and her shoulders relaxed. She clicked off the phone.

"Thank you," Drew said. "Let's go inside."

They did, but weren't two steps in before Gaby started speaking her mind.

"Why would he take our RV? *How* did he take it, first of all?"

Drew squeezed his eyes shut. Pinched the bridge of his nose. "I gave him the keys to keep it locked it up."

"Okay . . . Gaby took a deep breath. "I feel like you two *still* aren't telling me everything that went on at that liquor store yesterday."

"What do you mean? I know as much as you do."

Gaby turned from him and walked to the kitchen. Drew watched as she affixed the sonogram photo to the refrigerator at eye-level with a sea turtle magnet. She then took down a glass and filled it with water from the pitcher in the fridge.

Returning to the living room, Gaby plopped down on the couch. She guzzled half the glass of water. Drew took it from her and placed it on the table.

"Something else happened in that liquor store. Had to for him to take off like this."

Drew crossed his arms. "Maybe he didn't steal it or take off. Maybe he took it for a joyride. We could be jumping to conclusions."

Gaby barked a laugh devoid of humor. "Kind of hard to ask him since he doesn't own a phone, huh?"

Dropping his head, Drew said, "Yeah, you got me there."

Gaby immediately softened her tone. "Sorry. I didn't mean to shoot you down like that." She took a minute in thought before speaking again. "Let's say for a minute that he did take off. Is there some other way he would let us know if he's coming back or not?"

Drew perked up. "Actually, yeah. He would leave a note." He held out a finger. "I'll look around . . . Stay here."

"Don't have to tell me twice."

Darting out the front, the storm door slammed shut. Drew ran around the house to the driveway and scanned the area. Nothing. He opened the chain link fence—Jake hadn't relocked the padlock—and hurried to the front of the Transit Connect. Damn. No note wedged under the van's windshield wipers. Nothing left on any of the tires, either. Hell, Jake hadn't even scribbled a little message in the dust on any of the windows.

Drew skulked back to the front porch. "Hey, babe. Was there a house key on that ring for the Chinook?"

Gaby said, "I think? I don't know though. That's your deal."

"What's that supposed to mean?"

"Nothing."

Drew shook his head. Decided to focus on one problem at a time.

He went back inside and checked all around the couch and on and around the TV. Nothing in the kitchen, on the built-in by the front door, or in Drew's dresser drawers, either.

Exasperated, he went back outside where he thoroughly checked the porch and the seating area. Still, nothing. No note held down by a rock or rubber-banded to one anywhere. Drew ambled up the steps and leaned against the porch railing on his elbows.

Behind him, the storm door opened and closed. A moment later, Gaby ran her hand up the middle of his back to his shoulder and rubbed it.

"If he didn't leave a note, what do you think that means?" she asked.

Drew turned to face her. "Hopefully it means he did go for a joyride, or at least is hanging around somewhere close."

It was closing in on 10 a.m. They didn't have anywhere to be until that evening, but Drew had envisioned walking up to Adams Avenue for lunch and a beer either after the three of them figured out a plan, or as a brainstorming break. Now, Drew's stomach twisted itself into knots.

"I still think we should call the police," Gaby said.

Drew pulled away from her. "No. I'm not calling the cops on my only family."

Gaby scoffed. "Excuse me. I'm your family, too, Drew."

"You know what I meant. Besides you and your parents, he's all I've got. We're not calling the cops or reporting the RV stolen, if that's what else you're thinking."

"What if he doesn't bring it back?"

Drew shook his head. "He's not a thief. He'll bring it back."

"Except for those warrants for robbing a Walmart. And you don't sound so sure."

"I'm confused, is all. I wish he'd left a note. Scares me for him. What if you're right and something else happened in that liquor store that he didn't tell us about, something he did wrong? I bet he ran 'cause you freaked him out, saying we should go to the police."

Gaby huffed. "Ay dios mío. Don't you dare put this on me."

Drew averted her gaze. "Maybe I should go look for him," he mumbled.

"No," she said, perturbed. "You have enough on your plate with work and preparing for the baby."

"Okay, but where does that leave us?"

Gaby dropped her hands from her hips, let out an exasperated sigh. It seemed like she'd never answer him, she stayed silent that long. Finally, she said, "I guess we can wait him out. Maybe you're right and he's out on a joyride."

Neither said anything for a few minutes. The tension between them relented.

Drew took a step toward her. Touched her arm. "And you won't call the police?"

She wouldn't look him in the eye, but agreed. "No, I won't."

Chapter Nine

That evening, they had plans for dinner at Gaby's parents' house. Gaby reminded Drew about it while they were at the OB/GYN earlier, but he didn't need a reminder. Drew always looked forward to visiting her moms. They usually tried to visit them two or three times a month, and Gaby went over after work if Drew worked late and on Sundays during football season. Drew had really wanted to bring Jake along this time, so his disappearance soured Drew's enthusiasm.

Pulling away from the curb, Drew noticed an unfamiliar four-door GMC truck parked on the opposite side of the street. It only caught his eye because of its hulking size compared to the other cars and SUVs parked on that side of the street, and the glow of the setting sun made its immaculate black paint job shine.

"Did you remember wine?" Gaby asked.

"What? Oh, yeah. In the back seat. I ran up to Vons while you were showering."

Drew drove them out of their neighborhood, jumping on the 805 on-ramp. Soon, they were headed west on the 8, the sun dropping steadily in front of them, saturating wispy clouds with a rosy, pink hue.

They drove in silence.

Neither had said much over lunch or while killing time that afternoon. Gaby continued reading *What to Expect When You're Expecting* on the couch, while Drew tried to catch up on Padres news on his phone at the dining table. A big four-game home series against the defending champion Atlanta Braves started tonight—the Padres' home opener—and he was curious to see how the media thought they would fare without superstar shortstop Fernando Tatís Jr., who was still on the disabled list from an off-season motorcycle accident. It took Drew all afternoon to read two articles though because his mind constantly strayed to Jake and his whereabouts.

Once on the 5, Drew glimpsed to his left at the shimmering Mission Bay and Fiesta Island. Palm trees rustled. The parking lots were full of RVs, Jeeps, and sport utility vehicles. He could still make out in the dusk a few paddleboarders cruising across the flat water. Drew had great memories of Jake taking him to Fiesta Island on summer nights when he was in high school. They'd hang on the fringes, waiting long enough to ingratiate themselves to a group bonfire. More often than not, Jake mooched them free beers or a joint, and Drew would watch in wonder as his brother made lifelong friends out of the strangers around the bonfire. The first time Jake took him to Fiesta Island was the same night Drew drank his first beer.

Drew took the Balboa Ave. exit, looped around onto Morena Blvd, and entered the neighborhood of Bay Park. They made a series of rights and lefts, climbing through the hilly neighborhood until they came to Brandywine Street.

Gaby's parents' house boasted an incredible view. Rolling hills of coastal scrub brush, the houses that terminated into the east side of the 5, and an infinite sky and Mission Bay in full panoramic. Sunsets were particularly special from their elevated back deck. You could track the sun as it sunk right into the Pacific. And on summer evenings, fireworks at Sea World lit up the night sky, much to the chagrin of his in-laws, but Drew found it magical. Whenever he pictured Gaby having grown up in this house, he became slightly jealous. What a fantastical childhood she'd had.

Drew pulled the Kia into the driveway, shifted into park, and killed the engine. The house itself was simple, but beautiful. A one-story California Ranch they'd modernized the exterior with stucco, solar panels, high-quality windows, and a gorgeous redwood and frosted glass front door. The inside of the house was even nicer; elegant yet warm. Gaby's moms bought the house when Gaby was in kindergarten. They'd paid less than $250,000, a fact they shared often as a "can you believe it?" factoid that absolutely drove a hot poker right through Drew's heart. He couldn't imagine buying a house in San Diego County with a view of the water for so cheap.

Drew and Gaby were collecting their things when Vicky and Ester ran out of the house to greet them. They made a bee-line for Gaby.

"There's my love," said Vicky, wrapping Gaby in an embrace. The chunky black necklace she wore knocked against Gaby's collarbone. "This green dress looks so good on you."

Ester kissed Gaby's cheek. "Mija, you are glowing."

"Aw, thanks, Moms."

"Hi, Drew." Vicky gave him a wink. Gaby may have inherited her skin tone, hair color and eyes from Ester's family, but she'd received Vicky's grace and strength.

"Hey, Vicky. Ester. Thanks for having us over."

Ester scrunched her nose. "Stop. We love when you two visit."

Vicky smiled at him, too. "Come on, kids. Let's go inside." With one arm still wrapped around Gaby, she escorted her daughter to the front door.

Drew and Ester exchanged a smile. Both followed their spouses into the house.

"We brought wine," said Drew, holding up the bottle so Ester could see it. She took it from him with a smile.

"Ah, sangria. How thoughtful."

"It was Gaby's idea. I hope it's good."

Ester patted him on the shoulder. "I'm sure it is." She closed the front door once they were inside. Drew laid his and Gaby's jackets on one of the couches. The living room, dining room, and kitchen were one combined great room, tied together with bleach-blonde wood floors running throughout and every wall painted seafoam green. High-concept paintings hung on every wall, and the accessories on side tables and the bookshelves said fancy, even if Drew didn't quite "get it."

On the other end of the space, directly across from the front door, stood a wall of French doors leading out back. The waning sunset still lit up the yard with a pale pink glow.

"It smells amazing in here," Gaby said, easing into a chair at the fully-set dining table. "What's for dinner?"

"You mean you can't tell?" asked Ester. "Vicky made enchiladas."

Drew loved how Ester pronounced enchiladas with her slight accent. Every syllable dripped off her tongue like warm honey. "Oh, man. That sounds excellent," he said.

"The only man here is *you*." Vicky raised an eyebrow, puppeting her oven mitts at him.

Gaby rubbed circles on her stomach. "Not for long . . ."

Vicky and Ester giggled.

Drew sat down next to Gaby and stroked her arm. She feigned a smile.

He looked to the kitchen, the most recently upgraded space in the home. A couple years ago, they'd installed gray granite countertops and a white subway tile backsplash, maple cabinets, and stainless-steel appliances. The space was clean and comforting. Adding to that vibe, the window over the sink provided a view of a plumeria tree in the front yard, and when in bloom and the window open, its tropical fragrance enveloped the kitchen.

Ester showed the bottle of sangria to Vicky, who was plating the enchiladas. "Look what Gaby and Drew brought."

"Ooh, sangria," Vicky said. "Thank you, kids."

"What do you want to drink, Gaby?"

"Water's fine, please."

"Drew, dear," Vicky said. "Could you get the sour cream out of the refrigerator, please?"

"Sure."

"Thank you."

While Drew retrieved the sour cream, Ester asked about Jake.

"Wasn't he going to join us?"

Gaby sighed.

Drew took a deep breath. "I thought so. But he took off while we were at the doctor."

"That's too bad. We were looking forward to seeing him," Ester said.

"Where did he go?" asked Vicky.

"No clue." Drew set the sour cream in the middle of the table and sat down.

"It's a long story," Gaby added.

Vicky and Ester carried the plates over to the table. They sat. Neither inquired any more about Jake. It was a quality they both possessed that Drew recognized early on when first dating Gaby.

They never pumped a person for more information if they showed resistance. Most times it worked, like silent reverse psychology or something; the tactic usually caused the person to spill their guts. Maybe Vicky and Ester employed the strategy in their elementary school classrooms. Whatever the case, it wasn't going to work this time.

"Dig in," Vicky said.

They did.

The first bite of gooey, cheesy enchilada burned the roof of Drew's mouth, but he didn't care. It was that delicious. Soon, the only other sounds besides the four of them moaning were clinking forks, sour cream being dolloped, and sips of sangria.

After a few minutes, Ester spoke. "We have a bit of big news we wanted to share with you two."

"Oh yeah?" Gaby said, mouth half-full.

Ester looked at Vicky, who motioned for her to continue.

"Your Mom and I have filed some pretty monumental paperwork . . . We will be officially retired at the close of this school year."

"Wow, congratulations," Drew said.

"That's incredible." Gaby extended her arms across the table and Vicky and Ester each took one of their daughter's hands.

"Thank you, both," Vicky said. "I wasn't sure it was what I wanted, but once we turned in the papers, it really felt so freeing, like it was time."

"Well, I know the last couple years with the pandemic have been really tough on you both," Gaby said.

They nodded.

"I'm excited about what's next," Ester said.

Drew swallowed a bite, wiped his mouth with his napkin. "What are you thinking?"

Ester took a sip of sangria. "Nothing set in stone. Maybe we'll start with some regular hiking, go to the beach more often—maybe do some traveling."

"That sounds nice," Gaby said.

Vicky raised an eyebrow. "You kids have the right idea with that RV of yours."

Gaby and Drew groaned in unison.

"Did I say something wrong?"

"No. It's nothing," Gaby said.

"Jake took off in our RV . . ." Drew said.

"Oh, no," Ester said.

Gaby set her napkin on the table. "Yeah."

"I'm sure he'll bring it back soon though." Drew poked at his last bite of enchilada with his fork.

"I'm sure you're right," Vicky said.

"Drew, do you want more to eat?" Ester asked.

"No, thank you. I'm good," he said.

Silence fell. A slight awkwardness began to build until Vicky cleared her throat.

"Gaby. When do you think you'll be able to resume your RN classes?"

Gaby wiped her mouth with her napkin. "Good question. The pandemic threw a wrench in things as it was, and then—" She rubbed her stomach. "I guess it depends on what our schedules look like after the baby comes. There are a lot of factors."

"I hate that you weren't able to complete your course work," Vicky said.

Gaby pursed her lips, and scooted her chair back from the table. "Excuse me. Speaking of the baby. He's doing jumping jacks on my bladder."

Drew got up and assisted Gaby with her chair.

He waited until she was across the living room on the way to the hallway bathroom to sit back down.

Vicky propped her elbows on the table. "So, Drew. Getting excited?"

"About what?" he asked. Vicky gave him a suspect expression. Drew instantly felt foolish. He should have given the question a beat, thought about it for a half-second longer and he would have gotten it. He tried to recover. "Shoot, sorry. My mind's a little preoccupied with my brother. Yes, I can't believe we're going to have a baby in less than three months."

"But are you looking forward to being a father?" Ester asked.

"For sure."

His in-laws stared back at him, unblinking, as though they saw straight through the lie and into the heart of his worry and hesitation. Several painfully long seconds elapsed. The longer they all sat there saying nothing, the more Drew's insides twisted. Thankfully, Ester let him off the hook with a question he didn't anticipate.

"Do you know I have a brother?"

"Uh, yeah. Of course. Ernesto, right? Gaby's biological father."

"That's right."

Vicky and Ester had been very open and honest with Gaby as a child about how she was conceived, given the fact she had two mothers. To ensure she shared blood from both Vicky and Ester, Vicky provided her eggs, while Ester's brother donated his sperm, effectively providing Ester's family DNA to Gaby.

"I don't know if you know this about him though," Ester said. "Ernesto went missing when Gaby was four—a year before we moved into this house. For a while, we thought maybe he moved back to Tijuana, but none of our family ever saw him there. I know he had some money problems . . . After we didn't hear from him for a year, we filed a missing persons report. I thought for sure the police would find him, so I didn't look for him myself."

"Don't blame yourself," Vicky said. "You—we—were busy raising a child."

"I didn't know all that," Drew said. "Gaby doesn't talk much about him."

"My point is this, Drew. You know your brother best. If you are worried about him, don't sit around until you've built up a lifetime of regret because you didn't do something when you had the chance. Take this from me."

Vicky wrapped her arm around Ester, rubbed her shoulder.

Drew didn't know what to say at first, mainly because she'd verbalized everything he'd been wrestling internally with all day, and so succinctly.

"Thanks, Ester. But Gaby would kill me if I went running all over looking for him."

"Ah, mi mujer fuerte." She put a finger to her lips and stared past Drew into the middle distance for a few seconds. Once she looked at him again, she said, "Gaby is hard-headed, she gets that from me. But she's also understanding. Tell her how you feel. I'm sure she will soften."

Drew nodded. He appreciated the sentiment, but he wasn't as sure Gaby would budge.

Over her shoulder, Ester caught a glimpse of Gaby walking back into the living room from the hallway and jumped out of her chair. She shuffled over to meet Gaby.

"¿Todo bien?"

"Yeah, Mom. I only had to pee. What did I miss?"

"Nothing. Drew was telling us how excited he is to become a father."

Gaby's eyebrows raised. Her amber eyes grew to huge disks. Clutching her chest, she said, "Aw, really?"

"Of course," Drew said.

Fibbing to his wife caused a small pang of guilt. He didn't like the feeling, so he told himself he better be upfront with Gaby about the thing he was planning to do.

Chapter Ten

I t was after ten when Drew pulled Gaby's Kia into an open street spot a few houses down from where she normally parked. The brakes only squealed slightly.

"Fun night," he said.

She squeezed his hand, having held it most of the drive home. "I thought so, too."

"Hey, I need to run something by you."

"What is it?" she asked.

"I was talking with your mothers tonight, and, well, I really feel like I need to go track down Jake." Gaby screwed her face and Drew held out a hand. "Let me explain."

"I'm listening."

"What if I check with the friends of his that are in town? He could actually just be hanging with them. It's not going to take too much time to ask around a little. I'm getting worried, Gaby."

Her face softened.

He continued. "Obviously, we've both got jobs and a baby on the way. Those are my priorities. I just—he's just—he's my brother, babe."

Gaby drew him in, hugged him. "Do what you have to do. I understand."

"Thank you."

After the embrace, they walked hand-in-hand up the sidewalk, a cool breeze swirling between the two. When they reached the gate, Gaby realized she'd left her purse in the car.

"I'll grab it," Drew said. "Go wait on the porch."

She agreed and made her way there.

On his way back to the car, Drew looked up at the sky and marveled at the number of visible stars. He breathed a breath of fresh air. It felt like a weight had been lifted off his chest. He could look for his brother and figure all this out.

Drew thought of the GMC truck that had been idling when they left, then, so he scanned the street. It was nowhere in sight, but he did notice another car lurking—a newer Chevrolet Impala parked in Gaby's usual spot with its daytime running lights on. Drew chalked it up to being a rideshare driver or food delivery person.

He retrieved Gaby's purse and squawked the key fob. Halfway up Bernie's driveway, a voice behind him called out his full name in the form of a question. Then repeated himself.

"Sir. Are you Drew Jones?"

Drew turned around.

A white dude about two decades older than himself stood 10 feet or so away staring back with intense focus and holding himself with authoritative posture. The moonlight reflected off his receding hairline. As he approached, Drew saw he had a thick gray mustache, and wore navy blue khakis, a striped button-down, and a solid navy-blue tie. Drew had seen this look before, sending a shiver up his spine.

"Who's asking?"

The man stuck out his hand. There was a gun holstered on his hip and a gold badge on his belt. "Detective Timothy Billberry from Mid-City Division. Now a good time to talk?"

"Uh . . ." Drew panicked inside. A detective? "Fine, I guess. How can I help?" *Don't admit anything. Volunteer nothing.*

"I appreciate that. Won't take long." Up close, Billberry's clothes were disheveled. How long had he been waiting in his car?

"Do you frequent Hoppy Time Liquor over on University, in North Park?"

Fuck. Fuck. Shit. "Uh, yeah, from time to time. It's sorta on my way home most days."

"What do you do?"

"Drywall contractor."

"And when was the last time you were at Hoppy Time?"

The walls felt like they were closing in on Drew. This detective knew something. There must be surveillance video of him and Jake driving off from the liquor store. Drew's eyes flashed to Billberry's hands set on his hips—so close to his handcuffs.

Drew rubbed his chin, looked off like he was giving it some thought. Risk it and lie? Or come clean? No. Make him earn it, a voice said.

"Tuesday. I bought some beer and a slice of pie."

Billberry reached behind his back with one hand. Came out with a notepad. Flipped it open and jotted down some notes. "And you haven't been there since?"

"I'm not an alcoholic, Detective."

Billberry laughed. "That's funny. Okay, well, here's the part where I have to inform you of some not so good news."

Shit.

Billberry reached behind his back again. This was it. Cuffs were coming out this time. Instead, he whipped a piece of plastic at Drew like a magician revealing a person's playing card.

Drew took it and stared. It was his debit card he'd given to Jake before the shooting.

"You must have dropped it on Tuesday after your purchase. Was found while we were investigating a crime that occurred there yesterday."

"Oh, wow."

"Yeah." Billberry squinted.

"I saw on the news there was a shooting there. Hope everyone is okay."

Billberry straightened his posture. Didn't say a word.

Drew swallowed. "I know Ahmed, one of the clerks there. Is he okay?" *Let him be okay.* Drew knew he had a family, but felt shitty he couldn't remember if he had two kids or three.

The detective let the question hang for a few long seconds before answering. "I'd love to tell you he is, but I can't share anything about an open investigation."

"Sure, I get that."

"So, to clarify: You did not visit Hoppy Time Liquor at any point yesterday?"

Either this cop was trying to catch him in a lie—which, why would he bother if had surveillance video?—or he was fishing.

Drew shook his head. "No, came straight home after work yesterday."

Billberry thrust out his hand, startling Drew. "I'm gonna need that back. You'll receive it after we conclude our investigation. Probably quicker if you order a new one from your bank."

Drew handed his debit card to him. Billberry pocketed it while staring Drew down.

"All right, sir. Thank you for your cooperation." He handed Drew his business card.

Drew accepted the card. "No worries," he said, but he had worries. Plenty of them.

***

"What took you so long? Did I hear you talking to someone?" Gaby asked when he finally met her on the porch.

"Pete next door. We got talking about the Padres." It was the best he could come up with. He couldn't tell her about the detective. She'd insist Drew call him back, throw Jake to the wolves before even hearing Jake's side.

"I'm freezing and have to *go*. Let me inside."

"Sure, babe," he said, fumbling with shaky hands to grab the house key on the key ring.

Once inside, she hustled to the bathroom. Drew made for the kitchen. He swung open the freezer door, yanked out the bottle of Campo Azul tequila, and took a long pull. After swallowing, he gasped.

The tension in his shoulders relaxed slightly.

He could do this. He had a couple rooms of texture to finish out his work at the La Jolla house in the morning, then he would find his brother and get some fucking answers out of him.

Chapter Eleven

He started at the first place that made sense. The Ocean Beach Pier. It was where Jake said he'd been when he called Drew three days earlier. Hopefully his friends were still camped there before pushing on to Yellowstone like Jake had also said.

Regardless, the people who hung around the pier and the vibe they set were definitely Jake's scene. If Drew's hunch was correct that he hadn't left town, the pier seemed as good a place as any to start.

Drew pulled the Transit Connect into the pier's small parking lot at 10 a.m. He'd already swung by the La Jolla remodel and got in and out. Textured the last two rooms before Mon could finish her second cup of coffee. Now he had the rest of the day for his pursuit.

After cautiously moving past two SDPD patrol cars parked sixty-nineing at the entrance, Drew found a parking spot surprisingly easily. He backed in between a ratted-out gold Toyota Tercel packed to the headliner with personal belongings and a clean silver Prius.

He stepped out of the van. The sky was clear and the temperature already at sixty degrees on its way to a high of sixty-five. Over the sounds of traffic on Abbott and Newport and people shuffling all around was the ever-present dominance of crashing waves.

The wind shifted and the strong odor of pot caught Drew by surprise. Sure, weed had been legal in California for seven years now, but not in public. With cops lurking nearby it struck him as weird. Then again, OB was weird. Fun weird. He always enjoyed that about the neighborhood. When he and Gaby first moved in together, they lived in an apartment a few blocks away on Brighton Ave. A 400-square-foot closet. Didn't matter to them though. It was less than a two-minute walk to the beach in one direction and a little more to the row of bars and restaurants in the other. Hard to believe that was six years ago. The place probably rented for three grand a month these days.

Drew scanned the parking lot, deciding where to begin. No RVs, and all the vehicles in the interior weren't occupied, so he headed toward those parked in the beach-facing spots.

On the way, a Black guy with gold dreads rollerbladed through the lot, right in Drew's path. He paused, let the guy pass. To his right, near the cop cars, a faded blue Chevy Astro van sat with every door wide open; two bros drying off and peeling off their wetsuits after a surf session, talking about their recent "scores." They didn't look like Jake's type.

The line of vehicles facing the beach was a mix. There were several sedans and small pickup trucks, all of which parked head-on, presumably to give the drivers a view of the ocean. Drew zeroed in on the four vans. Each one backed into their spots.

The van on the end was another Astro—silver, with bubbled-up tinted windows, a red handicap placard hanging from the rearview, and its dashboard littered with fast food containers and other random junk. Rounding the van, Drew pulled out his phone and brought up the selfie he'd taken with Jake at Hodad's when they'd met for lunch.

A burnout in his fifties sat in the back of the van staring at the water, his scabby legs dangling off the bumper. The smell of cheap weed flooded from out of the interior of the van.

"Excuse me, sir." Drew held up the photo. "I'm looking for my brother, Jake."

"So what?" The burnout's breath reeked of booze.

"Have you seen him? He's the one in the Padres hat."

The man gave a cursory look, and barked, "No."

Drew held up his hands and shuffled away.

Headed down the boardwalk, two young women—one Asian and the other a redhead—wearing shorts and sports bras jogged past him. Drew approached the next van, an old Dodge Caravan. The back hatch door was swung up, but no one was in the back.

He stepped off the boardwalk to peek inside the open sliding door on the side. There he found a young white guy sprawled out on his back on a sleeping bag.

"Hey, man. Can I bug you for a second?" No answer. Drew stepped closer. "Bro?"

"What, man?" The guy sat up. He was a kid—maybe twenty-years-old. Tops. Wearing a wrinkled teal knit shirt, purple swim trunks, and brandished more than two dozen friendship bracelets on his right wrist.

"I'm looking for my brother. Wondered if you know him?"

The kid looked at Drew's phone. "Nah."

"But have you seen him?"

"Nope, sorry. Good luck though."

"Thanks."

The next van Drew approached was a rusted-out, maroon-striped Ford. The back doors were shut. A splintered yellow surfboard was wedged behind the spare tire. Moving to the driver's door, Drew shielded his eyes and peered through the dirty window. It didn't seem like anyone was home, so he decided to move on to the last van in the row.

Drew got his hopes up as soon as he set eyes on the light blue Honda Odyssey. It was clean, with a luggage case on the roof. These weren't beach squatters. They traveled.

The back hatch was up. Seated on the bumper sharing a joint was a Latino man and white woman, both in their twenties. They were a matching set. Both wore 80s-style wrap-around, blue-tinted sunglasses and loud tie-dyed shirts.

"Hey, I'm Drew," he said to the man, who was stroking his thick beard.

"What up? I'm Jorge and this is Cody."

Drew held out the selfie. "I'm looking for my brother, Jake, and wanted to see if either of you know him."

Cody reached for the phone, and Drew's heart jumped. He handed it to her. She took her time inspecting the photo.

"Oh yeah," she finally said. "We don't know him, but he's cute."

Jorge elbowed her.

"What? He is, look."

"I seen," Jorge said.

Drew cleared his throat. "What did you mean, 'Oh yeah.'"

"Sorry, buddy," Jorge said. We don't know him, but we did see him."

Excitement surged through Drew. "Really? When? Where?"

"Right here, man. He borrowed our phone a few days ago to make a call."

Drew deflated. Realized that was probably when Jake called him to meet up. "Ah, okay. So, you two live around here full time? Cause I thought maybe with the travel luggage . . ." Drew pointed to the roof.

"Yeah, man. San Diego's home base. That's like, our dresser. You know?"

Drew nodded. "Cool." He held out his hand. After a nudge from Jorge, Cody gave Drew back his phone.

Jorge flicked his chin. Extended the joint. "Want a hit before you go?"

Drew waved. "I'm good, but thanks."

"Good luck finding your brother," said Cody.

Drew flicked his chin, threw them a half-hearted wave, turned around, and continued south on the boardwalk.

He made it a few steps before he stopped and turned to the water. His gaze followed the OB Pier to its terminus, then he scanned the ocean. Well beyond the less than a dozen surfers who looked bored with the every-flattening water, were two boats. Both too far away to tell what kind they were.

Where the hell was Jake?

The vastness of the Pacific gave Drew the demoralizing feeling that his brother could be anywhere. Past the jetty on his right were Pacific Beach and La Jolla, two more places Jake could be. San Diego wasn't a big city, but sprawling all the same. Finding his brother wouldn't be easy.

After a beat or two, Drew determined to get back to it. He took off toward Newport Ave. Once there, he turned east, toward OB's main drag.

A few restaurants were opening, and workers stirred in the bars as well, righting barstools and sweeping patios. Not paying attention, Drew dodged a man in a wheelchair headed the opposite direction. A few transients sat leaned up against a utility box wrapped in a beautiful mural of the ocean.

After passing a walk-up margarita bar, Drew hooked a right on Bacon Street. Both sides of the two-lane road were lined with vehicles, none of them a '94 Chinook Concourse, though. It would've been like Jake to park it somewhere in plain sight. Maybe if Drew explored a bit, he might get lucky. He wished he was driving to be able to cover more ground. He'd make a loop and grab the Transit Connect to do a bigger sweep of the area.

This section of Bacon St. he walked featured a hodgepodge of businesses. A pet supply place on the right; design studio on the left; cell phone store, yoga studio, and a trendy ale house farther up. Drew reached Niagara Ave. and inspected both ways. Not a free street spot in either direction. And no RVs.

Taking a right, which led back to the pier, Drew's stomach rumbled. He checked his phone. It wasn't even eleven yet. Maybe hunger wasn't the feeling his body was trying to convey. A breeze picked up, rustling the fronds of palm trees lining the street.

Passing apartments and single-family houses, it dawned on him that he was coming up on the Surfview Cottages. Drew checked his phone again. No missed calls. Lydia, the property manager, said they would be selecting the contractors today. Drew's shoulders tightened. Winning the bid would be ideal. Having finished the La Jolla house, he had a rare lull between jobs, with nothing on his calendar the following week. If he didn't land anything soon, he'd have to accept some of the smaller jobs he usually passed on. He really wanted—needed—the Surfview job.

With that, he'd completed a circle and was back at the pier.

Time to get the work van and cruise the neighborhood. He could swing by Sunset Cliffs too—another popular spot where van lifers liked to squat for hours on end. He hustled down the stairs to the beach, weaving his way around a fisherman climbing up to the pier, and a few transients hanging about.

Halfway across the parking lot was when he heard familiar voices. The couple with the matching sunglasses shouting his name.

"Bro, Drew," Jorge stood behind his van, waving at him.

Drew hesitated, but Jorge's excitement intrigued him.

"What's up?" he asked, reaching Jorge.

"Come here. This couple says they know your brother."

"Really?"

"Yeah, c'mon." Jorge waved him on. Drew followed. Jorge's flip-flops popped as he hurried to the boardwalk and juked right.

Behind the rusted-out Ford van stood Cody and another woman and man couple, probably closer to Drew's age or older, but still young.

"Hey, this is the dude we were telling you about," said Jorge.

The new couple didn't budge. Both held suspicious looks on their faces.

Drew nodded. Took a step toward them and extended a hand to the man, who wore frayed camo cargo shorts and a black hoodie. "Hey, I'm Drew."

The man let Drew hang for a beat or two before shaking his hand. "Kyle. Hey, man. This is Jaycee."

"Hi," Drew said.

"Are you really Jake's brother?" Jaycee asked in a vocal fry. She was pretty. Wavy light brown hair, green eyes. She wore black leggings and a blue hoodie. Drew suddenly felt dopey wearing his contractor whites amongst four chill nomads.

"That's me. I mean, we're foster brothers, but yeah."

"How do we really know you're the Drew that Jake talks about?" Kyle's face shifted back to sus mode.

"Uh . . ." Drew thought about it. "So, wait. Are you the friends he drove down with from the Bay Area, and you guys are heading to Yellowstone next week?"

Kyle looked at Jaycee, who dropped her arms and shrugged.

"That's us," Kyle said. "Guess you are him."

Cody let out a little squeal, and clapped her hands together repeatedly and hopped, while Jorge said, "Right on."

"Let me open up the van and we can talk some more." Kyle extended his fist to Jorge, who bumped it. "Cool to meet you two. Let's hang later."

"Sounds dope," Jorge said.

"We'll bring the—" Cody pantomimed smoking a joint with two fingers.

"Cool. See ya," Jaycee said.

Cody and Jorge shuffled off toward Newport Ave., hand-in-hand up the boardwalk.

Kyle opened the back doors of the Ford, revealing an inviting interior that looked like one big bed. A fluffy pink and cream comforter and a dozen pillows adorned the space, and a string of LED lights were strung along the perimeter of the headliner.

"We woke up an hour or so ago and went for a walk on the beach, else we'd have this rolled up. Sorry," Kyle said.

"No worries." Drew rubbed his chin. He took a seat on the bumper, following Kyle's gesture. The aroma of fresh laundry clung to the inside of the van, with a slight hint of weed. Kyle sat next to Drew, in the middle, with Jaycee on the other end.

"Have you seen Jake in the last day or two?" Drew blurted out.

"Whoa, man," Kyle said. "Let's vibe first. We're big on trust."

Jaycee nodded in agreement.

"Okay. What do you want to know?"

"It's nothing we *want* to know. We want to get to know *you*," Jaycee said.

Damn hipsters. Drew flashed them a tight, closed-lip smile.

"I mean, we do know you already, more or less, from all the stories Jake's told us over the years. Weird to actually meet this brother of his," Kyle said.

Drew bobbed his head. "Yeah, know what you mean. I haven't met very many of Jake's friends. He usually pops in a few times a year to say hi, and hits the road again."

"Why don't you ever go with him?" Jaycee asked.

Drew shrugged. "No time, I guess. Last time I went on a road trip with him was the summer I graduated high school. We went to Yosemite. Camped out for two months. After that, life just happened, you know?"

"Damn, that bums me out," Kyle said.

Jaycee pouted. "What do you mean life happened?"

"Oh, you know. I needed a job and got hooked up with this old guy who was a master drywaller. He became my mentor, and we worked a ton before he retired. Once I got my license and started my own thing, I really didn't have much free time. The only thing I did outside of work was play sand volleyball. That's how I met my wife. So, I spent all my free time with her, and now we're going to have a baby." Drew shrugged. "Life."

"A baby, that's awesome," Jaycee said. "Congratulations!"

"For real," Kyle added. "Spoiler alert, though. We already knew you were having a baby cause Jake told us."

Drew sat up straight. "So that must mean you've seen him recently . . ."

Kyle and Jaycee nodded.

"Was he in a Chinook RV?

Jayce giggled. "Uh, yeah. We were like, 'Who'd you steal that from?' We were totally kidding, but he said he borrowed it from his brother, and that he'd—you—would understand."

Drew contorted his face. "I'm confused. He still hanging around San Diego?"

"Okay, look." Kyle held up his hands, palms out. "He's still in town, I can tell you that."

"Did he seem like he was scared or in danger?"

Kyle turned to Jaycee and they exchanged a look that told Drew he was on to something.

"I don't know about that . . . but we did get the sense later that something was . . ."

"Off," Jaycee said.

"Did he tell you where he was going or staying?" Drew asked.

Jaycee leaned into Kyle and whispered in his ear. He whispered back in hers. A few seconds passed. Jaycee looked Drew in the eyes. "Sorry, trying to do what's right."

"I only want to find my brother and make sure he's okay."

Kyle bobbed his head. "Right on. Okay. He said he was going to go to the RV resort where we met him a few years back, south of here. Said he'd be there for a day or two, and if you came looking for him, to tell you that's where he'd be."

"He brought it up super caszh," Jaycee said. "So, we had no way of knowing he might be in trouble. Figured it was some game between you two, like, 'come find your RV.' You know?"

Drew took a slow, deep breath, trying to stay cool. "What's the name of the place?"

"Sun Outdoors," Kyle said. "It's in Chula Vista."

Three seagulls landed on the boardwalk in front of them and squawked. Drew wanted to take off running to his work van, but he had one last question first.

"So, hey. Can I get your numbers in case I find him or need to ask you something else?"

Kyle patted his pockets. "No cell phones for us. We live life in the moment—" He gestured out at the beach. "Enjoy being present."

Of course. Sounded familiar. "Ah, gotcha. Well, it was really nice to meet you both."

Drew hopped out of the van, and shook both their hands.

"Good luck, Jaycee said.

"Yeah, man," Kyle said. "We're taking off on Monday, so let us know if you find him before then."

"Oh," Drew exclaimed. "Is Jake still planning to go with you?"

Kyle shook his head. "No, that's the whole reason he swung by. To tell us he wasn't going with us, that he was hanging around San Diego for a while, but couldn't say how long."

Chapter Twelve

After quickly cruising by Sunset Cliffs—figuring he was too close not to at least check—and finding nothing, Drew drove home.

Turned out he was hungry. And if he planned to drive all the way to Chula Vista to follow up on the lead from Jake's friends, he'd need to eat a free meal to offset the cost of gas.

He should have made himself a lunch before heading out in the morning, same as every workday, but he'd been too amped up and not thinking straight. Maybe he'd skip lunch. He didn't want to do anything to irritate Gaby, not after she was so understanding about his need to look for his brother. He only hoped he could find him before that detective. Not telling Gaby the police had shown up asking questions was probably not the best idea, but again, Drew didn't want to worry her if he didn't have to.

Drew guided the Transit Connect into its spot behind their home. After cutting the engine, he held up his hands. They were shaking. A mix of anxious energy and hunger.

A gust of wind blew as he entered the property through the chain-link gate. The wooden fence gate at the other end of the yard banged. Like it hadn't been latched properly. Drew went over and pulled the gate shut, shaking his head. Gaby must have been running late when she left for work. Then another noise grabbed his attention, like a picture frame falling off a wall.

"Bernie?" Drew gripped the top of his landlord's fence, stood on his toes and looked over. Bernie's back door was closed, a sure sign he wasn't home.

There was another loud noise, and this time Drew immediately clocked it as coming from his own house. He whipped around to see their storm door was wide open.

"What the—" He darted there. Bounded up the porch steps to the front door, where he stopped cold in his tracks in the threshold.

Dead ahead, at the other end of the house in the hallway, stood a tall, thin man in dark blue pants, matching jacket, and a black ballcap tipped up on his head. He heard Drew and turned. Stared daggers at him with deep-set eyes.

Drew shouted. "Who are you? Get the fuck out of my house."

The man didn't flinch. Instead, he turned back to where he'd been looking—in the bedroom and barked. "Shaw."

Before Drew could understand what was going on, an enormous man wearing jeans and tan boots burst from around the corner and rushed him. In a split second, he slammed into Drew, driving him out of the house and tackling him onto the front porch. Every ounce of breath in Drew's lungs exhaled in one violent ejection when their combined weight hit the wooden floor. His vision went black with pulsating streaks of light. Ears rung with a shrill, deafening tone.

Next, a hot wave of shit breath filled his nose and mouth. Drew peeked. Shaw's face hovered over his, the man's eyes those of a rabid animal. Drew tried to speak but didn't have enough breath to do so. Then, what little air remained in his lungs was expelled when Shaw pressed himself off Drew with two meaty fists to his chest.

Grimacing, Drew flailed his arms to his sides. Blood rushed into his fingertips. His head lulled to the side, and he rolled over in the same direction. Next came involuntary coughing.

Shaw leaned over him. Growled. "Stay down."

"No," said the other man, his voice low, menacing. "Get up, Drew." Shaw kicked the sole of Drew's work boot.

Who were these thugs, and how the fuck did they know his name?

Drew's cough persisted, but slowed gradually into jagged spurts. He pressed a hand to the deck and worked to get up. Shaw grabbed his forearm and yanked, pulling Drew into an awkward slumped sit-up. The big man yanked him again, this time bringing him to his knees.

"Stop." Drew pushed Shaw away. Slowly, he made it to his feet. He doubled over and squeezed his knees. Sucked wind. "Who . . . who . . . are you?"

Shaw got in his face, putting his nose within a centimeter of Drew's. "That's Zan West, motherfucker. And that's your last question."

Drew straightened up, but before he could right himself fully, Shaw shoved him hard with both hands. Drew lost his footing; his momentum sent him flying backward into the porch railing. The wood creaked and splintered. A sharp pain shot up his spine. Then, hands were on him again. Shaw manhandled him by the shoulders, pulling him away from the railing. He patted Drew down. Shoulders, chest and back; down to his waist and pockets. Shaw pulled out Drew's cell phone and keys, slammed them on the porch rail. The pat-down continued to his thighs, quads, and down to his calves. Shaw finished up with his meaty fingers prodding around Drew's ankles, above the tops of his work boots.

"He's clean." Shaw stepped aside.

The thin man in dark blue took three methodical steps forward. He possessed a surfer's frame with long limbs, and a deeply sunken face. Cheekbones as hollow as an ocean floor trench. His wasn't a face born of malnutrition or substance abuse. No. This face held haunted horrors. A simmering violence that drove a spike of fear right through Drew's chest.

Zan bore his creepy eyes into Drew's. Without breaking concentration, he pointed at his Latino muscle, whipped his arm across his body. "Search his van."

Shaw lunged in front of Drew and snatched his keys off the porch railing.

Whatever they were looking for in his van didn't matter right then. Catching his breath was Drew's sole concern, so he offered no objections. Shaw stormed down the porch steps, and disappeared around the corner of the house.

A few seconds passed with Zan doing nothing other than staring down Drew. It was enough time that Drew was finally able to catch his breath.

"The big black GMC truck parked out front last night was yours." Zan smirked.

Drew decided to press his luck.

"I know your bodyguard said no more questions . . ." Drew paused to cough. "But I could give you what you want a lot quicker if I could, you know, ask questions."

Zan pulled his ballcap down tight on his forehead. "What I want . . ." He jabbed a finger into Drew's sternum and rose his voice. "Is my motherfucking money back."

"What?" Drew's brow knitted with confusion. "What money?"

Taking another deliberate step forward, Zan flashed gritted teeth. "The money you and your partner stole from me at my fucking liquor store three days ago."

Drew's mind reeled with the events of that day.

Sitting outside Hoppy Time Liquor. Gunshots. Jake running out, bloody. Squeezing his backpack. Fleeing the scene. Jake shutting down on the drive home. Hugging his backpack. *The backpack*. Shit. Is that why Jake ran away so suddenly? Did he rob the liquor store?

"Liquor store?" Drew said.

"Drop the fucking act, kid. I have you both on surveillance. You, waiting in your work van out front. Your partner running out and you both taking off." Zan's face reddened as he spoke. "Not to mention frame by fucking frame of what went down inside the store."

Shit. At the mention of surveillance video Drew thought of the police detective, Billberry. Didn't seem like he had video and only found Drew because he recovered his debit card from the crime scene. This Zan guy must have withheld the video from the police or scrubbed it before they arrived. But why?

"Look," Drew said, holding up his hands. "All I know is I heard two gunshots and next thing I know, my brother ran out saying the clerk shot a robber. I don't know about any money. And now you're saying my brother robbed your place?"

Zan's lips parted and a sick smile spread across his face. "Brother, huh?"

Drew tensed. What did Jake do?

"How did you and your *brother* know about my place?" Zan asked.

"It's not like that. I go by there on my way home from work. Buy beer. Lottery tickets sometimes. Shit like that. My brother—"

"What's his name?"

Drew tucked his chin, averted his eyes.

Zan pressed his hip to Drew's body and a hard object dug into Drew's side. "His name."

"Jake."

Zan eased off him. "Keep going."

Drew shook his head to regather his thoughts. "Uh . . . Oh, yeah. My brother, he doesn't even live here. He's never been to the liquor store until I took him."

Shaw rounded the corner then, climbed the porch. His forehead beaded with sweat. "Nothing. Construction shit. That's it."

"No backpack? No straps?" Zan asked.

The big man shook his head no.

Eyes back on Drew, Zan ran his tongue across his top teeth. Sucked. Took a step back and crossed his arms. "Well, we've got a real problem, Drew. Your brother sure as fuck robbed me. Not the store. *Me*. Which is way fucking worse. And I want it back." He flipped his jacket and shirt tail up to reveal the butt of a black pistol sticking out of his waistband.

"How much did he steal?" Drew asked.

"Why the fuck you asking that?" Shaw said. "Don't you know, motherfucker?"

Zan waved him off while keeping his eyes on Drew. "One-hundred grand."

Drew choked, the coughing returning.

When he could gather himself, he asked, "How?"

"How what?"

"How was there that much cash in your safe?"

Zan advanced, slammed his chest into Drew's. "That's my fucking business, bitch."

Drew nodded.

"Since you insist you don't know dick, *your* business is to tell me where your brother is at so I can get my money back."

Sweat rolled down Drew's back. Stomach tied in knots. He didn't know how to respond.

"Where is Jake?" Zan said. "Call him up. Get him over here right fucking now."

Drew retreated as far as he could until the porch railing dug into his spine. He had nowhere to go. No one to cry to for help.

"He doesn't have a phone. And . . . he . . ."

"What? He what?"

"He took off two days ago in my RV."

Zan stepped back, threw up his hands, and barked a humorless laugh. "Of course." He rested his hand on his gun. "You lying to me? Where is he, really?"

"I'm not lying," Drew pleaded. "Not sure. But I think he's still in town."

Zan moved, pointed to Shaw, then at Drew.

Shaw lunged and punched Drew in the stomach, doubling him over.

Pain coursed through his core: locked up his abs, spread another aching wave radiating through his already tender back. If Shaw or Zan were saying anything, he couldn't hear it over the ringing in his ears. He dropped to a knee and hugged his stomach.

The coughing returned, and some blood along with it. He spat it off the porch.

Shaw grabbed his arm and pulled him to his feet.

"Sup, Drew? What are we going to do about this?" Zan readjusted his ballcap.

With absolutely no reason to feel so bold, Drew, wincing, said, "How do you know my name anyway?"

"Fool . . ." Shaw cocked his fist.

Drew flinched, shielded his face with his arms.

Zan laughed. Waved off Shaw. "I already told you I have you on video. Pretty easy to track down the owner of DJ's Drywall."

"Sorry. Guess you've turned my brain to mush."

"Imagine what will happen if I don't get my money back."

Drew didn't want to imagine. People killed for a lot less than $100k. Brain foggy, he tried to think of a way out of this but nothing came to mind.

Zan cocked his head. "What are we going to do about this, Drew?"

Blood rushed behind Drew's eyes and pounded. He held a hand to the side of his head and felt like he could puke. He knew he needed to choose his next words carefully. One idea he could offer pushed to the front of his mind. While he hated to, his brother put him in this position and Drew had no other solution.

"I—I just started looking for him earlier today, to get our RV back. But San Diego isn't so small when you're looking for one person. So, it might take me a while since he has no phone and I have no other way to contact him."

Zan straightened. Rolled his neck. "You love your brother, Drew?"

"What kind of question is that? Of course."

"Tight. I thought so. Here's what's going to happen. You're going to track down your brother and deliver him and the money to me."

Drew's stomach tightened as Zan continued.

"You bring your brother *and* the money—IN TACT—and I'll show Jakey mercy."

Drew covered his mouth, felt his hot breath against his fist.

"Don't look so concerned." Zan smacked Drew's shoulder, making him flinch.

"What do you mean you'll show him mercy?"

Zan laughed, head jerking back. "I'll be straight with you. He's gonna get fucked up. Bad. He won't die, as long he can get to a hospital fast."

The words cut through Drew like a razor blade. "I'll find him, I promise."

"Damn straight, you will. And I'm giving you until end of day Monday to get it done."

Drew's stomach dropped. "Three days? I've got work, and do you know how many places there are around here to camp with RV? I need more time than that."

Zan stared at Drew, through him. Shaw didn't move either. The three of them completely motionless, as if someone had paused the world. Drew tensed. Had he pushed this mad man too far? Would Gaby come home to find him shot to death on their front porch?

Then, Zan snapped to life.

"I hear what you're saying and I'm not an unreasonable man. I'll give you ten days. Bring Jake and the cash to me by midnight next Monday and we'll be straight."

"What happens if I can't find him?"

"Good question . . . If I have to find him myself—I'll shoot that thieving piece of shit in the fucking head, Drew, and leave him to rot out in the desert." Zan let his words hang thick for a several long moments. "We straight?"

Nerves buzzing, Drew nodded furiously.

Zan elbowed Shaw. "Go get a burner for Drew here."

Shaw took off toward the front gate to get to the street.

Zan smoothed his clothes. Tipped his ballcap up on his head.

"I'm going to give you a burner phone and if it rings, you pick up. You find Jake, you call me. You find your RV—you call me. I want updates so I know we're on the same page about this. That's the only way I'm giving you ten fucking days to get this done. Straight?"

"Yes," Drew said. His hands shook, so he stuffed them in his pockets.

"So there's no misunderstanding: Jake and my money. Not one or the other. Both."

Drew gulped. "Okay."

"One last thing." Zan reached into his jacket, causing Drew to flinch. Zan didn't pull his gun, however. Instead, he retrieved a small, square piece of paper, gave it a look, then flipped it around to show Drew the sonogram photo that Gaby had displayed on the refrigerator. Drew's body felt like he'd been set on fire, and the taste of blood filled his mouth from biting down hard on his lip.

"No, man, please, no!"

Zan waved the sonogram photo like it was a developing Polaroid before sticking it back in his jacket pocket. "Don't make me regret giving you and your brother this opportunity, Drew. I may look like one of your "brahs," but I guarantee you I will destroy everything you love in this life if you fuck this up."

Chapter Thirteen

*W*hat the fuck, Jake?

He'd robbed the liquor store? Scratch that. Jake apparently stole this Zan West guy's huge stash of cash? One-hundred grand? It felt unreal. Like a movie.

Drew didn't want to believe it, but it made sense based on Jake's behavior following the shooting. Now he was in the wind, and Drew left behind to carry the burden. Familiar story.

The house was a mess. Couch cushions tossed, framed pictures broken on the floor. Same scene in their bedroom. Everything rifled through without regard. In the kitchen, drawers and cabinets were slung open; pots and pans littering the floor. And no sonogram photo on the fridge. How would he explain where it went? There was no way he could tell Gaby the truth about that.

Standing in the bathroom, Drew stared at himself in the mirror. Stunned. Trying to process what happened. A flood of questions now came to him that he wished he would've thought to ask, but probably wouldn't have anyway, given the violent, imposing, menacing nature of his assailants. Whoever Zan was, Drew whole-heartedly believed every threat he spewed. Goddamn Jake and for whatever he'd gotten them involved in.

Drew gingerly peeled off his shirt, revealing splotches of redness: the beginnings of bruising to his chest, sides, and back. The back of his head throbbed too: a delayed pain response to having his head bounce off the porch deck when Shaw tackled him.

Not finding any blood or wounds on his body needing attention, he put his shirt back on. Made a mental note to ice the more painful areas after cleaning up the place. Gaby wouldn't be home for several hours, and Drew would need every minute to get things back in order. She couldn't know Jake's actions lured two violent criminals to break into their home, or that Drew now had a gun to his back—and to hers and their unborn child's.

Starting in the bedroom, Drew gathered up the clothes strewn all over and piled them on the bed. As he refolded the laundry, he tried to convince himself that he wouldn't be betraying Jake by finding him and bringing him to this lunatic, Zan. He'd be saving his life. It sounded ridiculous, but Drew needed to believe it. Otherwise, what kind of brother was he?

Once he got the bedroom in order, he moved to the living room. Not much damage done here due to their minimalist tendencies. The built-in was in disarray with books scattered all about and picture frames knocked over. Drew saw one of the pictures on the floor by the TV. He picked it up. Pain shot through his ribs. Behind a spiderweb of broken glass, their younger selves smiled back. Gaby and him on their wedding day.

They'd married on Pacific Beach in a small ceremony more than four years ago. Gaby, her parents, a dozen or so of her closest friends, two or three of Drew's that he didn't keep up with these days, and a non-religious officiant.

Goddamn, they had big dreams back then.

If they had come true, Gaby would've been an RN by now, Drew bringing in six-figures, and they would be living in their own beautiful slice of the San Diego dream, preferably within walking distance to the ocean. That's the thing about dreams, though, Drew knew. You can wish for them all you want, but life usually kicks them from out of your grasp when you want them the most.

Drew set the picture on the coffee table, and stacked others with broken glass on top. Those that hadn't been broken, he placed back on the built-in where he thought he remembered them being. He pulled the vacuum cleaner out of the hall closet and vacuumed the living room.

After that, Drew moved to the kitchen. Before attempting any clean-up here, he decided to take a break. First, he popped five ibuprofens. Next, from the freezer he pulled out two bags of green beans and a five-pound bag of strawberries from Costco, returned to the living room, flopped on the couch, and iced his bruises.

It was 3 p.m. If he worked quick enough, he would get everything in order before Gaby came home. He would also need to come up with an explanation for the broken picture frame and several shattered dishes.

Drew eased back against the bag of strawberries he'd wedged between him and the couch. The cold felt good. Knowing what he would have to do to ultimately save his loved ones did not feel good in the slightest.

INTERLUDE

Zan sat seething in his truck. Starving from the adrenaline dump. He was waiting out front of a closed wine bar across from Handy Liquor, just a few blocks from Drew Jones's place.

Shaw would be back after pulling the clean cash and heating up a frozen burrito for Zan. But Zan's stomach was ablaze. He needed something now.

Stretching for the glove box, he opened it, fished out some beef jerky.

Biting off a chunk, he hung his arm out the window. Adams Ave. Busy as fuck for a weekday. Vehicles flew by in both directions. Pedestrians crowded the sidewalks, passing restaurants, bars, and shops. Normal Heights. More like *Normie* Heights. Least the liquor store gave the corner cred.

Of his eight liquor stores across the city, this Jake and his working-stiff brother had to hit his biggest money maker. Infuriating. He should've collected that morning. Stretch told him the clean was good to go. Instead, Zan had wanted to surf a few more sets. Stretch got shot as a result, and Zan lost a hundred grand. Fucking bullshit.

He ripped off another bite of jerky. Banged his palm on the truck's door, but Shaw didn't hear him. Head buried, he probably was still heating up the burrito.

Stretch's fate wasn't on him though. One of those series of unfortunate events things. What Zan hadn't been able to figure out yet was if Ahmed was being truthful. That he'd accidently shot Stretch—aiming at Jake while the two wrestled—or if Ahmed intended to shoot Stretch. The video showed nothing conclusive. He counted on the loyalty of the store owners and clerks who funneled his dirty money through their businesses in exchange for upgrades and protection. First, though. He needed to hear Jake's side to know precisely how many bullets he would fire.

Shaw was wrapping up. Had the cash in one hand and a plastic sack with Zan's burrito in his other. About time.

Rarely did it cross Zan's mind to wonder how different his life would have turned out if he hadn't sunk his professional surfing chances by blowing out his knee at fifteen. Not sure why it did now. He'd been climbing the world rankings. Would've banked. Not a single doubt. He was predestined—his skills handed down through his blood. On a board since age two, it never occurred to him he would do anything else.

If the injury wasn't enough, when Zan was seventeen, pancreatic cancer tagged his father. He kicked the bucket six months later. Choices were few after those two colliding events. Caring for his mother on minimum wage jobs was never going to cut it.

So, he reinvented. Hustled. Scrapped. Built what he had now all on his own.

Maybe that's why his past came to him now: No fucking way in hell two punks were taking off with any piece of his hard-earned present or future.

Shaw jogged across the street, dodging a couple cars. Zan snickered. Big fool wasn't built for running.

"Want me to drive so you can eat?" said Shaw, standing outside the passenger's door.

"Nah. I'm good. Get in."

Shaw did. Handed Zan the sack with the burrito. He pulled it out, along with a couple paper towels. Spread the plastic bag across his lap. After wrapping one of the paper towels around the burrito, he took a huge bite. Moaned. Put the truck into gear and gunned it, cutting off a honking car.

Shaw shot the driver the bird out the window.

Zan eyed the other sack at Shaw's feet. "How's the take?"

"All there."

"Hound good?"

Shaw made a confirming sound in his throat. "He's had zero issues. Nothing like at Hoppy Time, if that's what you mean."

The truck fell silent. Zan worked his way out of Normal Heights. Whipped a right onto the 805 on-ramp, headed to the 8.

"Hey," said Shaw. "You're not really gonna show those bitch-ass boys mercy, are you?"

Zan snorted. "The fuck you think?"

Chapter Fourteen

"Want to put together the baby's crib when I get home?" Gaby stood in the doorway with her purse draped on her arm.

Drew leaned in, kissed her. His back and ribs ached with the movement, reminding him to take more Ibuprofen. "What time will you be home?" She'd picked up a Saturday shift at the clinic, and he knew they closed at noon. Gaby raised an eyebrow at him.

"Maybe two? The girls were talking about going to lunch after we get off, and Sherissa said she'd buy me lunch."

Excellent. Drew tried not to smile too big. "Nice. Text me when you're headed home."

They kissed again.

"So . . . the crib?"

"Yeah," Drew said. "We could do that."

"Hope you get a call about that job."

Drew pursed his lips. "Same." He tried not to think too hard whether her words held subtext that he should be working today. She wasn't like that; it was his own guilt pushing his mind there.

"Where did you say you're going to look for Jake today?"

"Chula Vista. Friends said he may be at this RV park."

"Ok, let me know how it goes."

After she left, Drew looked around the small living room, took a deep breath and let it out. Gaby had bought his explanation for the broken stuff yesterday—his clumsiness brought on by dizziness, which he *did* experience when he didn't stay hydrated. He promised her they'd go buy some replacement picture frames and dishes when they came into more disposable money. Whenever that would be.

For now, he needed to find his brother before the cops could, and certainly before Zan's deadline.

***

Drew took the 15 south to the 5 and arrived at Sun Outdoors RV Resort in ten minutes.

Situated in South Bay—more precisely the city of Chula Vista—the resort sprawled southeast of the National Wildlife Refuge, with a breathtaking view of the San Diego Bay. Even in April, the saltwater glistened like a warm summer day.

Tall palms surrounded the property like sentinels posted around a fortress. Locating the main entrance, Drew guided the Transit Connect over a series of speed bumps and parked in front of the one-story office: a cozy structure with gray wood siding and bright white trim.

Drew killed the engine. Took a deep breath. "C'mon," he muttered, lazily willing the universe to show his search favor.

Entering the office, a very tan woman with a nose stud standing behind the front desk asked, "Have a reservation, hon?"

"No." He stepped up to her, folded his arms on the desk. A dull roar of lingering pain flowed through his bruised body, the pills he'd taken before leaving the house yet to fully kick in. "I'm looking for someone, my brother. Friends of his said he might have stayed her for a night or two recently."

The woman—who wore a gold name tag reading Darlene—turned to her computer with no further prompting and tapped a few keys. "Name?"

"Jake Dwyer." Hopefully, he'd used his real name.

Darlene hemmed and hawed, tapped away on the keyboard. "Not . . . seeing that name. Do you know if he stayed in one of our vacation rentals, or did he rent an RV site?"

"RV site. He would've been in a Chinook Concourse, if it helps."

"Okay."

Drew bit the inside of his cheek. Felt cautiously optimistic about her willingness to help.

"Not seeing anything like that, hon. Sorry."

Inhaling deeply, Drew decided to try a different tactic. "Do you mind if I take a look at the RVs, see if he's over there?"

Darlene took a defensive posture, though her tone remained calm. "We've got security cameras covering the entire resort. Squatters don't last long here," she said. "Besides, our visitors don't like freeloaders, so I'm sure I would have heard if we had a squatter."

"I don't doubt that, Darlene." He smiled. "Thing is, my brother's a charmer. Mooching off others is kinda his specialty."

"You're quite the charmer yourself." She blushed. "Tell you what. Since you seem genuine—" Darlene laid her hand on Drew's. "Go ahead and look. Just don't disturb the guests."

"That's so nice of you. Thank you."

She gave Drew a big smile. He said goodbye, but Darlene followed him outside onto the office's porch. A twinge of panic went through Drew, hoping he hadn't led her on, but then felt embarrassed when she'd simply come out to point him to the RV hookups.

He thanked her again and they parted ways.

Drew plodded down a freshly blacktopped street with campers parked on either side. The sheer number of RVs sent a sinking feeling through his core.

If he couldn't gather another lead here, Zan's deadline might as well be a month, or an entire year. Jake could be anywhere. The city of San Diego provided free parking galore that RVers took advantage of at parks and beaches. Even more places up the seventy miles of San Diego County coastline. Jake could hopscotch from Fiesta Island one day to Torrey Pines the next, to Moonlight Beach in Encinitas, and any of the other dozen or so coastal state parks from Mexico up to Carlsbad—and many, many more spots out east. And, oh yeah. Drew now knew Jake had $100k, which increased the number of places he could camp out, exactly like this RV resort. Shit. If Jake dipped too much into Zan's cash, they'd both be screwed.

Drew breathed deep. Pull it together. It's day one, and still early. Besides, Jake is cheap. He probably hadn't spent any of the cash yet. Please, god.

He refocused on making progress this morning—whatever that meant—because he'd be pinned at home tomorrow with Gaby having Sundays off, playing the dutiful husband. Meaning his deadline from Zan had a minimum of two dead days when he could do nothing.

A few camper doors were open, but Drew didn't see any guests outside them yet.

He continued along.

The breeze off the bay was chilly yet refreshing. The only sounds were rustling palm fronds, and the chuckles, clicks, and croaks of ravens perched in those palm trees.

Not every hookup was booked. Seemed about half to three-quarters were occupied. Still, an impressive collection of campers. Winnies, Airstreams, Gulfstreams, Coachmens, vintage RVs, and several fifth-wheels. Drew hadn't yet seen a single Chinook.

Ahead on his left about 100 yards, someone moved about at a clean-looking Minnie.

Closing the distance, Drew heard Darlene's instruction not to bother the guests echo in his head. He felt conflicted, but told himself if a guest greeted him, all bets were off. Jake's life and his family's lives were on the line, and Drew would never see Darlene again anyway.

The owner of the Minnie turned out to be an old white man with a long gray beard, wearing nothing but a powder blue bathrobe and a pair of yellow Crocs.

"Morning," the man called out.

Invitation accepted. Drew strode over.

"Good morning, sir."

"Sir?" The man chuckled. "Well, I guess everyone is a sir to someone your age. Name's Frank; what's yours?"

"Drew." He shook Frank's outstretched hand.

"Nice to meet you. Just get in?"

"Sorry?"

"You're staying at the resort, right?"

"No, sir. I'm looking for my brother." Drew produced the same photo on his phone he'd shown to people at the OB Pier. "Jake. Wonder if you've seen him?"

Frank stroked his beard. "Hold on a second." He stepped over to his RV, leaned his head inside. "Susy-Q? Bring out my readers, would ya?" Looking over his shoulder and holding up a finger, he said to Drew, "Need my eyes first."

Fried bacon wafted out of the camper.

A few seconds later, an arm stuck out of the doorway holding a red pair of glasses.

"Thank ya, dear." Frank put on the readers, waved Drew to him. "Jake, you say?" Frank inspected the photo.

"Yes. He would have been staying in a Chinook."

Frank straightened up. Took the glasses off. "Sorry, Drew. Haven't seen him or a Chinook. But we only got in last night, so maybe I'm not the best person to be asking."

"Ah. No worries." Drew closed his phone and pocketed it. "I appreciate your time."

"Hope everything is okay . . ."

Drew gave a thin smile. "Thanks."

"Want a cup of coffee?"

"That sounds great, but I'm running short on time."

"Rain check." Frank held out his hand. Drew shook it, said goodbye, and left.

Drew passed two more RVs with guests stirring outside, but neither so much as looked in his direction. Drew figured he'd give them time to wake up and approach them later, if needed. Turning the corner to a new row, the sun blinded. Having forgotten his sunglasses in the van, he shielded his eyes with his hand.

More guests were making their way out of their campers and milling about. Under awnings, sitting in front of their vehicles in lawn chairs, and even one young couple perched on the roof of their Winnebago. Leading with the photo, Drew dispensed with greetings and pleasantries in favor of getting to the point with these guests.

"Have you seen this man?"

The young couple wanted to know if he was a cop, and a gray-haired woman asked if he was tracking down his runaway romantic partner. For the most part, though, Drew received a lot of shaking heads and lackluster nopes.

Turning on to another row, Drew checked the time. 10 a.m. Four hours remaining. That sinking feeling came on again.

"Taking a morning walk?" The question came from a Latina with a shock of silver running through her hair. She gripped a mug of coffee and sat on the doorstep of a huge rig with *Sunny Times* airbrushed in pink on the back end. "Much prettier down on the beach."

Drew walked over to her. "I believe you. I'm looking for my brother Jake, though. He stayed here a couple nights ago, and I'm trying to find him."

The woman clicked her tongue on the roof of her mouth. Shook her head slowly when Drew showed her the photo.

"Sorry, doesn't look familiar."

"That's okay, thanks." Drew stared past her, the view a serene one. Rows of RVs and cabins, with the blue bay beyond. Present circumstances excluded, Drew could see the appeal of staying at a place like this, and he hadn't even set eyes on the restaurants, fitness center, pool, or other top-notch amenities being promoted back in the office. The thought of spending a night here, lounging outside his Chinook with Gaby and Jake, feet up with a small fire going between them . . . stars and moon shining, the bay glistening . . . Sounded like a dream.

"Well, I'll get out of your hair," Drew said to the woman.

"Good luck—"

The sound of flip-flops or similar steadily smacking against pavement interrupted them.

Looking over his shoulder, Drew saw a silhouette jogging toward them, the sun blinding his complete view. A second later, he realized it was Frank, the bearded owner of the Minnie. He did his best to move quickly while keeping his flapping robe from unveiling too much of his body. Thankfully, he wore boxers.

"Drew," he said, out of breath. He bent over, clutched his knees.

"Take it easy, Frank. You okay?" Drew asked.

"Yeah . . . yeah. My neighbor . . . he has something . . . you will want to see."

Chapter Fifteen

nticipation rose in Drew's chest like a Southern swell.

Frank said his neighbor had something for Drew to see. Jake? The possibility of seeing his brother churned in him a mixture of emotions—primarily excitement and anger.

"This way," Frank said.

They cut through rows of campers. Through vacant lots. Sand or grit crunching under their hurried steps. "What's he have to show me?" Drew asked.

Winded, Frank held up a hand. Dismissed the question. Waved Drew on.

When they reached Frank's Winnie, his wife—a tiny woman with a huge curly mop of dyed red hair—greeted them.

"Carl said he'd be inside waiting," she said to Frank. Smiling at Drew, she said, "Hi, dear. I'm June."

"Hi, ma'am. Drew."

"So polite for a California boy."

Drew had no idea what that meant, so just gave her a thin smile in return.

"C'mon," Frank said. He led Drew to the Airstream on their right. Door was closed. Bistro lights were strung along the awning extending from the side of the trailer. Frank rapped on the aluminum door. "It's Frank. From next door. Found the kid I told you about."

Footsteps sounded from inside. Slight creaking, but the trailer didn't wobble one bit.

The door swung open, sending a waft of dirty laundry and moldy cheese into Drew's face. Standing there was a skinny white man probably in his fifties, judging by the gray dominating his stubble. He had a shiny dome on top with long, greasy brown and gray hair on the sides flowing past his shoulders.

"You Drew?" he asked. Spit off to the side, climbed down the steps.

"That's me. Frank said you have something for me to see?"

"Not so fast." He whipped out his hand. "Carl." Drew shook his hand. "I'm gonna need to see some ID."

"Serious?"

"Not exclusively. But certainly right now," Carl said.

Frank chuckled.

Drew reached in his back pocket. Jake had him playing some sort of game? Why? Oh, could it be because the dumbass was on the run with $100k of stolen cash?

"Here." Drew extended his license to Carl.

"Drew Jones. Forty-eight fifty-four, Thirty-Fourth Street, San Diego. Where's that?"

"Normal Heights."

Carl let out a low whistle. "What do you do?"

"Rent."

Carl and Frank looked at each other and laughed. Drew hadn't meant it as a joke.

"You're all right, kid," said Carl. He wiped his forehead with the back of his hand, and gave Drew his license back. "Hang here for a second."

Drew watched Carl until he disappeared inside the Airstream. "Does this guy know my brother?" he asked Frank.

The old man shrugged. "All he said when I told him you were here looking for your brother Jake is that he had something for you to see. I went looking for you right after."

"Okay."

He didn't have to wait long. Carl came out of the trailer as quickly as he had gone in. Stomped down the stairs, and thrust his fist at Drew, nearly punching him in the sternum. He slowly opened his hand to reveal what he'd retrieved.

Drew's heart jumped into his throat. There was a piece of paper rubber-banded to a potato-colored and shaped rock. The sight flashed Drew back to the note Jake stashed in Drew's underwear drawer when he was fourteen.

"Who gave this to you?" Drew asked, knowing the answer.

Carl spit. "Your brother. Jake. We've known each other for a few years now. Crossed paths a few times. He gave me the rock, said, 'Give it to my brother, Drew Jones. He should be coming by soon.'"

The rock was completely smooth, and dense. Its weight anchored the feeling of hope building in Drew's chest.

"Excuse me." Drew stepped away from Carl and Frank. Neither objected.

The brittle rubber band broke before he could undo it. The paper was a scrap. Unfolding it, the edges were torn. Scribbled on it in print letters, three lines of text.

Drew, sorry I took the Chinook. I had a good reason. Go to Balboa Park and find an old Ford van that used to be an ambulance: white on top, orange on the bottom. -Jake

Drew read the note three times. No mention of the money, Zan, or the liquor store. The lone reference Drew had to go on that Jake possibly knew he was in danger consisted of five letters: *I had a good reason.* "Goddamn it, Jake."

"Everything okay?" called Frank.

Folding the note and stuffing it in his pocket, Drew muttered yeah. Flipped the rock to the ground. The dull thud it made reminded him of the sound drywall mud makes when you plop some into a mud pan.

"Guess I'm going to Balboa Park," Drew said.

***

Drew started on the western edge of the world-famous Balboa Park. Host to two World's Fairs and planted with exotic trees from all over the globe decades before Drew was born, the park had also been where Millers' Kids held their annual reunions. Sadly, that all ended when Joe and Rose went down.

Taking a right at Upas off Sixth Street, Drew entered the park, proceeding onto Balboa Drive. It was a well-paved road that cut through this side of the property, providing extensive parking and access to expansive grassy fields, shaded plots, and well-groomed gardens.

Jake telling Drew to find a van at Balboa Park was about as helpful as instructing him to find a surfer in a wetsuit at one of San Diego's beaches. Thankfully, the van Jake described sounded unique. An old Ford painted like an orangesicle.

It was Saturday, closing in on lunch time, which meant the park was packed. Every street parking spot and painted lined spot was taken. Families gathered on the lawns for parties; young adults drank out of paper bags hanging about; people of all races sunbathed on the grass; and old ladies strolled the gardens.

Drew's pocket buzzed, so he slowed to a stop and retrieved his phone. A text from Mon. "Get the OB gig yet? Pulling for you."

He texted her back. "Not yet. Thanks."

Driving again, Drew kept his speed under control, despite wanting to tear through. But cops always hunkered here, ready to ticket drivers for the slightest infraction.

A familiar vehicle made Drew slam on the brakes. A Chinook exactly like his parked on the street on his left. Emphasis on *like* his. The sight still sent a thrill through him; he could see blood pumping through the veins in his wrist. He eased on the gas again.

By now, it was clear Jake was leading him along. He wanted Drew to find him. Jake's friends at the OB Pier led Drew to the RV park, and Jake left the note on the rock instructing him to go here. As encouraging as it was to know Jake was guiding him, Drew hoped the crumb trail would lead him to his brother in time.

Crossing El Prado, huge fig and Eucalyptus trees shaded Balboa Drive. The road transitioned to the Eighth Ave. loop. He followed the curve around. Passed the Fire Alarm building on the right, and was then driving back the other way. All the parking spots were taken in the three cutouts on the left, but none of them by an orange and white old ambulance. Drew decided to pull over to collect his thoughts before driving over the Cabrillo Bridge to venture to the eastern side of the park. As he slowed, his phone rang.

The number came up local. Maybe Lydia? Another gig? Drew answered it before it rang a second time. "Hello, DJ's Drywall."

"Is this Drew Jones?"

"Yes. How can I help?" Drew brought the van to a full stop.

"This is Detective Billberry."

"Uh, hi. What's up?"

"I'm in your neighborhood and need to stop by and talk. Are you home?"

"No, Detective. I'm . . . I'm working at the moment."

There was a long pause.

"Tell you what. Go to the Mid-City Division when you finish. I'll give you the address."

A police station? Drew thought fast. "If you can give me twenty minutes, I can meet you at my home. I was headed there for lunch soon anyway."

Another pause.

"That will work. See you then."

The detective hung up. Drew checked the time. Almost noon. What the hell did this cop want now? Or worse, what did he have on him? The possibilities chipped away at what little optimism Drew felt about finding Jake.

He'd have to pick up on this lead on Monday, though it killed him to.

And there was Zan to consider. Should he call him and let him know he made progress, or wait until he found Jake? Both options sucked. The back of his eyes began to throb and a huge weight descended on his shoulders. Drew tried to remind himself he was doing this to ultimately save his brother's life. But like that, the pain of every aching muscle and bruised bone Shaw had inflicted on him intensified until he could barely stand it.

Chapter Sixteen

P ulling behind the house, it occurred to Drew that Det. Billberry had first come to question him the same night Zan lurked in his truck on the street. Seemed likely now the cop deterred Zan from breaking into Drew and Gaby's house at that time. It made Drew wonder how long Billberry had also been waiting for him to return home.

Drew grimaced getting out of the Transit Connect. He crossed the yard and was unlatching the front gate to find the detective when he experienced a sinking realization. He wasn't wearing work clothes, though he'd told Billberry he'd been at work.

The detective was parked right out front. Drew side-eyed Bernie's house, hoping his landlord wasn't home to witness him being questioned by the police.

"Mr. Jones. Good to see you again." Billberry held a notebook in his left hand, and extended his right to Drew. They shook.

"Detective. What can I help you with?"

"Mind if we go inside?"

Drew hated to think that was probably best, since everything in him screamed not to welcome a cop into his home. The last time cops had been in his home was when they arrested his foster parents and dragged him out barefoot in the middle of the night.

"Okay," Drew said, trying to hide the reluctance in his voice.

As they walked, Billberry tried to make small talk: the weather, gas prices, even a throw-away comment about the latest COVID variant.

Drew unlocked and opened the front door. He guided the detective to the couch. Billberry sat. Drew dragged Gaby's ottoman over in front of him and sat down.

"I'll get right to it," Billberry said. "We recovered some footage from a Ring camera across the street from Hoppy Time Liquor . . ."

Drew's orifices clenched.

The detective continued. "Seems you—or at least your work van—was parked outside Hoppy Time around the time of the shooting. And what's more, a man is seen running out of the store and jumping in your van."

Drew opened his mouth, but Billberry cut him off.

"AND, your van, with DJ's Drywall clearly visible on the side, is seen fleeing the scene."

"Fleeing?" Drew blurted, defiant. "Since when is driving away considered fleeing?"

Billberry sat up straight. A stern look anchored his doughy features. "You told me you weren't at that liquor store on the day in question. And who was the person who got in your van?"

"What exactly are you accusing me of?"

"You're facing obstruction charges if you don't come clean right now, Mr. Jones."

Sweat trickled down Drew's back. Billberry had him. Obstruction? Shit. Then it occurred to Drew that Billberry must be fishing. If he was in real trouble, why wasn't he under arrest?

"You said my van was spotted at Hoppy Time *around* the time of that shooting. What time was that exactly that my van was there and what time did the shooting occur?"

The detective harumphed. "Officers arrived on the scene of the shooting a little later, after you left. It's an active investigation, so I'm not going to divulge much else."

"But call logs are accessible through public information requests though, right?"

"Don't get cute with me."

Drew felt he had Billberry on his heels.

"Who was riding with you?" the detective asked.

"Uh . . . A friend."

"Name?"

"Not sure I want to tell you that."

"What are you hiding?"

"Nothing," Drew said.

"Would you rather tell it to me after spending a night in jail?"

Drew took a deep breath. Feeling he'd been cornered and with no other choice, he caved. "Jake Dwyer."

"Good. And where is Mr. Dwyer right now?"

"I don't know." Drew caught a suspicious look on Billberry's face, and threw up his hands. "Honest."

"Are you two close?"

"Sure, you could say that."

"What do you know about what happened inside that liquor store?"

Drew cleared his throat. "Only what I saw on the news. Fine, I was there, but way before it happened. My friend grabbed a couple slices of Julian pie for us after work, is all. We couldn't believe what happened when we saw it on the news later."

Billberry rubbed his chin. "Why didn't you say that when I first came by?"

Drew shrugged.

Silence stretched out between the two. Multiple negative ways this could play out passed through Drew's mind.

Suddenly, the detective stood. Handed Drew another of his business cards. "In case you misplaced the first one."

"Thanks."

"Drew. I'll level with you. I know you're not telling me the full truth." A long pause. "But since I also know your friend knows more than you, here's what I want."

Billberry went on to tell Drew that he was to call him the second he heard from Jake and report on his whereabouts. He threatened Drew two more times with obstruction of justice charges if he was found aiding Jake or impeding the detective's investigation in any way.

When Billberry finally left, Drew couldn't have felt more overwhelmed. The pressure of one more person out to get his brother, and the threats of legal trouble. Both threatened to obliterate his hopes of a normal, stable life. But fuck if he was going to help a cop do his job, especially when it came to his brother.

***

Zan's burner nearly dropped out of Drew's shaking hand twice.

Pacing the kitchen wasn't helping to calm his nerves, but he didn't stop. Sweat beaded his forehead; his mouth went nearly San Diego summer dry.

Finally, he went for it—hit the call button.

Zan answered after the second ring.

"Find him?"

Drew gulped hard. "Not yet. But I'm working on a lead."

"Be better if you had him."

Drew fumbled to spit something out, and Zan spoke again.

"You were right to call. Stay in contact."

"Wait," Drew said.

"Yeah, what?"

Words spilled out of Drew with a dreamlike inability to control them. He told Zan about the visit from Det. Billberry. How he divulged Jake's name. How the detective knew they were at the liquor store the day the shooting occurred. How he instructed Drew to tell him where Jake was when Drew found him.

"Fuck that cop. He's got nothing. We called an ambulance—that's it—so he's in the dark. Stick to the plan and keep your mouth shut. Find your fucking brother and my money and bring them to me. Got it?"

"Yes." Drew said.

Zan hung up.

Drew stared at the burner phone. Set it face-down on the kitchen counter.

He squeezed the counter in a death grip. Dug his nails into the grout between the tiles.

Air became difficult to draw. He lunged to the side and threw up into the kitchen sink.

Chapter Seventeen

Gaby sat on the couch the next day, Sunday, reading *What to Expect* and snacking on Trader Joe's chili onion peanuts without having said much to Drew after breakfast.

He'd given her an update on Jake—leaving out anything about Det. Billberry and Zan. She nodded along, but was more distracted with finding the missing sonogram photo. When she brought it up, that it wasn't on the refrigerator, Drew played dumb, but he could tell she didn't fully buy it. That could also be his own paranoia. He couldn't tell her the truth—that a violent criminal broke into their home and stole the photo as a threat if Drew didn't find and deliver his money and Jake to him. She didn't press him on it, and he told her he would call the doctor and ask for a new one, but she declined, only wanting the original. Ever since it felt like a gulf had grown between the two, even though Drew was stationed ten feet away at their small dining room table. He'd spent a couple hours calling back all the potential small-job clients he'd shrugged off in previous weeks, but now needed desperately to keep from falling behind on bills. To his dismay, they'd all found other contractors.

Chin propped on his fist, he glazed over at his wife. Sunlight poured through the front windows, drowning Gaby in a golden aura. Lit her auburn hair aflame.

Her hair.

As gorgeous as she was, as athletic and toned her body, her hair is what caught his attention the first time their co-ed volleyball teams squared off. She played with a ponytail, and with every serve, every set shot she made, it bounced about, catching the sun's gleam. He fell hard for her. He wasn't sure she'd noticed him in the same way though, which is why it took him two more matches over a month's time to work up the nerve to approach her and ask her out.

Gaby coughed. Tripped Drew from the dream.

"Why don't you take a break?" she said. "We could put the baby's crib together."

Drew dragged a hand over his stubble. "Sorry, Gab. I'm pretty distracted at the moment."

"That's the point. You're grunting and groaning over there like you're in pain, so I thought maybe you could use a break."

I am in pain. Like he couldn't even tell her. Some physical lingering from Shaw. Mental thanks to Zan and Det. Billberry. And emotional pain? That hurt most. His heart felt swollen; something dark and heavy filling his chest cavity.

"The end of the month is coming up fast, and if I don't schedule some work soon . . ."

"We'll be fine. Your last job and my overtime will cover rent."

"And what about savings?" Drew asked. "We've got to get ahead if we ever hope to buy a house of our own."

Gaby gave a little huff. "I know that. I'm only saying, we're okay right now. There's two weeks left in the month, and you could still get the Surfview job, right?"

Drew interlaced his fingers behind his head, stretched. Blew air to the ceiling. "I guess so. I don't know. The property manager said she'd let me know end of last week—Friday."

Gaby turned off her tablet. Set it on the couch. "C'mon. Let's set up the crib and focus on happy things about our future." She rubbed circles on her stomach.

Drew's throat tightened. How could he dream about their future when he was so mired in this huge mess of the present?

His phone buzzed. A text message.

"It's Mon. Hang on, babe." Mon was in the neighborhood. She wanted to pop in on them and say hi to Gaby, see her baby belly. "Let me call her, see what's up." Drew said.

Dialing Mon's number, he rushed out of the house to the yard—as far from Gaby's earshot as he could get.

"Hey, Mon," he said when she answered. "Now's not a good time. Gaby's napping, but if you want, I could meet up for a beer on Adams."

She agreed. He told her to meet at The Rabbit Hole in ten minutes.

Back inside the house, he fed Gaby a line about Mon wanting to meet up to talk about potential jobs. Gaby bought it, told him to get going and buy the drinks if Mon was hooking him up with work.

He hated to lie to her, but building a crib and talking about raising their baby were the last things on his mind.

***

"Why did you get pregnant then if you don't want to have a baby?" Mon had already knocked back half the pint of her sour lager Drew paid for. The two of them sat in a booth meant to seat half a dozen in The Rabbit Hole, a bar and grill that catered to the younger, hipster crowd of Normal Heights.

He took a gulp of beer, and sighed. "It's not that I don't want to have a baby. It's just not the best time. That's all."

"Don't they say there's never a good time to have kids?"

Drew shrugged.

The music playing over the house PA was way too loud for the small pre-lunch crowd. Some Machine Gun Kelly song forced Mon and Drew to lean in across their table and nearly shout to hear each other. Drew eyed three empty patio tables, wondered if they should move.

"I'm just saying. Between trying to save to buy a house, and grow our careers, it's not the best timing. And now I'm focused on trying to find my brother. Besides, I want to be a good dad and I'm worried that if I'm not ready, I'll end up fucking our kid up."

Mon drained the rest of her beer. Rubbed her arm. "So, what you're saying is . . . It's not that you don't want to have a baby, it's that you're *scared* to have a baby."

"Terrified," Drew said, throwing up his hands.

"Still? I mean, I knew you were scared early on, but I have to think that's true of most first-time parents."

Drew flagged down a passing waitress. "Can we get two more, please?" She nodded and headed to the bar. Drew weighed how much he should divulge to Mon about his childhood for her to understand his point of view. The memory of Special Agent Tony barging into his bedroom flew to the front of his mind and sent a chill up his spine.

Mon said, "And what's this about looking for your brother? Where did he go?"

"Fuck. That's a long story."

"Short version it."

Drew paused while the waitress approached the table and set their beers down.

"Thanks," he said to her. She smiled and left. Drew looked back at Mon. "The short version is he saw or did some shit he shouldn't have, took my RV and bolted. Now I'm trying to track him down."

Mon wiped beer foam off her lip, bulged her eyes. "What did he do?"

Drew looked around. Jutted his chin toward the patio.

They picked up their drinks and walked outside.

Once settled, the sun warming Drew's skin, he told Mon in a hushed tone about the liquor store, the money, Zan's threats, and Drew's search for Jake.

"Shit." She drew out the word. "That's messed up. You call the police?"

Drew scoffed. "No. Not the biggest fan. Anyway, haven't you watched a movie? The bad guy never lets you call the cops, or else."

"And how's that usually play out in the movies?" Mon said.

"I'm not saying I know what I'm doing. I'm doing my best to find my brother, so this maniac doesn't kill him."

Mon got briefly distracted by two Corgis being walked down the sidewalk before giving her attention back to Drew. "What's Gaby say about all this?"

Drew sat up straight. "She wants me to focus on the baby."

"Sounds reasonable."

"Yeah, but that can wait. I can't let my only brother get killed over one mistake."

"So, she knows you're running around town with a gun to the back of your head, right?"

"Well, Jake's head, and not really. She's cool with me looking for him and our RV. I just haven't told her any of the rest of it."

"Why not?"

Drew inhaled deeply. "I don't want to worry or scare her."

"She's a lot stronger than you're giving her credit, Drew."

Dropping his head, Drew rubbed the back of his neck.

Mon rubbed her face all over like she was wiping away spiderwebs. "Shit, dude. I don't know what to tell you, other than you should probably be open with your wife. I'm sure—"

"Hold on," Drew said, checking his phone. It was ringing. "It's the Surfview—Hello? Yes. Hi, Lydia . . . Uh-huh . . . Oh, that's excellent, thank you. Yes, I can start first thing tomorrow morning. Thank you so much. Right. Sure. Okay, thanks again."

A big smile stretched across his face as he ended the call. "At least I can stop sweating finding some work for a minute."

"Good for you," Mon said. "That gig's a good get."

"I know, right? It's all good now."

Mon made a face. "Well, not *all* good. For real, dude. Talk to Gaby about all this."

"Okay, okay." Drew sneered. "You're bossy even off the job."

Mon snorted. "Screw you, Jones."

Chapter Eighteen

Measure, measure, and remeasure.

Jacked on iced coffee, Drew moved from cottage to cottage the next morning, following the first lesson he received half a decade ago from his drywall mentor, Harry Staubs. The man set Drew on the path to self-sustainability and provided his life purpose, and his lessons still pinged in Drew's brain. Especially during times like these: when his skin tingled and mind wandered with anxious energy—that schoolboy feeling of wanting to be somewhere, anywhere else. In these moments, Harry's instructions compelled Drew to buckle down, focus on the task at hand.

He'd arrived at the Surfview Cottages at 4 a.m. The area had been pitch-dark, the methodical crashing of waves the lone sound. Surfers would show up in another hour or so, but no other life rustled.

Lydia had no problem with him getting such an early start, and left him a master key in the office mailbox to access the cottages.

Inside, the units had been demo'd. Bare floors and naked studs. The sight gave Drew an idea of what the inside of a hollowed-out skeleton might look like. The paltry lighting added to the creepy vibe. Regardless, he worked quickly, but diligently, measuring and remeasuring each unit in order to place a materials order.

By arriving so early, Drew gave himself at least three hours until materials and supplies would arrive after he completed the order. Three hours to find the orangesicle van in Balboa Park. Three hours to find the next clue in the scavenger hunt that was locating his dumbass brother.

After collecting the measurements, Drew sat in his work van with the windows rolled down, finishing his order. The sun crested the eastern edge of Ocean Beach, bathing the area in a wash of tangerine. Seagulls squawked nearby. The smokey bite of fried bacon floated along on a gentle breeze. Out of the corner of his eye he saw the roofers there, unloading their gear. Drew ended his call after providing his preferred drop site for the materials.

He took a deep breath.

The air had a sharp bite to it, an energy he couldn't place. Yet, it felt invigorating. He'd been up for hours by this point, and the brightening day gave him the mixed sensation of being ahead of the game while also feeling like he was running late.

Drew cranked the engine, crammed the van into drive, and hit the gas.

Balboa Park was about a fifteen-minute drive away from here, ten with no traffic and if he booked it.

Along the way, Drew couldn't help but let his mind wander. Jake, Zan and Shaw, Det. Billberry. Ahmed—god, he hoped he was okay. All of what he'd found himself mixed up in danced on the edge of his brain, but one person pushed forward.

Gaby.

He'd left the house with her asleep in bed. She'd been thrilled when he came back from the bar yesterday with the good news that he scored the Surfview gig. All he wanted was to give her what she deserved—a home of their own. To do that, he had to work harder than ever. This job would definitely help. He'd be able to get it done in a couple of weeks, even with using his lunch breaks and before and after work to track down Jake.

Drew disliked keeping Gaby in the dark about Billberrry and Zan. He wasn't used to lying to her.

Well, that wasn't exactly true, was it? She knew nothing—at least he didn't think so—about how he dreaded becoming a father, about his fear of screwing up their child. No, he'd kept that from her too, and for good reason.

Jumping on the 8 from Sunset Cliffs, Drew gunned it.

A boundless clear sky greeted him in the east, while in the rearview stood a wall of thunderheads. Reminded him how the forecast called for cooler temps at the end of the week and into the weekend. They were even saying a rare county-wide April rain was likely starting Friday, with a Southern swell set to cause erratic waves from South Bay up to La Jolla.

Old Town passed by unseen on his right, shrouded here by tree cover, and USD stood high on the hill to his left. Soon, the Hotel Circle exit came up next. It provided access to the row of shitty old chain hotels. Drew wondered whether they were ever choice spots back in the day.

Going the opposite of rush hour, he made it to the 163 in no time, took the south exit.

Thinking back to yesterday, Mon's advice to talk to Gaby nearly took. Drew worked himself into a sweat on the walk home, practicing what he'd say to her. To come clean about everything. To ask her if she thought he was doing the right thing. When he got to the front door, however, he pushed it all down and remained silent.

Hopefully he would find Jake soon and get this all resolved.

Then he'd be able to tell her everything.

Then he could focus 100 percent on Gaby and their future.

He blinked his eyes slow and hard.

The University Ave. exit came up fast.

He turned on the radio, tuned it to 94.9. Billy Corgan screamed about being a rat in a cage. Gooseflesh bloomed on Drew's arms as he screamed along until his throat burned.

Chapter Nineteen

B alboa Park was quiet.

Drew decided to start by retracing the parts he'd already searched two days earlier.

This early on a Monday, the park hadn't fully woken, including the many unhoused who sought shelter in its vast cover. A few dog walkers and older folks strolling along were the only things moving.

A benefit of arriving early meant far fewer vehicles parked along Balboa Drive compared to Saturday, hopefully making Drew's job of scanning for the old ambulance quicker and easier. Those parked appeared to be people living out of their rides, as well as a choice few go-getters.

One such group gathered between tall pine trees further up on the right. A bootcamp setting up. The lead trainer, a musclebound, Black guy, outlining an obstacle course with little orange cones, while an attractive woman with short red hair hauled battle ropes from the back of a Honda Pilot to the course. Participants loitered at the fringes—yawning and sipping coffees.

Drew continued along, intent on finding the contact as quickly as possible. He just hoped having to split the search across three days wouldn't mean the owner of the ambulance had already moved on from the park.

Crossing El Prado, Drew whipped his head left. The view down the Cabrillo Bridge to the museums in the distance looked celestial. Sunlight poured through cuts between the buildings in striking beams, bathing the bridge in a warm yellow hue. But no ambulance.

Drew sped up slightly as he passed a swath of empty curbs on the southernmost end of Balboa Drive. Continuing on to the loop, he did spot two sedans parked next to each other in the lot uphill to the right. A possible early-morning affair meet-up?

The Transit Connect groaned slightly as Drew took the loop a little too fast. A commercial airliner roared above head, making its final descent into the airport. The downdraft of air it created rustled the Mexican fan palms violently. A couple dead fronds broke free and speared the ground below.

Up on his left he saw three parked vehicles. A Prius, a faded red Tacoma, and a dope cream Dodge Coachmen with brown and gold striping—Padres colors.

Drew rubbed his face, continued on.

Down past a large field on the right, under a grove of sprawling fig trees, there were three different colored lumps: three people huddled in sleeping bags. Drew jolted as the road cut sharply back toward Balboa Drive. He turned right, came to El Prado. After another right, he entered the Cabrillo Bridge.

The sun had climbed in the sky, and the lampposts lining the bridge flickered, dimmed, and shut off. More people showing now, too. Some walking dogs on the sidewalks on either side of the road; a rail-thin guy powerwalking; two scraggly dudes in their early twenties riding electric bikes from the opposite direction; and a Goth girl with black hair riding a skateboard, gumming up his progress.

Drew slowed to give her breathing room. Impatiently drummed on the steering wheel. Many San Diegans wanted the Cabrillo Bridge to be transformed into strictly pedestrian-only access, but proposals to do exactly that had always failed. Drew was thankful in the moment they had, for the bridge made it easy to cut-through to the other side of the park. The girl glanced over her shoulder, threw up her arms. He had no clue what her reaction was about, so he slowed even more to create additional space between them.

Traffic way below on the 163 hummed.

Soon, they approached the entrance to the museums and plaza. When they reached the Museum of Us, the girl jumped her board onto the sidewalk, allowing Drew to continue solo through the tight tunnel ahead.

Once through, banners for an exhibit called Cannibals hung from the Spanish-Colonial buildings. And on his left, the ornate carvings and sculptures carved into the museum's towers glowed from the morning sun. Into Drew's head popped the framed picture they kept in the living room of Gaby and her moms posing in front of this very spot.

In 2015, they rushed down to see a display of rainbow-colored lights flooding the museums in celebration of the Supreme Court legalizing gay marriage. The photo wasn't the best quality due to it being taken in waning twilight, but if you looked closely, all three women wore huge smiles on their faces. Drew smiled himself, noting the connection.

There was no traffic through to the plaza. Drew followed the narrow road around, leaving the Museum of Art and Botanical Building behind him.

The Prado restaurant and the Japanese Friendship Garden passed by on his left.

And further up, the sun cast the heavy tree cover in a warm brightness. The sound of another airliner broke the tranquil scene as it cruised across the cloudless blue sky.

A large parking lot emerged on his left. He slowed to scan it, but it was nearly empty and he saw no vehicles matching the ambulance's description.

Ahead, the road opened to a massive open parking lot. Right off, he saw more than a dozen vehicles spread over the area, but the lot was too enormous to see it all at once. There were hundreds of parking spots, from the entrance all the way to the Air & Space Museum in the distance. The lot provided parking for it, a gymnasium, the Puppet Theater, the Automotive Museum, Recital Hall, and many other museums and buildings, and on weekends you'd be hard pressed to find an open spot.

Drew took it slow around the perimeter. The vein on the side of his neck pulsed.

Mumbling to himself, he checked off each vehicle he passed. "Chevy Volt, charter bus, Ford F-150, Nissan Altima . . ." If this lot didn't come through, he planned to cut over to the other large ones at the Natural History Museum and the art village, before doubling back and checking them all again in reverse. "Toyota Camry, Nissan Frontier, a beat-up 4Runner . . ."

Drew threw his arm out the window, felt the cool wind funnel up his arm, into his face.

A second later . . .

"Hell yeah."

Drew yanked the wheel, gave the Transit Connect some gas, and aimed for the far corner of the lot.

There it was.

The old orange and white ambulance. Parked in the long shade cast by hundred-foot-tall eucalyptus trees, near the entrance to the Air & Space Museum.

Pulling into a spot three over from the ambulance, Drew parked and cut the engine. He could hear his pulse, and looked to see his hands shaking slightly.

He took a deep breath.

When he felt himself relax a bit, he climbed out of the van.

The ambulance didn't look like one at all, really, other than retaining a topper with multiple strobe lights affixed to it. The Ford was jacked-up several inches, and sported heavy-duty all-terrain tires with thick tread set on matte-black wheels. The paint job was bubbled and cracked at the door seams and along the running board, though the colors still popped. White topped the van and carrot-hued orange cut it in half horizontally. The van definitely stood out.

Drew poked his head around the back quick enough to find a surfboard strapped to the spare tire, and the windows littered with stickers. The first one he saw read, "Zombie Apocalypse Vehicle." And that's what it looked like—an old ambulance turned into an assault vehicle you'd see in an apocalyptic movie.

He checked the time. 6:47 a.m. He bit his lower lip. No lights were on inside the van. Nothing moved in the three windows on the side—passenger's door and two back doors.

Approaching slowly, Drew could hear himself breathing loudly. He paused. Fuck it, he thought, and knocked on one of the back windows.

Nothing stirred inside.

He gave it another couple seconds, then rapped on the window a bit louder.

He heard a put-off groan.

Drew stepped back.

"Who's there?" came a froggy female voice.

"Uh, I'm Drew Jones." Said it like a question. "Sorry it's early. My brother Jake Dwyer sent me here."

A few seconds passed. A light inside flicked on. Drew felt awkward about now being able to see inside the van, so he averted his eyes. He wondered why she didn't use curtains.

"Hang on," the woman said.

Ravens clucked in the tops of the eucalyptus trees, giving Drew something to focus on while he waited to meet the latest holder of clues to Jake's location. Two of the ravens hopped branch to branch in what appeared to be playfulness. Another perched caught his attention. Its black eyes stared through him. Perfectly round and shiny. So beautiful—in a frightening way. Like Zan's eyes.

Drew shook his head to rid his mind of the comparison.

A metal click sounded. Drew turned around. The back side doors of the van opened like French doors, but no one emerged or appeared.

He stepped closer, angling for a glimpse.

"Who's there?" said the woman.

"Drew Jones."

"Been expecting you. Come on, then."

Drew stepped up and inside. The space was nothing like he'd expected. Right off, he took note of a laminated wood floor, an orange couch, floor lamps, and large potted plants.

A petite Black woman, probably his age or a little younger, with a purple scarf covering her hair stood in a breakfast nook on the side he'd entered. She motioned for him to sit on the other side in a vintage-looking wooden chair with fire engine-red cushions.

He sat. Folded his hands in his lap.

"You want to see ID, or anything?" he asked.

"Nope, I'm good. You look exactly how Jake described you. Coffee?"

"Oh, yes please." He watched as she dragged a turquoise Makita toolbox from the back of the counter forward. From the cabinet above, she retrieved an aluminum canister. Next, she grabbed a full plastic water bottle and untwisted the cap. She lifted a lid on the toolbox, and poured the water inside.

Drew nodded. A battery-operated coffee maker.

After scooping grounds into another compartment, she took two ceramic mugs off a metal rack anchored to what would be the backsplash area in a house. She inserted one of the mugs below where she'd added the grounds.

She clicked a button, turned around and faced Drew. "I need to run to the bathroom. If I'm not back when this is done, switch out the mugs for me. First cup's all you."

"Thanks."

She grabbed a leather case off the round side table next to Drew, stepped into purple flip-flops by the doors, and left.

Soon, the rich aroma of coffee filled the van.

Drew extended his legs. The heels of his work boots rested on a small, blue area rug. If he didn't know better, he would have thought he was in a studio apartment in PB or an artist's loft in Little Italy, not an old Ford van that used to be an ambulance. Looking around, there were a lot of indoor plants in the van, including a large one in each of the four corners of the "living space." They gave the van a lush, lively feel. Separating the front seats from this area rested a low, horizontal bookshelf lined with hardback books and paperbacks of titles Drew didn't recognize. To his right, a gray patterned curtain divided the van in half. Must be her bed, clothes and other personal belongings, he figured.

Leaning forward, he checked on the coffee. The mug was about three-fourths full. Drew got up to monitor the machine's progress.

Standing there, he realized the space totally calmed him, or maybe more accurately, distracted him. Wasn't a bad thing. Now that he'd found this contact, he had plenty of time to find out what he could from her. He wondered if she would tell him directly where to find Jake, or if she only possessed another rock with a note rubber-banded to it to give him.

The mug was full. He moved carefully, switching out the mugs without spilling any, and was quick enough not to let any spill from the maker. He cradled his mug—a blue metal one used on camping trips—and blew steadily on the liquid. Taking a sip, he moaned.

A minute later, flip-flops slapped on asphalt outside. Drew sat back down in the chair. The woman climbed into the van, not wearing a scarf on her head any longer. She had short blonde hair she wore in springy curls, and she was dressed in a matching teal top and leggings set. Moving to the coffee maker, she checked on the second mug as it filled.

Turning to Drew, she said, "Careful. Sometimes it can come out pretty hot."

"Thank you." He took another sip. "It's tastes great."

She leaned back against the counter. "Renata."

"Sorry?"

"My name. Renata." She grinned. "Sorry if I was grumpy earlier."

"You weren't—I mean, I woke you up. I would've been grumpy too."

"So, you're Jake's brother, huh?"

Drew nodded. "That's me."

"Funny. You two don't look alike. I mean, you both white boys, but aside from that . . ."

Drew snorted. "Yeah, well. We were actually foster brothers when we were teenagers, but we've always had a strong bond. So we consider ourselves real brothers, even if we don't share the same blood."

"Cool," Renata said. "I don't have any brothers or sisters."

Drew sipped his coffee. His heart began to race a little—a combination of too much caffeine this early in the day and the low-humming nervousness of wanting to find Jake. "How long have you lived out of this van?"

Renata smiled a smile that showed how much she loved talking about this subject.

"This van? About six years. I had a legit beater before this one though. Always broke down. This girl? I won her at an auto auction in the middle of Nebraska. No one wanted her. But I saw the potential. I didn't have to spend much on it mechanically—ran like a dream from the start. I beefed her up some, and hit the road. She's taken me to thirty-three states, Mexico, and Canada. We've got many more adventures planned."

"Nice," Drew said. "And all this?" He waved his arms at the interior.

"Thrift store finds and curb grabs," she said with a bright smile.

"That's awesome. It's definitely one of the coolest interiors I've ever seen."

"Yeah, I can't imagine being cooped up in some house my whole life. Clock in to work every day, and can only go traveling once or twice a year—"

"If that," Drew muttered.

"Right? Pssh."

Drew dropped his head.

"Oh, sorry. I hope I didn't offend you," Renata said.

"You're cool. No worries."

"You sure?"

"Yeah." Drew's coffee cooled enough for him to take a gulp. After, he set the mug on the side table next to him.

"So," he said. "How long have you and Jake known each other?"

Renata blushed. Adjusting her stance, she sipped her coffee. "Coupla years, I guess."

"Are you two . . . an item?"

"An item? How old are you, Drew?" She laughed hard at her own joke.

"Okay, okay. Sorry."

"You're sweet. No, we get together whenever our paths cross. We're not exclusive though, or anything like that."

Light crept in through the windshield, casting beams straight down the center of the space. Drew stared at them to distract from the awkwardness he suddenly felt.

"Why you ask? Makin' conversation or something?"

Drew exhaled a big breath. "Or something. Sorry. Guess sometimes I feel like I don't know much about my brother other than what he tells me the couple, three times a year he swings into town for a quick visit. He's never brought a girl—woman—with him. Guess I was curious if he had someone special in his life . . ." Drew looked around. "Also, you must make him smoke weed outside when he's staying with you, cause this place smells great. Not like the other vans and RVs I've come across. They all smell like weed—or beer."

Renata threw out a palm. "No, no, no, no. First of all, no. Jake does not stay with me. This is my space—"

"Oh, okay. I get that. He can be a mooch," Drew said.

"You got that right. I let that boy stay with me one night, and it'd turn into thirty-straight. Hell no. Second, thank you." She pressed her palms together. "Ain't nobody smokin' nothin' inside Foxy Green."

"Foxy Green?" Drew stifled a laugh.

"Vivica A. Fox's character in Kill Bill—Vernita Green. I combined her last names: Foxy Green. Cause my baby is a fierce bitch just like Copperhead."

Drew laughed. "I like that. I would have thought something orange in the name since—"

"If she was Vernita Orange, I would have gone with Foxy Orange. Oh! I kinda like that . . ." Renata moved to the couch by Drew and sat down, leaving her coffee on the counter. She waited for Drew to stop chuckling before she spoke again.

"Anyway, your brother's a nice person, despite his faults," she said.

"So, you saw him recently," Drew said.

She nodded. "Saturday. Early. He didn't stay long at all though."

"Did anything other than that seem odd to you?"

"Oh, hell yeah. He was driving a clean-looking RV."

"A Chinook?"

"Yeah." Renata pointed at him. "I asked where he got it. Said he loaned it from a friend."

Drew smiled, pointed at himself with both index fingers.

"Seriously?"

"Yep."

"I'm guessing he didn't really borrow it?"

"Nope," Drew said. Renata made a disappointed face, and Drew quickly added, "It's fine, though. He might be in trouble, so the RV's not a big deal right now."

"If he stinks up your ride with weed, let me know. I'll make him fix it for you."

Drew grinned. "Thanks, I'll do that."

They both got quiet. Drew could hear leaves rustle in the breeze outside, and dried, fallen ones skipping across the parking lot. He checked the time on his phone. Plenty remaining until he needed to be at the Surfview for the materials delivery.

"Anything else you can tell me about my brother?"

"I mean, not really. He's your brother, so . . ."

"No, sorry. I mean, about what he might have said to you to tell me, or . . ."

"Oh. Duh. My bad." Renata pointed. "Open that drawer right next to you."

Looking down at the side table, Drew hadn't noticed there was a semi-circular drawer built into it. He opened the drawer.

Inside sat a rock with a note rubber banded to it.

He pulled it out. "Uh-huh. That's Jake," he mumbled, rolling the rock over in his hand.

"I didn't read it. Swear. I put it right in that drawer soon as he gave it to me," Renata said.

"Thanks." Drew kept rolling the rock in his hand. Staring at the white notebook paper. At the blue rubber band. Feeling the weight of the boring gray rock.

"You okay? I can give you some privacy if you want to read it."

Drew snapped out of it, looked at her. "Yeah, sorry . . . No, it's cool. I'll get out of your way. Thanks so much for being cool about me waking you up. And for the great coffee."

She waved a hand at him. "Pssh. Ain't nothing. I can make you another for the road . . ."

Drew stood. "No, thanks. My heart's beating out of my chest already. Think it's time to grab some food before I get the coffee shakes."

Renata stood up from the couch. "Cool. I have to move this girl anyway so I don't get a ticket. Not supposed to park here overnight, but I didn't know when you were coming by."

"Thanks for waiting me out."

She smiled and walked him to the doors. Drew stepped down, boots hitting asphalt.

"Hey, Drew," Renata said. He turned to see her gripping the doorway with one hand, the sun shining on her face. "You said Jake's in trouble. Is it bad?"

Drew shoved his hands in his pockets. In his mind, he briefly wrestled with how much he could divulge. "It's definitely not good. I can tell you that much."

She frowned. "I hope you find him soon."

"Same, Renata."

Chapter Twenty

"Good luck on your first day. Sorry I didn't get to see you this morning but you know how much I love my sleep."

Drew read Gaby's text while he sat parked at the Hillcrest McDonald's, biting into a second breakfast burrito. He sent her a response:

"Thanks baby. Hope you have a great day at work too."

Seagulls and ravens fought for position outside his door for another hand-out. He'd pulled off the ends of his first burrito and stupidly tossed the tortilla scraps to the birds. Now their incessant squawking and violent wing flapping made it painfully obvious why you weren't supposed to feed wildlife.

"Go," he shouted with a full mouth, waving at a seagull that hopped up on the hood. Drew hit the wipers to try to scare it off. It worked.

He took another bite.

Chewing mindlessly, his vision fell to the passenger's floorboard where Jake's rock sat. It had rolled off the seat as soon as Drew turned out of Balboa Park.

He kept chewing and looking at the rock.

It was too far of a reach to grab—he'd have to go around to get it.

Jake and his notes.

On one hand, the note held promise. The possible next clue of where to find Jake. Or maybe even his actual location. Hell, maybe a phone number if Drew was lucky.

The note also held the promise that by reading it, Drew would most certainly have to update Zan, while also keeping the same information away from the persistent Det. Billberry.

Drew devoured the last quarter of his burrito in one bite. Balled up the wrapper and dropped it in the paper sack, and retrieved the third and final burrito. One of the best cheap trash breakfasts you could buy.

The food did its job, soaking up the caffeine and warding off the shakes.

Unwrapping the last burrito, he spread the paper across his lap as he had the previous two. He looked at the rock again, huffed a long, slow breath.

He moved the burrito and wrapper to the passenger seat. He got out of the van, walked around to the passenger's side, and retrieved the rock. The Seagulls and ravens followed him around. They all flapped and hopped at his feet. Drew kicked at them in an attempt to shoo them off, but it didn't work. Exasperated, he snatched the burrito off the seat, turned, and chucked it across the parking lot so hard pain shot through his shoulder. The birds went nuts, flying after it.

Drew pulled the rubber band off the rock. He unfolded the piece of paper. Inside, the note was longer than the previous one.

Hey Drew. Isn't Renata great? Anyway. Go to this little taco stand in Dulzura, just before the turnoff to the road up to Otay Mountain. It's also a convenience market. Go in and order three pork tacos with extra hot sauce and they'll know it's you. Oh. Don't go until lunch time on Wednesday. See you soon little bro.

Another clue. Another hoop to jump through.

Chapter Twenty-One

Having to wait fifty-two hours to get the next clue to find Jake ate away at Drew the rest of the day. Aggravated the shit out of him, if he were being honest.

He went on autopilot back at the Surfview; hanging drywall in a handful of the units. There was no care taken, no love for the work. He simply screwed sheet of drywall after sheet of drywall to studs until he got tired of working.

That wasn't exactly true. A few mishaps hastened quitting time.

Drew stubbed his thumb two separate times and managed to knock over the panel hoist by ramming his hip into it. The unintended upside: he had the cottage interiors to himself, so only the crashing waves outside heard his expletive-laced tirades—and perhaps the roofers too, if they would have paused their scraping and shoveling for one goddamn minute.

By three, he had checked out and left the jobsite.

Going home didn't help improve his mood as he hoped either.

If he had to wait to keep looking for his brother, then all he wanted was to spend a quiet Monday evening with Gaby when she got home. Relax on the couch. Watch the Padres game. Instead, she had plans of her own. Directly after dinner, she leaned into him, insisting he wasn't pulling his fair share with baby preparations.

"You haven't even cracked any of the books the doctor recommended."

She hadn't even changed out of her scrubs—she was in the process—before she came down on him.

"Can't you summarize them for me?" Drew sat on the edge of the bed, chin tucked to his chest, avoiding her gaze. "You know I'm the hands-on type anyway."

Gaby made an exaggerated "pssh" sound. "Drew Jones. First, do I look like YouTube? And this isn't a new tool or a home appliance or something. This is our baby."

"I know."

"Do you?" She was now down to her underwear, standing in front of him.

He looked up at her. "What's that supposed to mean?"

"What do you think it means?" Gaby waited several beats before continuing, as if she truly expected an answer in this clichéd game of campy family sitcom they were suddenly playing out. "You've been off in your own world through this entire pregnancy. I feel like I'm doing everything on my own." Her voice cracked. "The least you could do is read *a* flipping book and help me build the baby's crib."

She was right. He *had* been AWOL all pregnancy. No way he could admit it though. That would mean explaining why—having to come clean about his worries and fears. Which, he knew sounded stupid, even in his own head.

"I take you to doctors' visits. I rub your feet. I remind you to take your vitamins."

Gaby huffed. "Jesus Christo. Yeah, okay. Good on you. But that's surface-level shit, and you know it. The bare minimum. We're having a baby in less than three months, Drew."

"I know that."

"You sure?" Her question hung like a noose. "What's really going on with you?"

"Nothing."

"It's Jake, isn't it?"

Drew cringed, but ignored her. Got up, smoothed the comforter where he'd been sitting.

"I'm on to something, aren't I?" she said.

He shrugged. "Maybe that's part of it. If I've been distracted—or whatever you think."

"Distracted," she murmured. Turned and rifled through her dresser drawers, grabbing out a change of post-shower clothes.

"Yeah, I know you weren't happy with me buying the Chinook, so maybe I've been anxious—and distracted—wanting to find him, or for Jake to bring it back on his own so we're not out that investment, too."

Gaby scoffed. "Investment . . . No, you're distracted *by* Jake."

Drew dropped his head.

Gaby continued. "You're completely obsessed with him, which fine. I get it. He's your brother . . . I know you'd like to be out there twenty-four-seven looking for him. But something tells me that's not all. Maybe you want to take off with him, and hit the road? Is that it? You want to go off and live another life instead of building this one with me?"

"What? No."

"Admit it, Drew. He's your drug."

"Stop it. He isn't."

"You have any idea where he is yet?"

Drew stared at the floor. Mumbled, "Not yet."

"Tell me the truth," Gaby said, her tone wounded. "Do you even want to be a father? Do you want this baby?"

Drew hesitated, fumbled with his words.

"Tell me," Gaby pleaded.

"Yes, I mean—"

"You *mean*?" Gaby threw her clothes on the bed. Crossed her arms over her belly.

"I do . . ." Drew said. "I do want to be a father."

Quieter now, tears welling, Gaby said, "You sure sound convinced."

He reached out to rub her shoulder, but Gaby dipped out of reach. She gathered her clothes and hurried to the bathroom, slamming the door. Next, he heard the click of the door lock, followed by his wife's muffled crying.

Drew struck his temple with the heel of his palm.

He paced from the bathroom door to the front door, trying to think how he could make things better. The water to the shower turned on. The white noise it created slipped Drew deeper into thought.

Was Gaby right? Did his love for Jake border on obsession? No. He felt obsessed with this search, with finding his brother. But only because he could save his life. There was no desire to leave Gaby and take off with Jake, like she accused. He decided to do the opposite the day he married her. So, why hadn't he been able to express that, to tell her how deeply he loved her?

A clunk came from the bathroom and a small yelp. She'd dropped the soap, was all.

Why couldn't he tell Gaby about his fears? Of becoming a father, of fucking up their child. He'd been able to tell Jake and Mon . . .

But what if he told her and Gaby left him because he wasn't ready to become a father?

Suddenly, Drew couldn't catch his breath. Pacing wasn't helping. He needed air. And he needed to channel all these frustrations and this panic into something physical.

Grabbing his wallet and keys from the bowl on the built-in, he dashed outside. Once he took some deep breaths, he headed for the Transit Connect.

He got in, started the engine. Pulling out his cell phone, he texted Gaby where he was going and hit send.

***

A low tide lapped lazy waves onto the beach.

The methodical sound echoed off the sandy cliff and traveled up and into the open windows of the cottage where Drew had returned to work.

Demo would have been preferrable to work off his frustrations, but returning to screwing drywall sheets up provided a hypnotic effect that seemed to be doing the trick.

The only thing breaking his concentration, besides a flickering bulb on his work light, was the need to see if Gaby had responded to his text. He checked his phone for a fourth time. Nothing. Just SEEN visible under the text he'd sent two hours earlier that read, "Going to the Surfview to work. Be back late."

After hitting the back arrow, he clicked on his conversation with Mon. Tapped it, hit voice-to-text, and said, "Hey Mon. I'm working late at the Surfview. Want to swing by?" After hitting send, he stared at the screen, waiting. Ellipses appeared. Next, a reply. "No can do. In for the night. Hit you up tomorrow?"

"Sure."

Drew went back to work—himself, his tools, and the dual head work light with one flickering halogen bulb. "Shit." Good thing he kept replacement bulbs in the van. He shut off the light to allow it to cool. Then used the flashlight on his phone to light his way outside.

He'd parked a few blocks away. Figured the walk would also help clear his head.

The air was crisp. The sky glimmered with a bevy of stars. Drew turned off the flashlight. There were faint sounds of late-night revelers coming from OB's main drag. Drew hit the home button on his phone. Ten-thirty. Okay, not so late for them, but he and Gaby would have gone to bed a half-hour ago, normally.

The back van doors squeaked when he opened them. He retrieved the replacement bulb from one of the built-in compartments and closed up the van.

As he headed back to the cottage, he observed his surroundings again. Off in the distance, the surface of the black ocean gleamed from the moon and stars. Closer, but out of view, waves washed onto the beach. Hoots and hollers persisted from his right. And the brisk air carried the aromas of saltwater and jasmine blooms. A totally relaxing night in Ocean Beach.

Back in the cottage, Drew plucked out the faulty halogen bulb. He inserted the new one and turned the light back on. The dual head fixture flooded the tiny unit with bright white light. Drew's shadow loomed across the room on the far wall. He walked toward it, and his shadow shrank down with each step until it matched his actual size.

He resumed work.

Hoist, set, screw, screw. He hung one drywall sheet after another late into the night.

Chapter Twenty-Two

Drew woke up the next morning on the couch. A head full of regret. A body aching from the toll he'd put it through the previous day on the jobsite.

His cell phone read ten o'clock. The sunlight pouring in the living room windows confirmed it. What his phone didn't show were any missed texts or calls from Gaby.

He sat up, dragged a hand down his face. The odor of burnt coffee consumed the room.

Before checking the coffee situation, Drew went to their bedroom. The bed was made, and there were no scrubs laid out on the dresser. Gaby had gone to work. Walked right past him without waking him.

Something else in the room disheartened him even more.

The baby's crib was spread out in a hundred pieces in the far corner, where they'd talked about it going—the only place it would fit in the room. She had obviously tried to build it without him. Taking a closer look, Drew saw she assembled the header and footer—if that's what you called them. The side rails, bars, and tons of wooden pegs and screws laid about.

A pain racked his chest, a hurt echoing Shaw's tackle and beating. But this hurt emanated internally. He'd let his wife down; rejected her simple request. One simple thing she looked forward to, and he'd ignored it so many times that she took it on by herself.

He shook his head. Getting to his knees, he picked up the sheet of unfolded instructions to the white Graco crib they'd bought at Target. He failed her, but he could finish what she started and hopefully show her he did care.

Skimming the instructions, and looking at the state of the crib, Drew couldn't discern where Gaby left off. Screw it. He'd build the side rails, then figure out what to do next.

Each guardrail post needed a wooden peg inserted at both ends. Next, they'd all get sandwiched by the main rails. As he inserted pegs, he recalled when they picked out the crib months earlier. She wanted something the baby could continue to use well into its toddler years. Would also save them money that way. Building it themselves would also save them a small amount. Drew stopped working. Looked around. He slowly stood up. Gaby wanted to build this crib together. He couldn't take that away from her. An idea formed of what he should do instead.

First, coffee. Then, a shower. Drew checked the time again. Five minutes since he first checked. Plenty of time to drive to Gaby's work, take her to lunch, and apologize for last night.

***

The private practice Gaby worked for was located twenty minutes away, in La Mesa, a city bordering eastern San Diego. A strip mall on the far backside of the Grossmont Medical District housed the clinic, along with six or seven other medical businesses.

Drew pulled into the lot and parked. It was now 11:30. He had no way of knowing if Gaby's lunch break was coming up, but he'd wait for her regardless.

The day was gorgeous—clear sky, a high of seventy-one, and a cool breeze blowing.

"I'm so sorry about last night. I feel terrible. I'm at your work to make it up to you. Come outside when you get a chance." Drew looked the text over, hit send.

He got out of the van. Sat down on the curb next to his van. While he waited for her reply, or to come outside, Drew couldn't help but daydream about tomorrow. The latest note said to go to the taco place in Dulzura at noon. Roughly twenty-four hours from now. That excited Drew, but he also had to think through what to tell Zan, and when.

So far, he hadn't checked in, not since Det. Billberry interrogated him. He hadn't told Zan about getting the note from Renata in the park. Should he have? Probably. But what would he have told him? Hey, my brother left me another note that will likely lead to another note?

One of the clinic's glass doors swung open and out walked Gaby. Drew stood up. Once she left the shadow of the building and crossed into the sun, she squinted hard. She shielded her eyes with one hand and held her stomach with the other.

"What are you doing here?" she asked in a snappy tone.

Drew walked to her. They met at the rear bumper of the Transit Connect.

"I wanted to apologize. I'm so sorry about last night."

Gaby crossed her arms, didn't reply.

"I saw you started to assemble the crib . . . I was going to work on it, but then I thought I should come apologize instead and tell you I want us to build the crib together, tonight."

Her face softened, but she kept her stance guarded.

"You were right, Gab. About a lot of it. I have been checked out and distant. I admit it. I haven't been a good partner to you through this." He dropped his head. His hands shook. "I'm not making excuses, but when you asked if I want to be a father, I froze, cause . . . cause . . . I've been scared and haven't known how to tell you."

Gaby's hand pressed on his arm. He looked up. Her beautiful amber eyes were wet.

"What are you scared about?"

Drew shrugged. "Everything?"

"You've got to be more specific than that."

A solid lump resided in his throat. His palms went slick, and he felt somewhat dizzy.

"I'm scared of having this baby and being a shitty father."

Gaby squeezed his arm. "Oh, honey."

"Growing up, I didn't have the same parents for more than two years—what the hell do I know about how to be a good one?" Tears fell from his eyes and splashed on his shirt. "What if I screw up our kid? What if I ruin his life because I don't know what the fuck I'm doing? What if he hates me?"

"None of that is going to happen."

"How do you know?"

"Because, Drew. You're a caring, loving person."

He looked up at her. She wiped tears from his cheeks. He pulled back, embarrassed.

"And plus, I'll be there to help. You're not going to do this by yourself," she said.

Drew didn't reply.

"How long have you felt this way?"

Drew gulped. His heart slammed hard in his chest. "Since . . . day one?"

"Why didn't you let me know?"

A gust of wind tussled Gaby's hair. She smoothed it, keeping her eyes fixed on him.

Drew felt completely exposed, raw. Like his insides had been turned outside.

"At first, I thought I'd get over it. And I couldn't say anything because, what if you agreed and left me because of it?"

The words barely finished leaving his mouth when Gaby wrapped her arms around him. "I would never."

The two of them stood there and held each other in that small parking lot for what felt like thirty minutes. Their necks pressed together, Drew felt their pulses beat damn near simultaneously. Hard and fast at first, until gradually slowing down as each calmed. When he felt confident enough to pull away and look at her, she wore a big smile on her face.

"So, we're going to build our baby's crib tonight?"

Drew smiled. "Definitely. Just one catch."

Gaby arched an eyebrow. "And what's that?"

"You have to go to lunch with me first."

She lunged at him and kissed his lips. "Let me tell my lead I'm leaving. Be right back."

Drew watched her bound back to the clinic and go inside.

Hands propped on hips, he cast his face to the sky and exhaled a sputter of air. The tension in his shoulders loosened; the ball of angst in his chest felt smaller.

Now, if only he could find a way to tell her about the mess he was in and the threats against all of them.

Chapter Twenty-Three

The hour-plus drive out to Dulzura the next day gave Drew ample time to think.

After patching things up with Gaby, they'd shared a nice lunch at a cheap Mexican place, followed by a quiet evening of non-alcoholic beers, popcorn, and constructing the crib together. Then, lying in bed in the dark, Gaby took Drew by surprise by reaching down his shorts, taking command of him. After, he passed out faster than any night in recent memory.

As a result of all of it, Drew woke up this Wednesday refreshed, excited, and hopeful.

Drew clocked a few anxious hours at the Surfview before heading southeast, to Dulzura. He cued up Pearl Jam on shuffle the entire way. Eddie Vedder sang about being alive when Drew hit the 8; owning a pellet gun while he merged onto the 94; and wanting to be a star in someone's sky as he passed the Jamul Casino.

From there, the land opened wide. Grazing fields zipped by, backed by a topography of green rolling hills and jagged mountains, all awash in purple—California lilac in full bloom.

He thought hard to recall when he'd last been in the back country. Must have been with Jake. It clicked when he passed a sign for the turn off to Otay Lakes. Drew had met Jake at the base of Otay Mountain four or five years earlier, and Jake drove them up the Otay Truck Trail. Well, Jake didn't drive. They caught a ride with some of his friends who caravanned up the mountain every Sunday in Jeeps.

The two-lane road narrowed. Drew cracked the windows to circulate in some of that fresh, back country air. All around, wildflowers were in bloom and abundant, despite the pitiful rainfall the county received the previous winter. He spotted purple and white lupines in the ditches. Further out in the fields were mats of owl's clover, smatterings of California poppies, and a multitude of other flowers he didn't know by name.

Gaby would love this drive, he thought. Maybe when all this was over, he'd bring her out to see the wildflowers. They could be one of those cheesy couples who took pregnancy photos lying in them, laughing, both petting her stomach. Or they could each smell a flower while they gazed all dopey-like into each other's eyes. He snickered. Wasn't such a stupid idea, though. He could use the levity and release from daily life's pressures. And she absolutely could as well.

The mountains ahead grew larger the farther he drove. Partial cloud-cover now accented the blue sky and cast shadows and punches of light that danced across the green land. A message pinged his cell phone that he might incur international texting prices. Sure, if he went beyond his destination he'd hug the border, but that was still miles and miles away. The message disappeared like an answer to his skepticism, and 5G returned to the top of his phone.

Thin orange safety cones now lined the double yellow line in the middle of the road and continued well into the short distance. The opening guitar lick to "Rearviewmirror" played as a Border Patrol station passed on his left. The stop had a long line of vehicles headed the other direction funneled through one security check point. The sight shot a nervous pang through him. What if Jake did show at the taco place and agreed to come back with him, and what if the San Diego cops had him on a watch list that Border Patrol was checking against all drivers?

The road curved. Drew slowed. Once the road straightened out, a small green sign appeared reading, WELCOME TO DULZURA, AN UNICORPORATED COMMUNITY OF SAN DIEGO COUNTY. More signs followed. One cautioned to slow to thirty-five, followed by several yellow signs with black arrows warning of sharp curves ahead.

The road switch-backed from here. Towering oaks grew at the top of steep cuts. Decomposed granite and soil spread over the shoulder into the road; likely washed down the cuts by a long-ago rain. Drew kept his speed under control to accommodate for the constant right-left-right nature of the drive and because he couldn't completely see around each next curve.

Finally, the road straightened for good. Farmland whizzed by now on both sides with livestock fencing lining the road.

The view ahead was all bright blue sky with dramatic clouds, surrounded by lush green land and rolling hills, backed by a majestic mountain range. Sans the fencing, he wondered if all of Southern California had looked this beautiful before colonizers strangled the land.

The map app on Drew's phone took over the van speakers, muting Eddie's vocals. It informed him the Dulzura Mini Market would be on his right in less than one-thousand feet. He checked his mirrors and slowed.

There it was. A log cabin-type shack of a place—something out of an old Western.

Drew guided the Transit Connect onto the shoulder, and into the gravel parking lot. Pulled into a space shaded by a tall Canary Island palm.

He collected his things and exited.

Outside, it smelled like smoke and meat and sun—the latter of which Gaby always contended he couldn't smell, but he totally could. After stretching his chest and shoulders, and rocking side-to-side to loosen his stiff hips, Drew headed for the market's entrance. Out front, he found the source of the smoke and meat: a rectangular-shaped, raised metal trough. Half of it was enclosed, and gray smoke billowed out of a vent on the side, while an open grill took up the other half, with split chicken breasts sizzling on top. Drew's mouth watered and his stomach growled when he walked past and to the open entrance of the market.

Inside, no fluorescents or other artificial means lit the store. Windows on all four walls provided an abundant supply of natural light, however. In the middle of the store were shelves filled with randomness. Boxed foods, candy, junk food—all stocked alongside emergency car equipment, farming supplies, and cosmetics, such as lotions, lip balm, and even toothbrushes. Three cold drink cases lined half the wall behind the dry goods. And immediately up front was the register, with a food menu hung behind; choices and prices in blue dry erase marker.

"Morning," said a black-haired guy with a thick Spanish accent. He must have appeared from the back. "Drinks are back there. Let me know when you're ready to order."

"How do you know I want to order food?" Drew asked.

The attendant sucked his cheek. "No one comes here at lunch time and walks past the meat cooking out there and doesn't order something."

Drew chuckled. "Fair, and you're right. Let me grab a water first."

"Take your time."

The wood floors squeaked as Drew walked back. He selected a bottle of spring water.

Once back at the register, he set the water down. "Okay, I'm ready."

"Our California burrito is real good," the attendant said.

"Thanks, but I think I'll have three pork tacos."

"Three pork tacos," repeated the attendant, scribbling the order into a notepad.

"Extra hot sauce too, please."

The man briefly eyed Drew. Did he get the code? "Okay. A water, and three pork tacos with extra hot sauce. Eight fifty-two, please."

Drew paid with a twenty.

"There are chairs out front, but the picnic tables are nicer in the back."

"Okay, thanks." Drew took a step to leave, and the attendant spoke up.

"Maybe out back *would* be best for you."

Drew cocked his head. "Sure."

"There's shade, and traffic in front can get too loud to enjoy your food."

"Sounds good. I'll be in the back then."

Drew walked outside and around the building. He was pleased to find the seating area was indeed a lot nicer than the front. An ancient, sprawling live oak shaded six large picnic tables, all of which were empty. Chickens clucked, unseen, somewhere in the short distance, and butterflies flitted about.

He sat on a bench at one of the picnic tables, and faced the back of the market.

He wondered if Jake would come out and greet him like nothing had happened since he took off in the Chinook almost a week earlier. Or would Drew get handed another rock with a note rubber-banded to it after he finished his lunch?

No. For some reason, he didn't know why, Drew felt confident he was about to see his brother. Call it brotherly intuition or animal instinct. A smile tugged at the corners of his mouth. Why else would Jake have him come all this way? This long, winding scavenger hunt was nearing its end.

He could feel it.

Even seated in the back of the market, the traffic on the main road was distractingly loud. He couldn't imagine how deafening the noise was on the weekends when motorcyclists and hotrodders took to the back country.

A white blur exited the back of the market, breaking his thoughts. Walking his way, a young woman, possibly a teenager, dressed in white. She carried two red baskets lined with yellow butcher paper, one in each hand. Drew's heart sank. One basket was his tacos, the other had to be a note rock. *Shit.*

"Hola," she said, reaching him.

"Hola."

She smiled, and set the baskets down in front of him.

"De nada," he said.

The young girl left. Drew inspected the baskets. In one were three delicious-looking street tacos filled with shredded pork, diced onion, cilantro, and a heaping of red hot sauce. In the other basket, the butcher paper was wrapped tightly around an object, appearing like a burrito might, but this burrito had corners. Jake found a rectangle rock?

Drew tore into the paper. Not a rock. He jolted back when he discovered he'd unwrapped a burner phone.

"What the hell?" He turned it over. Affixed to the back of the black phone was a pink sticky note. Drew snorted. So, Jake *did* leave a note.

It was short. Two words.

Call me.

Chapter Twenty-Four

Drew gave the non-descript flip phone a once-over. Stared at it. Turned it over in his hand several times before reading the note once more—*Call me.*

He'd now been given two burner phones in less than a week. One from each side of this shit storm of which he found himself stuck in the middle. Every part of it made his skin crawl.

As he stared at those two words on the pink sticky note, he understood he wasn't going to see his brother after all. What's more, Jake planting this burner phone here to reach him was clear evidence he did do something wrong, knew it, and fled because of it. Drew cringed, imagining his brother shooting someone in cold blood. Even if it was one of Zan's henchmen.

Drew worked himself off the picnic bench. Paced.

What would happen now? What should he say to convince Jake to give himself up? He hadn't even thought that part through yet. He'd been so busy simply following the leads and covering his tracks. And what would Jake say? He better say a whole hell of a lot. Jake owed him that. He'd endangered Drew, Gaby, and their unborn child in addition to himself thanks to his stupid decisions.

Drew exhaled sharply. Took a deep breath through his nostrils.

A yellow butterfly swooped past him. Chickens clucked somewhere behind him. A dog barked in the distance. Life would go on regardless. The realization did nothing to quell the anger growing inside of him.

Drew let out a monotone blast of noise. Tried to right his train of thought.

This was the exact point he'd worked so hard to reach the past few days. Now, one call could fix everything.

Opening the phone, Drew fumbled with the buttons to find where Jake had stored his number. He finally found it, hit the green phone icon, and put the phone to his ear.

It rang. And rang.

"Pick up, fool." Drew sat back down at the picnic table. His tacos looked delicious, but he couldn't tell if the rumble in his stomach was hunger or anxiety. "C'mon, man."

The line connected.

"Hello?"

"Jake?"

"Who's this?"

"Fuck you."

Jake laughed on the other end. "Bro. You made it. How are the tacos? You don't have to tell me. I know they're the best in the county. They are, right?"

Drew felt the vein on the side of his neck pulse. "What the hell are you doing?"

"Whoa, whoa, little bro—"

"Seriously. What the hell, Jake? You take off, don't say a word, and have me running all over looking for you?"

"Calm down, Drew. Everything okay?" Jake paused. "You and Gaby . . . okay?"

Drew snorted. "Yeah, for now, no thanks to you."

"What do you mean? That's the whole reason I left."

Drew snorted again.

Jake continued. "It's true. I didn't want you caught up in what went down."

"So much for that, asshole. What exactly *did* go down?"

The line fell silent. Jake took his time. Drew could hear him breathing. Jake let out an exaggerated sigh.

"We can get back to that. First, I need to know if anyone came looking for me—"

"No, first I want to know why you played with me. Why you handed me off from one of your hippie friends to the next."

Jake chuckled. "I've never heard you so worked up. Listen, I wasn't trying to mess with you. I wanted to make sure you were the only one who could find me. And I knew you knew where to start . . ."

"Lucky guess."

"No, you always pay attention to everything I say. I knew you'd go look for the friends I rolled in with. Since I told you we squatted at the pier, I was pretty sure you'd start there."

Jake is your drug. Gaby's voice made Drew wince.

"How'd you know you could trust all those people?"

"Shit, probably cause I've known them for years," Jake said.

"Pretty convenient they were all in San Diego."

"If not them, I would have found others. San Diego's a choice destination, if you didn't know. And anyway, it's a big community out there, little bro. We all look out for each other. Like you do for me, like I'm trying to do for you and Gaby."

"You're looking out for us? Is that what you really think?"

"Uh, yeah, dummy."

"How'd you even know that I would go looking for you?"

"Well, that's the whole reason—one of them, anyway—I borrowed your RV. I kinda banked on you coming to look for it, and me."

Drew squeezed his eyes shut. "It didn't occur to you that I would try to find you when you disappeared one day after almost getting shot and killed?"

Jake didn't respond. After a long pause, he changed the subject from the shooting.

"Back to my original question. Anyone come looking for me?"

"You stole one-hundred grand in cash. What do you think?"

"So, you know . . ."

"I know, Jake. The maniac tossed our house and had his bodyguard beat the shit out of me made it pretty fucking clear."

"I gotta say, I thought you'd be happier to hear my voice."

"Sorry. Guess you being a burden in my hand, not to mention fucking with the safety of my family, fucked my attitude."

"Sick Soundgarden reference."

"Shut up."

"So, what's this guy's name?"

"Zan West."

"Scary motherfucker?"

Zan's sunken face and predator eyes flashed in Drew's mind. "Yes. Very much so."

"Okay. So, what did he say?"

"He thought we robbed him together. After I convinced him that I didn't know what the hell he was talking about, he told me how you stole his cash, and that you shot his guy."

"Fuck that," Jake said. "I didn't shoot anyone. I was the one who nearly got shot."

"What are you saying?"

"You know I'm not a killer, Drew. I've never even got into a fight. Listen, here's how it went down. The first day we went in there, I saw a safe in the back room wide open, full of cash. So, I planned to come back and steal it. And, yeah, I did. After you parked, I ran in the back room, hit the dude guarding the money on the back of the head with one of your tools—"

"What the fuck?"

"He dropped, and I grabbed the cash off the desk—it was just sitting there in a plastic grocery bag for anyone to take. So, I grabbed the cash and took off. But I guess I didn't knock the dude out cold or something, 'cause he caught me before I could get out of the store. We wrestled for my backpack—where I stuffed the cash—for a minute or so, and then a loud bang went off. My ears rang like hell. The dude let go of me. I looked down and saw blood all over me. I panicked, thought the dude shot me. But then *he* started groaning. He shouted, cussed. That's when I saw the real blood. All over his shirt sleeve, soaking it, running down from his shoulder. Out of the corner of my eye, I saw the store clerk holding a handgun in two hands, pointing it at us. Before I could jump out of the way, he pulled the trigger again. Shot the dude in the stomach. He dropped. Everything got fuzzy, but I heard the clerk yell at me to run, to get out of there. So, I did."

"What the actual fuck?" Drew held his forehead, elbow propped on the picnic table.

"So, no. I didn't shoot anyone."

"But you stole Zan's money. One-hundred grand. What were you even thinking, Jake?"

"I had my reasons."

"Tell me. Seriously."

"What else did this Zan guy say?"

Drew took a deep breath. If Jake was holding back, he could too.

"He'd forgive everything if I found you and you returned the money to him personally."

Jake chuckled. "Forgive everything? If that's true, then why do I need to give it back to him in person? Couldn't I just give the money to you to give back and be good?"

"I don't know. I'm guessing it's a respect thing. Where are you anyway?"

"Close."

"You need to give that money back, Jake."

"Mmm, don't think I do."

"What about me and Gaby? You're not worried he'll punish us if you don't give it back?"

"Did he say that?"

Drew paused before letting Jake have it. "Yes, motherfucker. He took our baby's sonogram photo and showed it to me when he threatened everything I love, including your dumb ass if I didn't return you and the money."

Silence all but for Jake's breathing for several long seconds.

"So, call the cops if he comes back around," Jake finally said.

Drew pounded the table. "Why the fuck are you still in town if you're set on keeping the money? Thought you were worried for us, wanted to take care of us?"

"That's not what I meant."

"What did you mean, Jake?"

A pause. "Not now."

"What?"

"There's more I need to tell you, but not now."

Drew thought the very same thing. Both of them holding out on the other. Maybe he could use that to get Jake to meet-up, make him see he needed to turn himself into Zan and give back the money. Drew had to convince him one way or another. It was the only way to save his brother's life and keep Zan from hurting his wife and child.

"What's tomorrow look like for you, Drew?"

"I'm around, but—"

Jake cleared his throat. "We should meet-up so I can tell you everything. Then you'll understand why I did what I did."

Make that two of us, Drew thought. "Yeah, sounds good."

"Bonfires. Parties. Your first beer. Know where I mean?"

"Of course."

"Cool. Meet me there tomorrow at four in the afternoon."

Drew still fumed but he tried to stay cool so he wouldn't spook Jake. "Got it. And Jake?"

"Yeah?"

"Can't wait to see you, man."

"You too, little bro. Feels like it's been forever. I'm sorry to put you through all this."

"Save it for tomorrow."

They said goodbye and ended the call.

Drew took a deep breath and exhaled.

Finally, he'd see Jake, get the full truth, and help him right his sins against Zan while keeping his family safe at the same time. Gaby didn't need to be worried by any of it, either.

He was going to save his brother's life.

Acknowledging this sent a wave of optimism through him.

He took another deep, cleansing breath.

The intoxicating aroma of smokey pork wafted up into his nose. He looked down at the basket of tacos. Gently picked one up. It was still warm. Drew bit in, and it was all he could do to keep his eyes from permanently sticking in the back of his head.

Chapter Twenty-Five

Drew kept the gas floored all the way back to the city. Forty-five minutes after leaving Dulzura, he cruised into Ocean Beach.

The atmosphere along Sunset Cliffs was low-key electric for a weekday afternoon in April. A kombucha stand, vegan fast-food joint, and coffee shops all packed. A parade of choppers rumbled down Voltaire. Skateboarders jammed sidewalks. People walked dogs on side streets. Farther down, a drum circle of hippies on a church lawn pumped rhythm into the scene.

Drew arrived and parked at the Surfview Cottages. His energy felt the highest in days.

As he crossed the grounds, Lydia approached from the property office, hand raised.

"Do you have a second, Drew?"

Smiling, he waved her on. "For you? How can I help, boss?"

Lydia produced a half-smile. "I don't want to put pressure on you at all—"

"Uh-oh."

She held up a hand, dismissed the comment. "I neglected to ask how long your work would take to complete."

"Oh, is that all?"

"Sorry, I'm new at this. There are so many moving parts I wasn't prepared for. Maybe I should have hired a contractor to oversee everything, if I'm being honest."

"It's never too late, and I know a great one."

"Thanks. I'll keep that in mind."

"To answer your question: I'm a one-man crew. That said, I'm also a fast worker. I should have the units ready for paint by end of next week."

Lydia wrinkled her nose.

"Did I say something wrong?" Drew asked.

"No," she said. "It's just, the painters I hired said they want to start early next week."

"Want or need?

"They said want," Lydia said.

"Okay. I'll see what I can do. Maybe I can cut a day or two off if everything breaks right." Like if Jake conceded and returned the money to Zan, and Drew didn't have to take long lunches to go look for him anymore. "No promises though."

"That's reasonable. If you can't, well then it's on me for not thinking of this before now."

"Be easy on yourself. You're doing great."

"Thank you, Drew." Lydia offered her hand, and Drew shook it. She smiled, and turned around and headed back toward the office.

Drew went to the unit he'd halted work at before leaving for Dulzura.

Inside, half the unit's bones stood exposed, but he'd get them covered in no time. In fact, he had only two more units after this one to call it a day. He hadn't wanted to overplay his hand with Lydia, but he knew he'd be on to tape and mud tomorrow. If all broke right, he'd wrap everything up by early next week, even if it took working the weekend, which he was willing to do for the potential good word of mouth.

Drew picked up his drill, squeezed the trigger twice in rapid succession to ensure a strong charge. It fired. Drew felt good about the set meeting with his brother—he buzzed, like the drill. Resolving his brother's mess meant he could shift his focus back to work again, and not to mention making Gaby and the baby a priority—his first priority.

Grabbing a handful of screws, Drew got to work.

***

The last sheet of drywall hung perfectly in the last cottage unit. Drew would have killed to watch a time-lapse of the past few hours. Watch himself hustle—hanging panels in three units and finishing zipping up every last skeleton on this property.

He checked the time—4:27. Gaby got off at five.

An idea sparked. A big smile spread across his face.

"Hey babe. Had an idea. What if we meet at Mission Beach when you get off and we find a pickup game?" Drew sent the text.

No dots appeared as he stared at the screen, so he pocketed his phone and began packing up his work equipment.

Halfway to the Transit Connect with the hoist laid across his arms, his pocket buzzed. Too excited to wait, Drew set the hoist down, dug out his phone.

Gaby's text read, "Aw, that sounds fun. But I'm wiped out."

Drew's shoulders drooped. Dots flashed on the screen—Gaby working on a second text. Drew fired a text back first: "Come. You could chill and watch."

Gaby's dots stopped. They blinked again a couple seconds later. "Nah, I'm so tired, but you should go."

"You sure?"

"Yes! Have fun."

Drew pumped his fist. "Sweet." He texted back, "Would be more fun with you, but thanks! Love you. Get your rest." Gaby "loved" the text message.

He'd probably play awful, shaking off the rust of not having played since February. He didn't care. To simply dig his toes into the sand and have the salty air blow through his hair while he dove for spiked balls—would feel damn near therapeutic. Almost as good as it would feel finally seeing his brother tomorrow.

Drew loaded the hoist into the Transit Connect. Spotted the change of clothes and shoes he kept behind the driver's seat. One good thing at a time.

Chapter Twenty-Six

"You should have seen me out there, Mon. Best play of my life." Drew switched the phone to his left ear, securing it with his shoulder. Scraped excess mud from the joint he'd smothered carelessly. "Every one of my spikes landed, and every one hit at me I returned."

"That's cool, Drew. Sounds like you really needed it."

"No doubt. I wanted Gaby to come, she's a way better player than me, but she was too tired." A moment of silence between them. "Anyway, I wanted to thank you for pushing me to open up to her about the baby. You're a good friend."

"You mens."

"What's that mean?"

"I didn't tell you anything you didn't already know."

"Yeah, well." Drew set the tape knife down, checked the time. "Hey, reason I called . . ."

"You mean, other than to regale me with your volleyball prowess?"

"Ha-ha. So, I mentioned to the property manager that I know a great GC—cause she's looking pretty frazzled. I can give her your name and number, if you want an easy payday."

"Sounds good. Send me her info, too."

"Cool. I'll send it right after we hang up, which, sorry I gotta let you go."

"More volleyball?"

"No . . ." Drew said. "Going to meet my brother at Fiesta Island."

"No shit?"

"No shit. Ready to get all this behind us."

"Yeah, I bet. Good luck."

"Thanks, Mon. Talk to ya soon."

"See ya."

After they hung up, Drew examined the mess he'd made during their call. He scraped off the remaining excess mud from the wall. Poured what remained in his mud pan into the five-gallon bucket and sealed the lid.

Next, he washed up in the kitchen sink. Shut and locked the windows and locked up the unit on his way out.

***

The drive to Fiesta Island took a quick fifteen minutes, it was that close and traffic light.

Drew had his choice of spots when he pulled into the park's dirt lot. Passing a few small pickups, a Jeep, and a Tesla, of all cars, Drew nosed into a water-facing spot. A jet ski whizzed in front of his field of vision. He cut the engine, flopped back in his seat. It was 3:30. Thirty minutes to kill. Grabbing a nap crossed his mind, but he was too amped to fall asleep.

This was what he'd been working toward for nearly a week, and with only a few days of the deadline remaining. He'd done it. He found his brother by himself. Not by reporting the Chinook stolen or ratting him out to Det. Billberry. He found him and this burden could come to an end, provided he could make Jake see reason. Which, now that he recounted their phone conversation when Drew told him about the threats Zan had made and how flippant Jake had been, reason probably wasn't in Jake's vocabulary. Jake likely never saw reason in any sense of the word, Drew knew deep down. It's why he led life he did.

Drew got out of the van, walked around to the other side, and opened the sliding door. Plopped down, dropped his boots flat on the dirt. The sun was warm, the breeze off the water cool. Birds chirped, and water sports vehicles and small boats zoomed around the island.

This dirt lot held many memories of him and Jake. After today, they'd add one more.

"Jake. Remember that time I talked you into giving back one hundred-thousand dollars and getting your ass beat so you wouldn't catch a bullet to the head?"

They'd laugh about it one day. Hopefully.

Twenty minutes later, the sound of heavy tires crunching on dirt grabbed Drew's attention. He turned to see his RV slow and pull into the spot right next to him; Jake wearing his Padres hat, riding high behind the wheel. Excitement edged with frustration filled Drew.

"Little bro," Jake hollered down through the open window.

Drew hopped out of the van.

The Chinook purred right up until Jake cut the engine. A few painfully long seconds passed as Drew waited on his brother to open the door and climb down. As soon as he did, Drew launched himself at him.

"Whoa, bro. No broken ribs." But Jake reciprocated Drew's hug, squeezing him in equal measure. "Missed you."

Drew pulled away, held Jake by his shoulders and shook him once. "You dumbass. I love you, but you're a dumbass."

Jake made a smarmy face, shrugged. "Should we get on with this?"

Drew gestured for them to go sit on the sand berm in front of the vehicles. When they were both sat, Jake patted Drew's back.

"First off," Jake said. "I'm not giving the money back."

Drew's chest tightened. "Well, I've got some serious shit to lay on you that might change your mind, but you said you wanted to give me the rest of your story, first. So, go for it."

"Some serious shit, huh?" Jake whipped off his hat, rubbed his head. Plopped the hat back on his head and pulled the bill down tight. "Yeah, I know you think I fucked up, but I had my reasons." Drew didn't budge, or so much as blink. Jake took the cue, continued. "When I saw all that cash, and the guy back there guarding it, I could tell it wasn't the liquor store's money. Way too much of it. When I worked with you that day, I saw how hard you work. I always knew you were a hard worker, but you really pour yourself into your work. I'm guessing Gaby's probably the same. It got me thinking."

"About what?" asked Drew.

"About how you two work so damn hard and can still only afford to buy a house. How all your dreams got put on hold because of a stupid pandemic. Living on the road is my dream. It's always gonna be my home. So even though I don't get you two wanting a bigger house, I *do* get you wanting a place of your own. That's your dream, and you've earned it as far as I'm concerned. Guess what I'm trying to say is, when I saw that money, I saw an opportunity to help you two get back what you lost without anyone getting hurt."

Drew shook his head like clearing cobwebs from his brain. "But someone did get hurt."

"Yeah, and that sucks, but I didn't shoot him."

"I know you said Ahmed shot the guy, but he's the nicest dude. I just can't see it."

"He did though, 'cause he was sick of those thugs controlling his store."

"He told you that?"

"I mean, not in so many words. But I had a lot of time since then to connect the dots. Your Zan guy is probably laundering money through there and obviously it's not a copacetic situation since that dude was guarding things in the back room. Why else would the clerk shoot him and tell me to run—*with* the money?"

Drew sighed. "Okay, setting all that aside, what did you think we would say if you dropped one-hundred grand in cash in our laps if you had gotten out clean?"

Jake adjusted his hat. "Thanks?"

A snicker escaped Drew. "Seriously?"

Jake stared into Drew's eyes. "You wouldn't take it? Seriously?"

"Well . . . that's a moot point now anyway."

"Cause of this Zan guy?"

Drew nodded. "Time for me to tell you everything now."

Jake waved his hands like come on.

"I told you they broke into our house and beat the shit out of me, right?" Jake nodded. Drew took a heavy sigh, continued. "This Zan West creep is scary as shit. He said the only way this could be made right, is for me to find you, and get you to come in and return the cash to him. Otherwise, he will find you himself and kill you."

Jake blew air from his bottom lip. Turned to look at the water. Two jet skis were doing whatever the equivalent of doing donuts in the water is.

"Not going to lie, Jake. When you return the money, he's planning on beating the shit out of you. Worse than I got."

Jake jerked his head, arched an eyebrow, but said nothing.

"I felt you should know everything," Drew said. "He said you would live . . . if I could get you to a hospital quickly."

"This deal gets sweeter by the second."

"Jake. If you don't do this, he will kill you. One-hundred percent." Drew got chills from his own words. He thought the message would prompt introspection in his brother. Instead . . .

"Fuck all that. I'm so out of here. That's all."

"You do that and you're also putting me and Gaby in danger. Remember? Zan threatened us, too."

Jake shrugged so casually you'd think he was deciding between soup or salad for lunch, not weighing the fate of his life or theirs. "Why not run? Hit the road, like I do."

"I can't believe you. You'd risk your life and ours over this money? I have to check in with this guy. If I tell him you skipped town, he's coming for us and then for you."

"What?" Jake jumped up. "You're *helping* this guy? Here I thought I was dropping you clues, and this whole time you've been hunting me down to turn me over to a guy who wants to kill me? That's really great of you. Way to look out. *Brother*."

Drew had stood up by now, and reached out for Jake. "It's not like that. I didn't have a choice." Jake ducked away from Drew's hand. He scanned the parking lot.

"Did you tell him we were meeting here? Is he coming?"

"No," said Drew. "Listen, I haven't told him about us meeting. But if you run, I'll have to tell him something. I have to protect my wife, Jake!"

"Like I said before, call the cops if he shows up. You know what? I can't believe this. The one time I try to do something good for you."

"Don't be stupid."

"Now I'm stupid?" Jake kicked sand. "You know what? Fuck this and fuck you."

Jake stormed to the Chinook, disappeared around the back. Stunned, Drew followed him.

When he reached the back of the RV, Jake hopped down in front of him, a new black gym bag in-hand. "What are you doing?" Drew asked.

"Here. Take the money." Jake shoved the bag into Drew's chest. Its heft caught Drew by surprise and knocked the wind out of him.

"What? No. I'm not keeping it. Zan will kill you, Jake. He wants you *and* the money."

"He can't have me. If he wants me so bad, tell him to come find me."

"No." Drew chest-passed the gym bag past Jake, into the Chinook, but wondered if that meant he was giving Jake permission to take the RV for good.

"Nope!" Jake grabbed the bag by its handles, and pushed Drew out of the way. He marched over to the Transit Connect, and slung it in through the open side door.

"You're being an ass," said Drew, meeting Jake at the van. "I'm trying to save your life."

Jake bodied Drew. "For once, could you let me give you something good."

"How about for once you not run from trouble and leave me holding the bag for you?"

The two pressed their chests against each other. Heavy breath and clenched jaws. Sweat ran down their temples. Drew balled his hands into fists. They'd never gotten into a physical fight, but there's always a first time for everything, Drew almost salivating at the prospect.

"What's going on over here?"

The voice startled them both. The question came from a cop in a patrol car. Pulled right up next to them without either of them noticing.

Drew took a step back. Unclenched a fist and held out his hand. "Nothing, officer. It's just a brotherly disagreement."

Jake stepped back as well, twitchy, failing to pull off looking casual.

The cop put his cruiser in park. "You two been drinking?"

"No, sir," Drew said.

"This isn't good," Jake whispered.

"No shit."

Drew stuffed his hands into his pockets. Jake turned to the cop.

"I was about to leave, officer. Like my brother said, simply a minor disagreement."

Minor, Drew thought. Putting his young family in danger. Fucking arrogant asshole.

After sitting silent for an eternity, the cop finally said, "All right. Both of you get in your vehicles and be on your way."

"Yes, sir," they replied in unison.

Drew waited for the cop to leave so he could give the bag of cash back to Jake, but the cop wasn't budging. Jake patted Drew on the shoulder. Leaned into his ear, and whispered, "Give it to Zan. Or keep it. Put it on me either way, but I really hope you keep it."

Through gritted teeth, Drew said, "Let's work this out. Zan's deadline is Monday."

"My mind's set, little bro." With that, Jake turned and climbed into the Chinook, fired it up. The cop started his cruiser as well, pulled forward and did a three-sixty. The Chinook reversed, then lurched forward and headed out of the lot slowly with the cop following.

Soon, Drew found himself standing alone in the dirt lot with half of what he'd promised to deliver to Zan West. What should he do now?

Tell Zan that Jake was in the wind with all the cash, to do what he had to do? Or give Zan the bag of money and hopes it buys Zan's mercy? Neither seemed right, neither seemed like plans that would work. Zan was explicit. Jake *and* the cash, with the threat to destroy everything Drew loved if he didn't get both.

His eyes ached. And it felt like a chain was looped around his neck, tightening.

Chapter Twenty-Seven

After parking the Transit Connect between the palm tree and the house, Drew flung open the door and tore out. He stomped in front of the van and over to the small utility shed attached to their rental. Shoved a key in the padlock. Once he'd opened the shed, he dug out the aluminum bat that lived on the side of the washing machine and skulked back to the palm tree.

Taking huge swings, he slammed the tree trunk with the bat again and again.

"Goddamn—*whack*—you—*whack*—Jake!"

Small chunks of the trunk flew in every direction as he continued to strike it, yet the enormous tree absorbed every blow without sustaining significant damage. Drew zeroed in on a spot and pummeled it. Tree debris struck his arms and chest. With each strike, the bat elicited a hollow sound that echoed off the houses across the alley.

After dozens of swings, Drew quit, exhausted.

He dropped the bat. It clanged when it landed on the concrete and tinged as it rolled into the alley. Drew collapsed against the base of the palm. Folded his knees to his chest. The Transit Connect was dinging endlessly about the keys left in the ignition.

What the hell was his brother thinking? If he was willing to give the money to him, why not listen and return it to Zan? Drew didn't want it; he'd made that clear. He only wanted his brother safe, his wife and unborn child safe.

Drew had chewed on these questions the entire drive home. The only reasoning he came up with was Jake feared getting curb stomped. Which, okay. Who wouldn't? And so, he'd rather bet on himself that he could outrun Zan? He probably also bet Zan would lose interest in him after a while by giving the money to Drew. Drew doubted both assumptions. That's all they were though, assumptions. How could he know Jake's thinking for certain? The dumbass wouldn't answer his phone. Drew tried calling him the entire drive home.

"Dumbass." Drew wiped sweat from his brow.

And what about Zan? Drew had to call and report his "progress" at some point. Not now, though. Not when he was this heated, pissed, and frustrated.

Drew worked himself off the ground. Slowly made his way to the van, and leaned in and pulled the keys from the ignition. The dinging stopped. The sudden silenced elicited a thought.

The money.

Back in the dirt lot, a hopeless feeling of failure settled on him. He'd wanted to give the money back to Jake so he could return it to Zan himself, but the cop's presence fucked that up. Coming away with the money meant he'd only secured half of what Zan required, which made him feel as if he'd accomplished nothing.

Now, though . . .

He'd talked his brother into relinquishing the cash. That was huge.

Maybe coming away with the money was in fact a win. It's why Zan was hunting Jake, after all. So maybe if he gave the money back and begged Zan to show him and his family mercy, he might?

Apparently, it had been Jake's plan to give it to Drew and Gaby all along, but that was neither here nor there. What a stupid idea, anyway. Like he could use 100 grand of suspected drug money on a down payment and not get caught.

Drew took a deep breath.

Maybe all wasn't lost yet.

He had the money. He also had five more days to convince Jake to reconsider Zan's offer of mercy. And unlike when Drew began this mission, or whatever it was, he now had a way to reach his brother. As long as Jake didn't ditch his burner phone, Drew could potentially set up another meeting between the two.

All he could do now was secure the cash, lick his wounds, and live to fight another day.

Drew shut the driver's door, walked around the van to the side. The gym bag was still where Jake had flung it, behind the driver's seat. Drew stretched his body into the van. Grabbed it by the handles and pulled. The heaviness of the bag gave him comfort. Drew positioned the bag on the floorboard in front of him, unzipped it.

Straps and straps of rubber-banded, well-worn dirty cash laid inside. Gathering them, Drew realized the straps were bound by denomination. He arranged them into piles according to each amount. When finished, he had four piles—two straps of hundreds, six of fives, eleven of tens, and twenty-two straps of twenties.

He took one of the twenties and thumbed it, like he'd seen done in the movies. The bills were the furthest thing from crisp, and reeked of sweat and booze. Pulling off the rubber band, Drew counted the

number of bills. There were one-hundred, making the strap worth . .
. two-thousand bucks.

While rubber-banding the money back together, he examined the
other straps of twenties—they were all roughly the same thickness.
Drew pulled out his phone and opened the calculator app . . .
Two-thousand times twenty-four straps equaled forty-four-thousand
bucks.

Figuring the other denominations contained the same number of
bills as the strap of twenties—one-hundred—Drew did some quick
math . . .

Once he had the amounts of the denominations, he added.
Forty four-thousand, plus eleven-thousand, plus three-thousand, plus
twenty-thousand, equals . . . seventy eight-thousand. Shit. He'd goofed
somewhere.

Drew counted the straps of each denomination again. Math was a
fairly strong skill of his, needed to be in his line of work. In order to
make sure he wasn't assuming too much, he counted the number of
bills in one strap of each denomination. One-hundred bills in each.

Drew ran the numbers again. Same total again: seventy
eight-thousand.

"Shit."

He added it all again. Same total. He made sure each stack
maintained the same denomination throughout. They did. No flaw
there. He added it again. Same total popped on the screen again.

"The fuck did you do? Fuck." A sinking feeling of despair shot
through him. How could Jake be so stupid, so fucking inconsiderate?
Drew felt his heart beating hard in his chest; sweat pouring down his
temples. Felt like a couple nights back on the front lawn. What would
he tell Zan? How could Jake be doing this to him?

"Drew?"

Drew startled. Cocked his ear. He wasn't sure he'd truly heard his name called through the fog of emotions.

"Drew? Are you out back?" Gaby.

"Shit," he muttered while frantically tossing the straps back into the gym bag. "Shit."

As he tossed the last two in, he saw out of the corner of his eye Gaby opening the chain link gate. "Babe," he said. Zipped up the bag. "It's me." He tossed the bag back into the van, threw a canvas drop cloth over the bag, and slid the door closed.

"Were you shouting?"

Drew turned toward her. "When did you get home?" He armed sweat off his face as he walked to the rear of the van where and they met. Gaby laid a hand on his chest and they kissed.

"Just now. I heard someone yelling and it sounded like you," she said. Something distracted her to her left. "Is that our bat in the alley? And why is the shed open?"

Stammering, Drew said, "Uh, I . . . I saw a rat on the palm tree and went after it."

"So that was you yelling?"

"Guess so. I was pretty focused trying to kill the damn thing, but it got away."

Gaby smushed her face. "Too bad. Maybe you should pick up a trap tomorrow?"

"Good idea."

"What's for dinner?" she asked.

Drew reached into his pocket, beeped the fob to lock the van. "Good question. Why don't you go inside, I'll put the bat away and come in, and we'll figure it out?"

✳✳✳

Gathering and putting the bat away created enough time for Drew to also grab the two burner phones from the van. He'd been keeping Zan's on him, or close enough to make sure he didn't miss any calls. Now with Jake running off on him again, and shorting Zan's cash by twenty-two grand, Drew needed to keep his burner on him as well. At least until Jake answered and they could arrange another meeting. Which needed to be soon. Before Jake left town. So much for living to fight another day.

The storm door barely clicked closed before Gaby jumped him.

"How was your day? We had another three positive cases. I don't know if I can handle another wave with the new variant. We're all convinced this is never going to end." She radiated enthusiasm that belied her stated annoyance with work. She kissed him, and they hugged. "So?"

"What?"

"How was your day—before coming home to a rat."

Drew blew an exasperated sigh. "Okay, I guess. Started on tape and mud." He fell back onto the couch. He wanted to tell her about Jake, but knew that would open a can of worms and he'd have to explain the money, Zan, the cops. The threat to their safety . . .

Gaby followed his lead. "It's going well then?"

"Yeah, easy." He picked at the dirt under his nails.

"Drew?"

"Yeah?"

"Have you thought of any names lately?"

"Names of what?"

She swatted his leg. "For the baby . . ."

"Oh, yeah. Sorry. Guess the day was longer than I thought."

Gaby rolled her eyes quickly—her jab eyes, Drew playfully called them. "I thought of three names today . . . Want to hear them?"

"Sure," he said.

She let out a tiny squeal. "Okay. The first one is Will . . ." She let it hang, and stared at him. "No reaction?"

"Just tell me them all first."

"Will, Mateo, and Hunter. Will for Wil Myers, but two ls, 'cause one is dumb. And two babies came into the clinic recently named Mateo and Hunter and I like them."

Drew slowly stood. Stretched. "Sounds good."

Gaby grinned.

He took his cell phone out. "How about Zia?"

"For a name?" Her tone was incredulous.

"No, for dinner."

"Are you for real right now?"

"What?"

"*Those sound good, babe?*" She repeated his words in a mocking tone.

"What? I have to decide now?"

She swatted the couch, and stood up. "Never mind. Just order a damn pizza." She walked around the couch and headed to their bedroom. She disappeared around the corner, but reappeared just as quickly.

Hands on hips, she said in a whip-crack tone, "Have you heard from your brother yet?"

"No. I would've told you if I had."

Gaby huffed. "Go pick up the fucking pizza. A walk might help you fix your attitude."

Drew threw out his hands. "Seriously? Fine, whatever."

Gaby went into their room.

"A walk does sound good," Drew said.

"Good," called Gaby.

A walk genuinely sounded good to him. He had shit to figure out, and a thieving, dumbass brother to get on the phone.

Drew left the house, and went through the front gate. Closing it behind him, he heard Bernie washing dishes through his kitchen window.

"Hi, Drew."

"Hey, Bernie."

"Getting the mail?"

"No, going up to Zia to grab a pie for dinner. Want anything?"

"No, thanks. I already ate."

Drew waved goodbye to Bernie. Headed down the driveway. Once he made it to the sidewalk, he pulled out Jake's burner phone and redialed him. It rang and rang. Drew ended the call, squeezed a fist. What exactly was he up to keeping more than a fourth of the money? The possibilities scared Drew, knowing if his brother spent it, Drew couldn't cover that amount to make Zan whole. Getting Jake on the line ASAP needed to be his priority.

Unfortunately, he'd really fucked up back there with Gaby. Right when they'd been clicking again. She was obviously trying to make the baby easier for him to accept, too. She even made an effort, offering up the name Will as a tribute to one of Drew's favorite Padres players. God, he was dense and knew it. He could make it up to her later, though.

Drew tried Jake again. No answer.

He threw his head back. A bank of thin clouds rolled across the blue sky. Scaly-looking, the texture of elephant skin. Walking past an overgrown yard, he wrinkled his nose at the pungent odor of lingering skunk spray.

Once he made it to Adams Ave., traffic was heavy. He ran across the street during a brief lull and hooked a right on the sidewalk. A couple blocks up, he reached Zia and realized he hadn't asked Gaby what she wanted. He went to text her, but figured he'd order their usual—pesto pepperoni.

When he grabbed the door handle, his pocket began to ring. The pocket containing Jake's phone. He ducked to the side, pulling the phone out.

"Jake?"

"Call much? Goddamn, you're like a teenage girl who got dumped by the star QB."

"We need to talk."

"See? This is why I don't carry a phone."

"Uh-huh." Drew walked down the sidewalk to ensure privacy. "What the fuck, man? I don't even know where to start with you."

"Well, you better, 'cause I've got an appointment to look at this sweet ninety-three Itasca this guy's selling on Craigslist. New shocks, new brakes, new generator—it's clean as hell."

"What are you talking about?"

"Talking about buying my own RV."

"With what?" Drew asked, knowing the answer but needing Jake to say it.

"I assume that's why you're calling. You counted the money, right?"

"Yeah. It's short. Really short."

Jake laughed. "I wouldn't say it's short."

"Why is this a game to you? Zan is going to kill you and possibly me and Gaby if you don't bring back *all* the money. He knows where I fucking live, Jake. What aren't you getting about this?"

"Listen, bro. I took that money to help you and Gaby out . . . and to help myself. Don't sweat it. When I buy my own RV, I'll get the Chinook back to you."

"I don't care about the Chinook. It's the least of my concerns—hell, keep it. Will that convince you to make the right decision? As long as you take all the money to Zan, you can have the Chinook for all I care."

"No, no, no," Jake said. "I finally have the opportunity to take care of myself for once and not take charity from you. Anyway, it's been too long since I've had wheels of my own."

"Jake—"

"Listen, Drew. You have no idea what it's like for everybody to see you as a parasite. Always bummin' rides and food; crashing on people's pull-outs. I'm a grown man. Time to get my shit together. I know it, you know it."

"By stealing drug money? Or whatever the fuck it is? Dude. You can sleep on my couch permanently, or hell, if you think buying your own RV will prove something, I'll sell you the Chinook for a dollar. But, please. Whatever you do, don't spend that money!"

There was a long silence. Drew feared Jake hung up. He fumed at the thought.

Then, Jake groaned. "I don't know . . ."

"I know you'll catch a bullet to the head if you don't do what's right."

"Jesus. Chill. Anyway, you think doing what this thug says is doing the right thing?"

"In this case? Yes, because it will keep you alive." Jake blew air into the receiver. Drew added, "We need to meet again. Please?"

Another stretch of silence.

"I don't know. Maybe. Give me a day or two to think about it."

"Fine. A day, but you have to promise me you won't spend the money."

Jake groaned again, and exhaled an exasperated sigh. "Okay, Dad. I won't spend it. Jesus. Telling you. You're gonna be a good father."

"Promise you'll stay safe and call me when you're ready to meet again."

"Okay. Hey, Drew?"

"Yeah?"

"You really don't want to keep the money so you can buy a house of your own?"

Drew took a deep breath and exhaled. "Not if it means risking your life and Gaby's. No. Hell fucking no."

Chapter Twenty-Eight

Drew woke Thursday morning in a sour-ass mood no amount of coffee would fix.

The night before, he and Gaby exchanged few words over the pizza; and after, she disappeared to their bedroom to read, leaving Drew to watch the Padres game. To think, fume, and chew on the predicament Jake had put him in. Even the series-sweeping win against the Reds did little to cheer him up, and he went to bed irritated as hell.

He only hoped putting in a solid day's work would clear his head and his mood.

Arriving at the Surfview Cottages at seven, he parked the van and told himself *enough*. No more wallowing. He pushed Jake and Zan and Det. Billberry and Gaby and the baby to the back of his mind. Focused on the work of the day. Taping and mudding.

Drew lugged his supplies to the first cottage of the morning and got to work. Right away, the monotony of taping joints dropped him into that hypnotic state he relished. He embraced it. Before long, he was on to mudding the unit—his favorite step of the job. *Smooth perfection.*

Feeling it, Drew popped in his ear buds, cranked up a Grunge playlist that kicked off with "Unglued" by Stone Temple Pilots. His internal rhythm took control, rocking his body, as the song's intro raced. Scott Weiland began singing and Drew mouthed silently along to the lyrics, scraping his tape knife down a joint, giving it a flick of the wrist at the end of the run. The fast-driving song flew and Drew's artistry kept pace. He got chills when Scott sang about all these things he was sick about and coming unglued. "Can relate," Drew muttered to himself.

When the two-and-a-half-minute song finished, "No Excuses" by Alice in Chains came on. The drums and Jerry and Layne's harmonizing kicked Drew into gear. He hit a groove, mind detached, and feeling a little better.

An hour-and-a-half later, Drew finished the unit.

He smiled as he looked over his work, gear in arms, headed out the door to the next unit.

Along the way, his pocket buzzed. He set down his supplies in the sandy grass, and checked his cell. A text from Gaby simply stating good morning. He was glad to see their tiff the night before didn't alter their ritual of exchanging morning hello texts.

"Morning. Sorry about last night." He hit send on his text. Pocketed the phone, gathered up his gear, and went to the next cottage.

Only a few steps inside, another buzz. Again, he set everything down, but this time kept his phone pocketed while he set things up. Next, he walked to the wall in the tiny dining room and slide open the two windows. A gentle breeze, holding the tang of ocean and fish, drifted in.

Drew wandered back to the living room, and checked his phone. Gaby's reply simply said, "It's fine." For some reason, the text struck him sideways. A germ of resentment sprouted in his chest, even though he knew he had no right to the feeling. He tapped out a response to prove his contrition. "I'll be thinking about the names you mentioned." Before hitting send, he stared at the screen. Then, backed out the message, locked the phone, and set it down on his fold-out step stool. He dug the burner phones out of his pockets, and set them on the stool as well.

The playlist rolled on with Pearl Jam's "Once." Drew sucked his cheek and went to work, taping. If he continued to keep his mind anchored on work, he could bust out nine or ten units today, maybe more. On that pace, he'd have the gig wrapped by Tuesday or Wednesday, and hopefully impress Lydia enough to prompt her to spread word of mouth through the property manager world. Of course, if Mon got added as GC, she'd garner the praise. That was fine by Drew; she championed his work constantly. It was only fair he hooked her up for once.

Drew taped up the living room, moved to the tiny dining area, and finished in the bedroom. After popping the lid on the five-gallon bucket of mud and giving it a quick refresh, he returned to the bedroom. Normally, he began mudding where he'd finished taping, and work backwards. No set reason why. Just flowed for him best that way.

Drew opened the bedroom window that faced the interior of the property. Other subs milled about, including a four-man solar crew. The roofers must have finished yesterday. Must be nice to have an actual crew. Maybe one day, he thought.

Drew stabbed his tape knife into the mud and slapped a generous amount on to the first seam, and got going. The mud spread evenly with his steady direction.

A while later, and about the time Chris Cornell's otherworldly vocals reached another octave at the end of "Say Hello 2 Heaven" and the music shrank, a noise from the other side of the unit garnered

Drew's attention. He paused the playlist, pulled one ear bud out to listen.

Nothing for a long moment. As he went to reinsert the bud, he heard the sound again—his phone vibrating on the plastic landing of the step stool. He set down the mud pan and knife, balancing them against the wall. Clapped his hands against his quads, and headed out to see who was texting or calling him.

Right when he reached the phone, the screen's light dimmed. He grabbed it, pressed the home key, and a string of texts from Gaby appeared.

"Have you seen the news?"

"I'm so sorry, babe."

Broken heart emoji.

"Call me after you read this?"

Next, she sent a link to a story in *The San Diego Union-Tribune*: "Rose Miller, tarnished former local charity worker, dies at 76."

A lump swelled in Drew's throat. He hovered his thumb over the link, unsure if he wanted to read the article. Rose died? Didn't feel real somehow. He took a step back, stumbled, but caught himself. Another text from Gaby came through: "Are you ok?"

He ignored it, and clicked the link. The page opened to the same headline. Below, a hero shot of Rose and Joseph in full color, standing arm-in-arm in front of one of their thrift stores, likely during their peak. Sure enough, the photo was credited to a U-T photographer, dated 2002.

Drew scrolled down and read the first paragraph.

Former San Diego celebrity charity worker, part-owner
of the Joseph's Home chain of nonprofit thrift stores,
and convicted felon Rose Miller, died peacefully at an

assisted living facility in Mira Mesa on Wednesday. She was 76.

The next graphs Drew skimmed because he knew what they'd relay. Her and Joseph's rise to prominence. Their history of selflessness, charity, and philanthropy benefitting the area. Next, how it all imploded—a rapid loss of everything upon their convictions as complacent participants in a drug smuggling scheme orchestrated by an East County gang.

He skipped to the last paragraph. It said there would be no memorial service. No survivors listed, either. No mention of Miller's Kids. And nothing about honoring her memory by donating flowers or a gift to the charity of her choice like most obituaries announced. Didn't she deserve that small gesture? For her crimes, she had done exceedingly more good for the San Diego community during her life. Even in death, did she need to be held to the worst of her actions? Yet, he'd carried around only the negative since that horrible night, hadn't he? The raid and the Millers' crimes all but erased the good they'd done for him, so who was he to say how a whole community should honor her life—or not?

Drew cleared the link. He took a deep breath and lost grip of the phone. It clattered to the ground. He bent down and picked it up but got dizzy. Sweat bloomed on his forehead. Standing, the space felt like it was closing in on him. Drew burst for the front door, in desperate need of fresh air.

Outside, the sun beat down, and the sounds of several construction crews working on the exteriors, seagulls squawking, and waves crashing all at once hit Drew like a wall. He shook his head, overwhelmed, frustrated.

His phone rang. He answered the call, turned and ducked back inside.

"Are you okay? Did you know?" Gaby's voice was soft, comforting.

"Had no idea."

"I'm so sorry, honey. I'm sure you're feeling—"

"Everything," he said.

"Totally." She paused for a moment. "Is there anything I can do? Want to talk about it? Doesn't have to be this instant."

Drew paced. "It's okay. I think I'll be fine."

"It's okay if you're upset. She was a big part of your life."

"Yeah."

Gaby moaned compassionately. "I know—" She stopped herself.

"You know what?"

"Nothing, sorry. What I think isn't important right now."

"Sure, it is. Tell me."

Hesitating, Gaby said, "I know you said you didn't want to go see her. And I understood. Now . . . I hope her passing can give you closure in time."

"Thanks." What else could he say? Gaby was right. He knew where Rose lived and never entertained the thought of going to visit her other than the times when Gaby asked him if he should. Maybe he should have. But for *closure*? His childhood was full of it. Stay with this foster family until they give you the boot. Closure. Never did him any good then, so why would it have with Rose? "Look," Drew said. "I better get back to work if I'm going to stay on schedule."

"Sure . . . It's okay if you're not okay with this news. You know that, right?"

He grunted a confirmation.

"We'll talk about it tonight, if you want," she added.

"Sure."

"I love you," she said

"Love you, too."

After they hung up, Drew slammed the phone back on the stool harder than he meant. The two burner phones caught his eye. He still needed to check in with Zan, and should he tell Jake about Rose? Fuck them both, he thought. He needed to worry about himself, and get his mind back on work.

Drew skulked back to the bedroom. Picked up the mud pan and knife, mixed the mud. He couldn't remember being this affected by Joseph's death. Was he experiencing stronger emotions about Rose because he'd already been in a foul mood earlier? Or maybe now that both Millers had died, would that period of his life, also? Or maybe because he was stressed as hell with the Jake and Zan mess? Who knew? He slapped mud on the next seam—way too much.

"Fuck."

Scraping the excess off, he smeared mud across the drywall accidentally. Looked like a toddler playing with paints for the first time, not the work of a professional. He tried to clean up his mess, but each attempt to corral the mud resulted in smearing more of it across the wall.

"Fuck."

Drew lost it.

He spiked the mud pan and knife to the ground. Mud splattered up on to him and the wall. "Fuck, fuck, fuck." A fire raged under his skin. He reared back his fist and punched the wall. Cursing, he punched over and over, his fist driving hole after hole through the drywall.

***

Wet sand oozed between his toes with each step. Contractor pants rolled up to his shins and construction boots in-hand, Drew ambled down the beach. He wasn't one to take a beach stroll with more than half a day of work remaining, but after completely winding himself by punching eleven holes in the wall like a bad stereotype, a break seemed necessary.

He'd set himself back hours—but the work could wait until he got a grip, cooled down.

It was close to 9:30 a.m., and only a handful of surfers remained in the water. "The Dawn Patrol" had long since cut bait to get to their jobs, or simply because the waves flattened, as they usually did this time of day. Drew was headed in the direction of Dog Beach. He wouldn't make it that far, but the thought of receiving dog therapy would've been nice right then.

He squeezed the burner in his pocket.

He couldn't put off Zan any longer. The first week of his 10-day deadline was closing fast. They hadn't spoken in days, and while Zan didn't require daily check-ins, he insisted Drew stay in touch. Maybe it was Drew's paranoia urging him to call. Paranoia about having possession of most of the cash, or from the fact that he'd tracked down Jake, met with him, and hadn't been able to bring him in. Whatever the case, Drew felt an uneasy itch telling him a check-in was overdue.

Gentle waves washed onto the beach. Drew cut away from the water, and headed toward the boardwalk. When he reached the low concrete wall, he plopped down.

Behind him, on the far end of Veteran's Park, four earthy types were unloading music instruments out of a vintage, baby-blue Volkswagen van. Drew pulled the burner from his pocket, and turned back to the water. Waves lapped lazily onto shore. The sound relaxed him. After taking a few deep breaths to try to calm his remaining nerves, he dialed.

Shaw picked up. "Find your brother yet?"

"Yeah, sorta."

"The fuck sorta mean?"

"Can I please talk to Zan?"

Shaw took the phone away from his ear—Drew heard jostling, a hum like they were driving, and indiscernible words. Then, Zan came on.

"Drew Jones. How goes the search for my money and Jake?" He punctuated Jake's name.

"Good." How much should he tell him? Not that he only had part of the cash, or that Jake intended for them to split it. "I found him."

Zan clicked his tongue. "No shit? So, when do I get to meet this brother of yours?"

Drew felt a stabbing sensation in his chest, as if Zan's words were somehow weaponized. "Soon. He just needs a little time."

"Oh, he needs some time, you say? He better be using that time to get correct, and not to take off with my money for good. Cause *that* would not be, you know . . . good."

"Good," Drew said a half-beat behind Zan. "He's going to do the right thing, I'm sure."

Zan let Drew hang.

"Are you still there?"

"Where are you, Drew?"

"What?"

"Sounds like you're at the beach."

"Oh, yeah. I'm in OB. Doing a job by the pier."

"Sounds relaxing."

Drew flashed on the holes he'd punched into the wall.

"I'm glad you called, Drew. I questioned if you were taking things seriously."

Drew stifled a scoff. "I've been keeping busy the last few days trying to find him, is all."

"Did you see my money?" Zan asked.

Blood pumped in Drew's ears. "Yes, for a minute."

"Was it all there? It better all be there."

"He hasn't spent any of it, he assured me."

"I have to say. It fucking pisses me off that he needs more time. If I were you, I would have gone aggro on his ass, slung him in your van, and driven him straight to me."

"There were . . . circumstances. A cop pulled up when we were talking. Spooked us."

Zan made an understanding groaning noise. "Well. That's a damn cop for ya. Always fucking shit up. That said, do I need to remind you of your deadline?"

"No. I'm on it."

"Ten days is pretty fucking generous, Drew. And I gave you that long cause I knew covering this entire county would be no walk in the park. Now that you found him, finish this. My offer has an expiration, and so will your brother if he doesn't return my money."

***

Drew worked late to fix the trashed wall and get back on track. Replacing the drywall took longer than normal because he had to run to a box store to buy several new sheets. After he finished the reinstall, he picked back up with taping and mudding, knocking out an additional six units. It was after eight o'clock when he finally arrived home.

The sun had set, but the sky held a darkening mauve color. Drew swung open the chain-link gate. The sudden smell of oven-roasted chicken and potatoes made his mouth water. He turned the corner, and the house looked cozy, all lit up. The front door was open, allowing Drew to see into the house through the closed metal storm door as he climbed the porch. Gaby beat him to the door and opened it for him.

"Hi, baby." She threw her arms around his neck, stood on her toes and kissed him.

"Hey," he said. "It smells good in there."

Gaby nuzzled his neck. "I roasted a chicken and Mexican potatoes."

"I can tell."

"Come on," she said, pulling him inside by his arm.

Drew carried his lunch bag to the kitchen and unzipped it on the counter.

"Here, let me do it." Gaby nudged him out of the way with her hip. "Put the game on."

"You sure?" Drew stood there, dazed.

"Of course. Go." She shoved him playfully, and began to unpack his bag. There was only an empty baggie from the baby carrots and a plastic container he packed his turkey sandwich in. Normally, she'd tease him that he could keep them in the bag overnight since he packed much the same the next morning, and it wasn't like he packed anything messy that needed to be cleaned. He liked to unpack it though, gave him a sense of order. She didn't tease tonight, however. He knew she was trying to be helpful. Same intention with dinner. The flip threw him a bit, but he appreciated her taking control. Felt good to be supported.

Drew went to the living room and plopped down on the couch. "Padres aren't playing tonight. They start a series at home against the Dodgers tomorrow night."

"Okay," Gaby said in a far-away voice. "Whatever you want to watch then."

He turned on the T.V. and flipped to a rerun of one of the network comedies Gaby liked.

Soon, she brought their plates in. They ate dinner in silence. Not out of animosity or friction like the previous evening, however. Drew was mentally and emotionally drained, and he could tell Gaby was simply giving him space.

Later, as they sat on their respective sides of the bed, setting alarms and Gaby finishing her lotion routine, Drew spoke.

"Thank you for everything tonight." He sat back against the headboard. Gaby turned to him slowly with a reassuring smile. "Dinner was delicious. You did a great job with it. Sorry I was so quiet."

Gaby stroked his chest. "Don't apologize. You had a rough day. I'm here if and when you want to talk about it."

"Thanks." Drew laid down and turned off the side lamp. Gaby followed suit. The bed creaked as she settled herself. She snuggled to his side, draping her arm across his chest.

Soon, her heavy breathing gave way to soft, consistent snoring.

Drew stared up into the blackness, waves of thoughts and fears rushing through his head. In a way, he was glad he'd punched holes in that wall today and created more work for himself in the process. If he weren't also physically exhausted, there would've been no way his mind would have allowed him to fall asleep.

Chapter Twenty-Nine

A thick gray system hung over Ocean Beach and the Surfview Cottages all day Friday. Unusual for April. And unlike marine layers that are the cause of Southern California's May Gray and June Gloom, this day's gray consisted of legit clouds threatening rain. Doubly unusual.

Drew kept the windows closed in the units as he worked, or else the humidity would wreak havoc on his timeline. He needed the mud to dry for the walls to be ready later to sand and texture, so he used large fans to expedite the process. Additionally, he was forced to light his work with his heavy-duty lamps because of the overcast nature outside.

Despite the challenges, Drew made significant progress, knocking out five units by lunch, and another two by two o'clock.

As he doubled back to the last unit he'd finished to grab the rest of his supplies, a familiar voice called out to him.

"Jones."

He swung around. Walking from the office—Mon. Drew expelled a sharp laugh and threw up his hands. "She hired you?"

"Yep. Thanks for the reference."

They met, and Mon clapped Drew's shoulder.

"You didn't need my help," he said, "but it was the least I could do."

She leaned in close, whispered, "Easiest money I'll ever make. Not sure why Lydia was freaking. She had everything pretty well under control."

"Yeah, but now with you supervising, she can get her actual job done."

"True. So, where are you at? Need anything from me?"

"Nope," Drew said. "Taping and mudding, then on to sanding and texture—provided this soup doesn't hold things up."

"That's why I like about you, Drew. You're your own GC."

He smiled.

"Everything else good?" she asked.

"Eh. Guess so."

"That good, huh? Get that sketch business with your brother worked out?"

Drew snorted. "Know what? He's kind of the least of my issues. Not really, but yesterday was a little rough."

"Sorry to hear that. Let me know if you need anything. Maybe we can grab a beer this weekend, or I can swing by and say hi to Gaby for once."

"We would love that."

"Thanks again, Drew."

He flashed a peace sign, said goodbye.

After retrieving his supplies, he situated everything in the next unit and began working. Drew thought how nice it was to see a friendly face. Especially since the lone thing he'd been dwelling on all day were last night's nightmares. They basically played out every horrifying scenario he could've imagined. Resenting his child. Gaby leaving him. Becoming a drunk. Him abandoning the baby and Gaby. Zan, ever present, always lurking nearby. Drew woke for work in a cold sweat. The nightmares emotionally drained him—more so than before he went to bed. And they caused a realization that stoked panic through his core all day: Rose's death had reignited his fear of becoming a father.

Seeing Mon, though. Her cheery nature distracted him. Freed his mind to focus on work the rest of the afternoon. By quitting time, he'd finished two more units.

He could have worked longer, but a nine-hour day felt solid enough, especially after following the twelve-hour the day before.

Drew was loading up the Transit Connect, resigning himself to the need to work the weekend, when he spotted an unwelcomed visitor.

Detective Billberry approached from down the sidewalk.

"Shit." Drew side-eyed him. Out of caution, he ensured the gym bag with Zan's money was still obscured, hidden under the canvas drop cloth he'd thrown over it two days earlier.

"Getting a head start, huh?" Billberry said.

Drew's stomach dropped. He turned around. "Sorry?"

The detective pointed to the sky. "May Gray rolling in a couple weeks early."

"Oh, yeah. Suppose so."

"How are you, Mr. Jones?" Billberry didn't offer his hand. He stood stern, smug even.

"Fine, and you?"

The old cop did something with his lips that made his mustache dance. "Good, good. Wanted to see if you've gotten in touch with that friend of yours yet."

Drew straightened but tried not to alter his facial features as to not give away anything. "Not yet. I told you I would let you know if I do."

"Sure." Billberry hooked his thumbs in his waistband like some Old West sheriff.

"How did you know where to find me anyway?"

Billberry chuckled. "I *am* a detective, son."

Blood rushed into Drew's face. Billberry's words mixed somewhere in the back of Drew's mind with the face of the FBI agent that dragged him out of his bedroom all those years ago. Drew took a step backwards, grabbed the van's sliding door, and swung it closed. "How's the guy who got shot doing?"

"I can't say anything about that."

"Anything else?"

Billberry scowled. "Not right now."

"Well, you have my number. Call me next time if there's something else.

"I'll contact you any way I see fit."

Drew exhaled smoothly through his nose. "You do that."

"Have a nice evening, Mr. Jones."

"You too, Detective."

***

The front door was open again when Drew got home, only this time it was 4:30 and Gaby normally didn't even get off work until then. He shot right to worries of health concerns.

He burst through the unlocked storm door. "Gaby? You here? Are you okay?"

She emerged around the corner, from out of their bedroom. She was wearing a brown Padres jersey, unbuttoned, over a blue shirt.

A Padres ballcap sat high on her head, her auburn hair bunched underneath. Her face beamed with huge smile.

"I'm fine. You better get changed if we're going to beat traffic."

Drew rushed to her. Touched her arm, kissed her cheek. "What are you talking about?"

She moved around him and went to the built-in by the front door. Change and keys rattled as she grabbed something out of the catch-all bowl. She turned around, flashing those perfect teeth of hers, and unfolded sheets of white printer paper.

"Doctor Sanchez gave us her Padres tickets for tonight's game."

"Are you kidding me?"

"No, look!"

Drew took the paper from her and looked them over. Sure enough. They were tickets to the first game of the three-game homestand against the Dodgers. Why her boss would have given up such prized tickets perplexed him.

"She and her husband have tickets to some opera tonight, so she put these up for grabs. I thought it'd be perfect to get your mind off everything."

"Gab, I don't know what to say . . ." He was hesitant to say yes. He still needed to get in touch with Jake since he hadn't called yet about another meeting. Billberry still lingered like a bad case of COVID long-haulers, and Zan's money sat in Drew's van, making him nearly breakout in a sweat every time he thought about it being out there. Still, wasn't like he could do anything about any of it tonight, and she had a point. A distraction would be nice. Besides, they hadn't seen a game in two years. And the tickets were choice, and against the freaking Dodgers.

"Let's go. And thank you so much, baby." Drew wrapped her up, squeezed her, and lifted her off the ground. Gaby squealed, and kissed him when he set her down.

Chapter Thirty

The gates to get into Petco Park were slammed. Security moved moderately, checking purses and bags, and moving people through a bank of metal detectors. Rain clouds smothered the sky, but so far, no moisture had fallen.

The line inched forward. Drew scanned the crowd. People of all races, all ages, the majority dressed in Padres gear, waiting to get in. A young Latino family—mom, dad, and two sons—caught his eye. The boys were probably six and eight, both with baseball gloves. The older boy was showing his younger brother how to shield his eyes with his glove if a ball got hit their way.

"Think they'll win tonight?" asked Gaby, biting her lip.

Drew looked at her. "You know what? Yeah. I think this could finally be the year we slay big brother."

"Damn straight, brah," shouted a white dude to their left who wore a flat-billed Padres ballcap and already looked hammered.

Drew flicked his chin at him.

"Hope it doesn't rain," Gaby said.

Pulling her into his arms, Drew said, "I'll keep you dry if it does."

The energy of the crowd surged with impatience even though first pitch was still fifty minutes away. Announcements boomed over the PA of corporate sponsors, the game's military hero, and other dignitaries participating in opening ceremonies.

Finally, it was Drew and Gaby's turn to go through the metal detectors. He let her go first. Unalarmed, they collected their things, had their tickets scanned, and entered the stadium. A chill walked up Drew's spine, and he couldn't help but grin.

Immediately, he clocked the smell of hot dogs, nacho cheese, and beer in the air.

"Did you plan on us eating at the park?" Drew asked, shouting over the crowd noise.

Gaby gave him an incredulous look. "Well, yeah. We have to eat, right?"

"Just making sure since everything's pricey here."

"We're here, so let's enjoy it. Plus, parking and the tickets were free . . ."

Drew gave her a thumbs-up. "Let's find our seats first."

They shuffled along until the mass of humanity broke apart when the concourse widened. The entrance to the Padres Hall of Fame stood to their right. Normally, they'd keep walking. And walking, until they reached the ramp leading to the upper decks. Not tonight. Doctor Sanchez's tickets were super close.

Drew pointed to the lower bowl on the first-base side. "Section one-seventeen," he said. "That's us."

They made it to the lip of the stairs and were greeted by a white-haired woman dressed in Padres-themed usher garb. Her name tag read Opal. "Tickets?"

Gaby handed the sheets of paper to Opal. "Row nineteen, seats twenty-nine and thirty are down there on the left, halfway down in the first section. Enjoy the game."

They thanked her and slowly made their way down the stairs until they reached the lowest section, the proximity to the field mind-blowing.

"Whoa, babe. Look how close we are," Gaby said.

"Holy shit," Drew said.

Gaby scooted into the second seat off the aisle while he continued gawking at the field.

The grounds crew was doing a final raking of the infield dirt, and Padres players tossed balls around as part of their warm-up routine. Organ music played old-timey baseball hymns through the PA, and the scoreboard in left was lit-up and ready to go, complete with a photo and stats of Mookie Betts, the lead-off hitter for the Dodgers.

Drew settled into his seat, patted Gaby on the leg. "Some view. I could get used to this."

Gaby smiled.

"Twenty minutes till first-pitch. What do you want to eat?"

"How about Cardiff Crack?" she asked. Cardiff Crack. The nickname for the absolute best tri-tip in San Diego County, and maybe all of Southern California.

"God, that sounds great," Drew said. "Want the sandwich?"

Gaby nodded emphatically. "A bottle of water, too, please?"

"Of course." Drew kissed her on the cheek. Then bounded up the steps.

The market wasn't far away, but the line was longer than Drew anticipated, everyone with the same idea. By the time he got everything, paid, and returned to their seats, he'd missed first-pitch. In fact, the Dodgers were down to their last out of the inning, no score.

"Here you go, babe." Drew handed Gaby her sandwich. He leaned across her and placed the bottle of water in the cup holder at her feet.

"Busy?"

"Yeah. Craft Row was even more slammed though, so I got water for now, too."

"We could grab something from one of the beer vendors." Gaby raised her hand.

Drew gently pressed a hand on her arm. "I'll wait. I want to see what's out there."

Gaby and Drew dug into their sandwiches, moaning and rolling their eyes at each other. Justin Turner grounded into a fielder's choice to end the Dodger's first inning.

The crowd roared in approval.

In the bottom of the 1st, the Padres went in order. Drew let out a low groan, less disappointed than normal since he was savoring his last bite of tri-tip.

Between innings, Drew and Gaby cleaned themselves up, took big gulps of water, and stood to stretch and scan the sold-out crowd. To their sides, the lower bowl hummed with activity. Men and women jumped up to make beer or bathroom runs. Kids laughed. Bros high-fived. And many others danced in place to "Let's Get It Started" by the Black Eyed Peas, playing over the PA. Friday night in Downtown San Diego at one of the most beautiful parks in the Majors. Drew took a deep breath, smiled, and soaked it all in.

"Look, babe." Gaby was facing behind them. Drew turned around. "There's that family we saw in line with the two cute little boys."

"Oh, yeah."

She turned to him, touched her belly. "Won't it be fun to bring ours to games?"

For some reason, that possibility never occurred to Drew before now.

"I take it by the big grin on your face, that's a yes?"

"Yeah, that will be fun." And he meant it.

In the bottom of the 2nd, Wil Myers came up to bat. Gaby nudged Drew with an elbow.

"You never told me if you liked Will for our baby's name."

Drew turned to her and realized it was the second time she'd made the offer. He kissed her on the lips, then said, "You're too good to me."

After two innings, the score was Dodgers 0 and Padres 1.

Drew sunk into his seat and stared up at the purple clouds hugging the skyscrapers behind the stadium, the sky darkening. This was nice, he thought. More than nice. He hadn't thought about his brother the entire night, or anything else.

He rubbed Gaby's back and she smiled.

"Thank you," Drew said.

"Thank Dr. Sanchez. They're her seats."

"No, thanks for being so good to me, even when I don't deserve it."

"That's twice you've said that. Everything okay?"

"Yeah," he said. "Everything is great."

The next few innings were inconsequential for both teams.

"Up one-nothing headed into the 5th. Can't ask for much more than that," Drew said.

"The game is flying by," Gaby said.

"Yeah. That's what good pitching does."

"Hey, I need to go to the bathroom soon, so you know."

"If you can wait another inning, I'll go with you so I can get a beer."

"Sure."

The top of the 5th began with Mookie Betts at-bat. Martinez got ahead on him early with a called strike, but quickly fell behind 1-2 with two straight balls. On the next pitch, Betts cranked a shot into the upper left field stands, directly in front of the scoreboard, to the right of the old Western Metal Supply Co. brick building. The game suddenly tied at one.

"Shit." Drew ripped off his ballcap and slapped his leg with it.

Martinez battled back, getting two straight outs.

But on the next pitch, Max Muncy knocked a fastball to right-center. The towering shot landed in the outfield stands, putting the Dodgers up 2-1 and ending Nick Martinez' night.

"Pitching change," Drew said. "Want to go now?"

"Yes."

Drew stood and helped Gaby out of her seat.

"My butt is numb."

Drew chuckled. "I bet."

Fans poured from their seats as well, and a train formed going up the stairs. The line moved at a steady rate, however, and after a minute or two, they reached the top.

"You headed to Craft Row?"

Drew said, "Yeah. There's a restroom right there if you want to come with."

"Sounds good. I could use some steps."

When they reached the women's restroom, more than thirty women stood waiting in line.

"Go get a beer and take your time," Gaby said. "I'm gonna be here a while."

"Good luck."

They parted ways, and Drew felt for her. Gaby would never use her pregnancy to jump the line, but Drew might have if he was in her shoes.

Craft Row was hopping. Each of the forty vendors had at least a handful of customers in line, and a stream of people navigated through the row going both directions. Drew didn't know what he was in the mood for, other than something with a high alcohol content.

He poked along, and every vendor looked great. Stone, Green Flash, Hodad's, Ballast Point, Karl Strauss. All of San Diego's best. Drew finally settled on a Green Flash. Only downside, the line was ten deep. Drew looked toward the restroom to see how the line looked, but there was no way to see it with him surrounded by a throng of people obstructing the view.

Stepping into line, he pulled out his phone to check on the game. As soon as he did, he noticed a monitor playing the game anchored to the side of the vendor stand. Drew tucked his phone back into his pocket. Made him think how he hadn't brought the burners, having kept them stashed in his work van. A true night off.

The line moved along, and soon Drew was next.

Then, he was yanked backward by his shoulder.

Expecting it to be Gaby, he turned snorting, and said, "You jump the line?" But it wasn't Gaby. Instead, a smirking Zan West stared back. A scowling Shaw at his side.

"Hey, Jones." The words slithered out of Zan's mouth like a rattlesnake through scrub brush. "Come with us."

Chapter Thirty-One

"What are you doing here?" Drew's words sounded whiney, even in his own ears.

Without answering, Zan and Shaw briskly escorted him to a service hallway on the opposite end of Craft Row, away from the restrooms. The hallway was dimly lit, with two industrial-sized rolling trash containers used to haul garbage standing against one wall. They cornered Drew behind them to obscure their presence from the concourse—it worked.

Shaw shoved him up against the wall. Spun him around and shoved again. Drew threw out his hands in time to keep from face-planting into the wall.

"Spread your legs, bitch."

"Why? You think I brought a weapon in here?" Drew said.

"Just spread." Shaw kicked apart his legs. Began patting him down in the same order he first had on Drew's porch. Heavy hands chopped Drew's shoulders. Brushed across his chest and around his back; patted down to his waist. Reaching his pockets, Shaw squeezed Drew's cell phone and keys. Continued patting. To his thighs, quads, and down his calves. Shaw finished up feeling around Drew's ankles, and declared him clean.

The big man whipped Drew back around by the shoulder, shoved him against the wall.

Drew asked Zan again, "What are you doing here?"

Zan shouldered Shaw out of the way. Tipped up his black ballcap. Got in Drew's face.

"What? Like I'm going to miss the opening series game against the Dodgers? Have you looked around? All of San Diego is here, including *you*." Zan jabbed a finger into Drew's sternum. "What the fuck are *you* doing here?"

Drew opened his mouth to respond, but Zan cut him off.

"First, you're hanging out on the beach the other day when you called, and now you're casually taking in a game? With three fucking days to get your brother to me or you know what, and you're taking it easy. Am I missing something? Swear to Christ, I thought we had an understanding, a deal."

Drew gulped. "We do, it's just—"

Zan punched him in the throat with a quick jab.

Drew dropped to his knees. Began choking uncontrollably. He covered his throat with his hands. His vision narrowed, the borders bleeding white.

Zan said something, but he couldn't make it out the first time over the ringing in his ears.

"Hear me? Get a hold of yourself. You're gonna draw attention."

Shaw yanked Drew to his feet.

Drew tasted the tang of snot and tears running down his face.

"Christ's sake. Go get some napkins," Zan said to Shaw, who listened and rushed off.

The jab had been forceful, hurt well enough. But it was the suddenness of it, the surprise that rocked Drew most.

His coughing tapered off some. Turning the tail of his shirt inside-out, he wiped his face.

"Gross," Zan said. "Shaw's getting you a napkin."

"Fuck . . . *cough* . . . Shaw."

"So fucking bold." Zan stepped to Drew. He smelled of mustard and beer. Shaw showed, extending a wad of crumpled napkins. Drew took them, but didn't take an eye off Zan.

"Where is Jake and my money?"

"Close. I think. I don't know exactly, but he's close."

Zan's deep-set eyes pierced Drew's. His face featured so many sharp angles, held so much terror. There was a smear of yellow—that mustard, likely—on the corner of his mouth. Under other circumstances, the messy spot might have eroded the power his glare held. Not in this moment. Drew felt as if he was staring into a demon's eyes, into this hellion's very soul.

"You better fucking hope so, cause I'm tired of the bullshit fun and games. It's over."

This man wanted his money back more than anything Drew had ever wanted anything in his entire life—Zan's eyes spoke this truth.

"My . . . wife got us . . . the tickets," Drew said. "We needed a night out, is all."

Zan didn't budge. His lips spread into a sickly smile. "Hope you enjoyed yourself, Drewie. Cause now it's sink or fucking swim time."

"What's that mean?"

"Don't you think I'm getting to that, asshole?"

Drew averted his eyes.

Zan sucked his teeth, continued.

"Fuck three more days. You've now got twenty-four hours to round-up your brother and bring him and my money to me. I want them both by midnight tomorrow night, or I will kill both you dumb motherfuckers. No more nights off."

Drew choked, like he hadn't been breathing.

"You hear me, Jones?"

Nothing would come out of his mouth, so Drew nodded vehemently.

Shaw made a guttural noise and shoved Drew for good measure. Drew lost his balance and slid down the wall and into one of the trash containers. His left elbow struck the hard plastic of the container, getting him on the funny bone. An uncomfortable, painful laugh spilled from his lips. Echoed down the hallway. There wasn't a goddamn thing funny about any of it, but Drew couldn't stop laughing while rubbing his spasming elbow.

"Get a hold of yourself, you fucking kook," Zan said.

Through teary eyes, Drew watched as his two aggressors backed off, heads whipping toward the concourse. It took what felt like thirty minutes, but his laughing fit finally stopped. That's when Shaw lunged forward and kicked him in the ribs.

"He's not fucking around."

Stars exploded behind Drew's eyes, and he gasped for air. Just like when Shaw tackled him on his porch.

"Damn right. Come through or else." Zan said.

With that, the two men stormed off, leaving Drew crumpled in a heap next to a garbage container. Even as he worked to gather himself and catch his breath, Drew wished he had Jake's burner on him. Not only so he could call and coordinate a resolution to all this, but so he could rip his selfish, asshole brother a new one.

Chapter Thirty-Two

Gaby was wandering Craft Row when Drew emerged from the hallway. Many of the fans who had previously been in the concourse had gone away, making her easy to spot.

Holding his stomach with one hand, he waved for her with the other.

"Drew!" She ran, or rather walked as fast as her pregnancy belly would allow, to him. "Why are you grimacing? What's wrong?"

"I'm fine. We've got to go. *I've* got to go."

"Why? The game isn't over yet."

"Forget the game. I have to get home now and get something out of my work van."

"You're not making any sense."

"I'll tell you on the way, but we need to go right now." He pulled her arm. "Please."

"Humble" by Kendrick Lamar began to play over the PA, with the game announcer coming on to intro Manny Machado to the plate.

Gaby looked at Drew over knitted brows. Suspicion etched all over her face. But she didn't resist and went with him. "What happened to you? Did you hurt yourself?"

Drew righted himself as they walked. Wiped away the sweat that dampened his brow. "Sorta. But I'll be fine. I have to get home though and make a call."

"Don't you have your phone?"

Drew quickened their pace. "C'mon," he muttered. He shook his head, flustered. "I'll tell you everything when we get back to the car. Promise."

The crowd cheered, the sound echoing though the concourse that was devoid of many others besides vendors and a few other fans hustling back to their seats.

Gaby did an admirable job keeping pace with Drew and didn't fight his continued hold on her arm. Suddenly realizing the cringy optics of manhandling a pregnant woman, Drew loosened his grip, and let her go.

"Can we slow down? My feet." she said.

"Sorry, we've got to keep moving."

"You're scaring me, Drew."

He gave her a quick glance. "I'm sorry. I'm not trying to, really."

They reached the escalator that led to the street level. Drew gestured for Gaby to get on first. As they descended, Drew blew a skittering breath to the sky. Ink black, with thick clouds rolling across. The air humid and thick with the smells of concession food, while the sounds of the cheering crowd grew fainter, like a song's volume being turned down.

At the bottom of the escalator, a male usher thanked them for coming and gestured to the gate through which to exit the ballpark.

They made it outside the gates, and Drew lost all sense of direction. He threw out his hands, swinging his body side-to-side. "Where did we park?"

"Down Eleventh, on E Street," Gaby said. "By that green Victorian—"

"Got it." He turned to her. "Stay here. I'll run and get the car and pick you up."

Before Gaby could respond, Drew ran off.

He dodged a few loitering cops and cut over to Eleventh. The homeless had already staked claim to the street corners and under the eaves of high-rises, so he swerved into the street to avoid running into them.

Drew jogged and bit his lower lip. Goddamn Jake. Why couldn't he have listened? Now, both their lives were at risk because of his reckless actions. One glimmer of hope. Surely, Jake would give up the rest of the money and bring it all to Zan once Drew told him Zan intended to kill them both if he didn't.

He didn't slow at each light he came to if there wasn't traffic. A Californian's mindset of pedestrians always having the right of way emboldened him. That, and Zan in his head.

A thought bloomed—a worry. Jake said he'd call Drew in "a day or two" about possibly meeting again, and he hadn't. That was on Wednesday when they met, and later talked on the phone. Why hadn't he called? Had he taken off for good? If so, where would that leave Drew? "Fuck." He screamed into the night between heavy breaths.

The money in Drew's van was twenty-two grand short. He and Gaby didn't have that much in savings to cover the difference. There would be a fat check from the Surfview gig when he finished, but that would only account for roughly half. And, he couldn't get the job done in twenty-four hours anyway. Not even with his speed and skill. Not a chance in hell.

Drew saw the two-story green Victorian house on the corner of the next intersection, and hooked a left on E St. Gaby's Kia Rio was parked two cars back.

In one smooth motion, he unlocked the car with the key fob, swung open the door, and slid behind the wheel. His lone hope of putting all this behind them rested on reaching Jake and convincing him to do what Zan wanted. What had been the plan all along. Inserting the key, he paused. A voice in his head said to leave Gaby, head home alone. That's what he's wanted to do ever since finding out they were having a baby, right? *You're not cut out to be that kid's father.*

Drew growled, shook his head.

He turned the key and the Rio started right up, but the engine oil light blinked on.

"Of fucking course."

Drew whipped the wheel and stomped the gas.

After three left turns, he pulled up to the stadium. He honked over the squealing brakes as he looked for Gaby, not spotting her. A second later, her head popped up; she'd been sitting on a bench. When she opened the car door, Drew said, "Get in, get in."

"I am. Jesus Christo. What's gotten into you?"

She barely closed the door when Drew gunned it.

"Shit. I'm not even buckled yet."

"Well, c'mon."

Drew navigated his way through Downtown, fortuitously catching all greens along the way. The light to access the 163 was green as well, and he sped up to get on the on-ramp.

"Okay, tell me what's going on. Spill it," Gaby said.

Maybe it was the adrenaline pumping through his veins, his sheer fear of Zan, or maybe Drew simply did want to finally come clean to her. Whatever the case, he did spill it all.

"I've been running around the county this past week, trying to find Jake."

"Yeah, I know."

"Just let me keep talking. At first, I wanted to find him to make sure he was okay, to get some answers, and get our RV back, like we talked about. You know? Then, this . . . this violent maniac and his bodyguard broke into our house looking for the cash they say Jake robbed from his liquor store."

He stole glances at Gaby while speeding twenty miles-an-hour over the limit. She looked confused, upset. Drew went on to tell her everything in full detail. How they'd beaten the shit out of him. How Zan threatened to kill Jake unless Drew found him and got him to bring back the hundred grand. That he found and met up with Jake, but Jake shorted the money, and how Zan now wanted Jake and the money in the next twenty-four hours, *or else.*"

"Or else what?" Gaby asked.

Drew squeezed the steering wheel with both hands.

"Or else what, Drew?"

"Same thing. He'll find Jake and kill him," he partly lied.

Maybe he'd garner her sympathy if he told her Zan also threatened his life, but he'd no doubt also frighten her, and he didn't want to do that unnecessarily. For the same reason, he couldn't tell her the truth about the sonogram yet either. If Jake cooperated, this would all end, and she'd never need to know his own life and possibly hers and the baby's were also at risk.

"Why didn't you call the police?"

"Sure, sounds easy, but there was no way that was or is an option."

A long second of silence.

"Why didn't you trust me enough to tell me any of this before now?" she asked.

"It's not like that."

"What's it like then, Drew?" she said, raising her voice. "Because you've been running all over town, getting beat up, using burner phones like you're a drug dealer—"

"I know, I know . . ."

"And you've got seventy-eight thousand dollars hidden in your fucking work van? All this—ALL THIS—and you didn't trust me with any of it. So, tell me. What is it like, man?"

"Calm down."

"Do *not* tell me to calm down."

"Well don't call me man."

"They're not even in the same universe. And stop trying to change the subject. Why don't you trust me?"

This. This was why he hadn't told her about any of it before now. If Jake would have listened when they met-up, Drew wouldn't have to justify his actions. Totally justified actions, he'd love to point out, but knew he shouldn't.

"I do trust you, but I didn't want to scare you."

"So you thought you'd just be a big man and do this all on your own?"

"Well, you also wanted to call the cops, and that wasn't an option."

The car fell silent for a few awkward beats. Drew spoke again.

"When Zan showed up and shit got real, I really didn't have any choice."

Gaby was now looking out her window. The side windows all fogged up. Traffic on the 8 was clear. They'd soon come up to the exit for the 805, and would be home in about five minutes. Gaby muttered something.

"What?" Drew asked. "I was trying to protect you!"

"Bullshit" she said, waving. "You protected yourself. You didn't care about me."

"That's not true."

"All I've done to support you these past few days—hell, these past few weeks, months. And you're treating me like some kind of sensitive land mine you have to step around." She turned back to her window.

Drew shook his head, didn't reply.

He took the exit for their neighborhood. Looped around. At the three-way stop, the blinker clicked loud while he waited on a car to make it through the intersection. It wasn't far to get home from there, but it felt like an eternity as they remained in silence the rest of the way.

When he parked her car on the street in front of Bernie's house, he knew he needed to say something, anything,

"I'm sorry, Gab. Really. But I'm telling you everything now. That's got to count for something, right?"

Without responding, she opened the door and got out. She made it halfway up the driveway before Drew unbuckled his seatbelt.

Outside, the air was thick and brisk. No stars shone in the sky, or if they did, they were totally consumed by the thick blanket of clouds. Rain or not. Shit or get off the pot. Drew sputtered his lips, and trudged up the driveway.

As soon as he took one step onto their front porch, Gaby came out the front door.

"Here," she said, throwing something at him. Keys nailed his chest, and fell to the porch.

Drew bent down and picked them up. Standing, he gestured at her. "What's this?"

"You've got a brother to find. Better get to it," she said.

He took a step toward her. "Gaby . . ."

She stepped back inside and closed the storm door. Locked it.

"Are you serious?" He went to the door. "Let's work this out."

"No, Drew. You need to figure out what's really important to you."

"You are important to me. You're the most important."

Gaby held her stomach. Furrowed her brows. "Just me?" She looked mad or hurt. Probably both. "Go. We'll talk tomorrow."

With that, she closed the main door and turned off the porch light. He had his keys and could unlock the doors and walk in, but any husband anywhere knew that wasn't advisable.

Drew ripped the Padres hat off his head and flung it into bars of the porch railing.

"Shit."

Chapter Thirty-Three

Where was he supposed to go?

Drew rubbed his throat, still tender from Zan's jab.

He wasn't paying for a hotel, and while crashing at the Surfview crossed his mind, there was no way he'd go through with it with Mon as GC. Imagine her showing up early the next morning—even if a Saturday—to find Drew stumbling around in his boxers?

He'd figure out where to lay his head later.

First thing's first.

Drew retrieved both burner phones from the Transit Connect. He also checked that the gym bag of cash was still securely hidden. It was.

Closing up and locking the van, he turned to the back of the house. He purged a mixture of primal noises and curse words into the night sky in frustration. His throat went raw, his skin bristling with gooseflesh. While he didn't blame Gaby for feeling slighted, how could she say he didn't trust her? The words burned a hole through his chest. They'd been going so well lately, especially after he opened up to her about his fear of becoming a father. Now this? Trust wasn't the issue, as far as he saw it. How could she not see this was a matter of life and death? His brother's, and now his own too. She would've done the same as him if she had a sibling and the tables were turned.

He had a choice.

He exhaled deeply.

Later. He'd fix it later.

Drew flipped open Jake's phone and dialed his brother. A breeze picked up, rustling the canopy of palm fronds above him, breaking one loose. The phone rang and rang. He ended the call. Redialed. Same result.

"Shit. Where the hell are you, Jake?"

Squawking the key fob again, he took off down the alley with no idea where he was going. All he knew was he needed to move.

Security lights popped on at the back of every house he passed along the way. Made him feel like a trespasser in his own neighborhood. He checked the time. Nine-fifteen.

Way too early for Jake to be asleep, wherever he was.

The alley dumped Drew onto Collier Ave., so he took a left, then a right to head down 34th. Televisions glaring in a few homes he passed, the Padres game on. It seemed like an ancient forgotten interest now with everything that had transpired.

The fucking chances of Zan being at the same game. What were the odds? And to be in the same spot as Drew at the same time—damn his shit luck.

"Taking it easy," Drew muttered, mocking Zan's assessment of him being there. Couldn't change a guy's mind like that, so Drew hadn't even tried hard. *Taking it easy.* He wished.

On Adams Ave., a loud crowd hung out across the street on the patio at The Rabbit Hole. Drew decided to go left for some silence. First, he had to get past the Irish pub on the corner, which was also packed. The storefronts after the pub were dark and quiet. Soon, the noise from both bars dissipated to white noise behind him. He opened the flip phone, dialed Jake again.

The burner rang and rang and rang.

"Goddamn it."

He turned and faced the building. A security light flashed on and Drew caught his reflection in the storefront glass of a collectibles store. Disheveled. Frantic. His face a ruddy mess like he'd been drinking all night, when in fact he hadn't consumed a drop of alcohol. Yet. Time to change that, he thought. Would help him to relax. Maybe after a drink or two and some time, he could go home and see if Gaby had thawed enough to let him in the house.

Drew turned around, crossed the street, and headed toward The Rabbit Hole. Along the way, he called Jake two more times and got no answer. He closed the phone and looked up. The bar's neon signage bathed the patrons on the patio in a warm, marmalade glow. Through the open bay doors, he saw the game playing on several monitors above the bar.

He checked his cell phone. No missed texts or calls from Gaby. Only the locked screen selfie of her and him holding each other with La Jolla Cove in the background staring back.

Drew strode into the bar.

***

"Fucking turn this shit off already," Drew said.

The game had gone into the 8th, with the Dodgers taking a commanding four-run lead.

"It's almost over, bro. Chill," said a tool to Drew's left wearing a backwards Dodgers hat.

"It's been over going on two hours, *bro*."

"What's your problem, asshole?"

The bartender, a clean-cut white guy who looked like he prepared tax returns during the day, held out a hand to the tool, while approaching Drew.

"You all right, man?" he asked.

"Sure. As good as anyone can be with their favorite team *sucking* again, and their wife locking them out of their own damn house."

Giving Drew a look of pity, the bartender leaned in. "Look, buddy. Sorry you're going through . . . something. I'll turn the game off as soon as it's over. Until then, you could always take your beer outside to the patio if you're done watching."

Sliding off his chair, Drew said, "Sounds good to me. Air's a little too douchey in here for my taste anyway." He didn't make it two steps when he got shoved from behind. Spilling a little beer, Drew turned around, speechless but pissed.

"The fuck you say?" asked the tool.

Drew stepped to him, placing their faces within inches. "What? You can't hear? Maybe wearing your stupid-ass hat like that constricts blood flow?"

The tool's face darkened. He shoved Drew's chest.

"Hey," shouted the bartender. "Outside, both of you."

Looking around, Drew saw half the patrons watching them, and the other half still glued to their conversations, pool games, etc.

"That's where I was headed," Drew said incredulously.

The tool took it as a challenge. He shoved Drew with both hands, pushing him out of the bar—Drew taken by such surprise all he could do was backpedal.

Once outside, the tool took a swing, but Drew deftly dipped out of the way. While he avoided being struck, the attempt enraged him.

Blindly, Drew set his beer down on the patio railing, then hooked a fist into the side of the tool's head, connecting with his ear. Tool held his head and growled. Not giving him any time to recover, Drew dove and tackled him to the ground.

On the way down, time stood still, or at least moved in a glacial pace. The memory of Shaw tackling Drew on his porch ran through his mind; Zan's menacing voice and threats whispered in his ears; and Gaby's rejection of him—how she'd so casually and dismissively thrown his keys at him. It all burned behind his eyes.

The next thing he knew, Drew had the tool's arms pinned beneath his knees. His arms felt as heavy as anchors. Probably because he was swinging hard and fast. And yet, it didn't feel like a conscious decision. Like he was disconnected from himself. Next thing he knew, multiple hands grabbed at him, yanked him. A cacophony of yelling and begging him to stop, to get off.

Seconds later, stars exploded in his field of vision, and everything went black.

***

When Drew finally fluttered open his eyes, the world around barged full-force into his senses. There was again shouting, along with swirling red and blue emergency lights bouncing off all the glass storefronts and street-parked vehicles. His ears rang a deafening tone.

"He just attacked the guy," he heard a garbled, feminine voice say.

"He was pummeling the dude's face," said a man.

He flinched when black-gloved fingers began snapping in front of his face. Drew shook his head, hoping to clear his blurry vision. Slowly blinked his eyes. A dark-haired female cop came into view, squatted in front of him. "Can you hear me, sir?"

"Yeah. What happened?" Drew wiped saliva from the corners of his mouth. He looked to his sides. The Rabbit Hole's patio stood a mere ten feet or so to his right. All the people on the porch were huddled, staring his way, mouths agape. He squirmed, and the grit of brick scraped against his back. He was sitting, back to a neighboring storefront.

"You were beating up another guy."

He held out his hands. Rolled them over and saw blood and skin ripped open on his knuckles.

"You beat him up pretty bad," she said, with a flick of her head.

Behind her, Drew saw another cop, a nondescript-looking white guy, talking to a young woman dressed in club clothes. A hipster dude wearing pressed jeans, a gray blazer, and Bowler hat stood to the side. Both looked agitated.

Drew pressed his palms to the pavement, began to push himself up.

A firm hand on the top of shoulder stopped his momentum. "Stay seated, sir," the cop said. "A paramedic will be over shortly to evaluate you."

Ass on the ground, Drew rubbed his face. Still groggy. "Did I pass out or something?"

"Another patron hit you on the back of the head with a beer mug to get you to stop."

"Shit . . . How . . . how is the guy?" Drew touched the back of his head. Tender as fuck. He brought his hand back expecting blood, but his palm was clean.

"Paramedics are taking care of him." She thumbed behind her, across Adams at an ambulance. In his seated position, he could only see the top of the rig and its flashing lights. "Hopefully he'll be okay. You messed him up pretty bad."

Drew tried to stand again. This time, he made it to his feet, but the cop grabbed him by his left wrist and squeezed.

"What are you doing?" Drew asked.

"Sir, you need to cooperate."

It happened so fast. Call it panic. Call it his lizard brain bucking after connecting his current surroundings with the Miller raid from his youth—thanks to all the lights, cops, gawkers, and fevered activity. Whatever the cause, Drew ripped free of the cop's grasp, and bolted. Ran with long, heavy strides down the sidewalk.

"Get back here," the cop yelled. "I've got a runner!"

He hadn't made it fifty yards when he already could hear himself breathing heavy. The sounds of his sneakers stomping the pavement, followed by hers, struck next. He passed storefront after storefront. The teal neon NORMAL HEIGHTS sign that hung over Adams Ave. began to come into view. Then, a realization. He was weighed down by three cell phones. Not weighed down in the sense of them being heavy, but the threat of breaking any one of them if he were caught and tackled unnerved him. Where would he be if Jake's burner got crushed?

Drew slowed, threw up his arms, and shouted. "I surrender. Don't tackle me."

The cop's footfalls grew louder the more he slowed. Drew stole a quick glance over his shoulder to gauge her distance. In deliberate motions, he stomped to a stop, and dropped to his knees, interlacing his hands behind his head.

"Sorry, sorry, sorry," he said. Then his face ate concrete. "Shit."

"Shut up," said the cop. "You're lucky I don't tase your ass. Running from a cop? What the hell were you thinking?"

The male cop he'd seen interviewing the hipsters now ran up. Gun drawn, and aimed at Drew's face.

"Don't you fucking move, asshole," he said.

"I got him," the female cop said.

She cuffed Drew. Yanked him to his knees. Both cops pulled him to his feet. "Your friend back there wasn't going to press charges," she said. "But you can bet your ass I have a few of my own to file now. Dumbass."

INTERLUDE 2

Shaw got into his head. Bitched the entire rest of the game how Zan let Jones off easy, that they should've removed him from Petco Park right then. Taken him to Zan's place in Imperial Beach. Where the waves would deaden the sounds of beating him until he gave up his bitch-ass brother, Jake. Same as they were doing with Ahmed. Thing was, Shaw was completely right. Zan knew it but still hated the fact his muscle saw the situation more clearly than he had. Wasn't the way shit was supposed to work. A problem to solve later.

Right now, he intended to clear his foggy thinking.

They rolled into Normal Heights a little before 11 p.m. This being the third time going to Drew's house, Zan knew to cut into the neighborhood well before reaching the main drag on Adams Ave to avoid packed bars and the eyes of potential witnesses. Those two previous times, he'd played it safe, parking several houses down on 34th. Not tonight. Fuck every motion-activated light that popped on as they rolled down this alley. People didn't pay attention to shit these days with their faces glued to screens anyway.

Zan parked the truck right behind Drew's ugly-ass work van.

They got out. Pressed their doors closed, quiet as possible. No locking the truck. No flashing the lights. Shaw went over and touched his hand to the hood of the van. He mouthed, *Cool.* It hadn't gone anywhere in a while. Probably took his wife's beater to the game.

Zan flicked his chin. They met at the chain-link gate. It was unlocked, and even better, it didn't squeal when he opened it. Leave it to a construction worker to keep everything at home lubed up.

Inside, they flattened themselves against the side of the house. Both windows were dark. Moving slowly, Zan reached into his jacket. Retrieved the bump hammer and dummy key. When they reached the corner of the house, Zan held up a fist. Shaw stopped. Zan pointed at his ear, then across the yard to the back of the property's main house.

Shaw nodded that he too heard the noises of two people talking and laughing. The pattern of each was a predictable rhythm. Talk, talk, talk . . . big laugh. From this distance, the words were indiscernible, but Zan sat on that rhythm, fist held high, waiting . . . talking, talking, talking—go. They darted for the porch, reaching the top right as the pair's laughter petered out.

Zan tried the storm door. Unlocked. Again, lubed, with no squeaks or whines.

He paused for another round of laughter to bump the lock, but as he waited, checked the main door. Unlocked also. He shot Shaw a look. Tucked the tools away, and opened the door.

Inside, the house was pitch dark. No one on the couch or standing in plain sight. Zan gave Shaw the sign for sleep—pressed hands to the side of this face. Shaw nodded. They slowly, quietly made their way to the back of the house.

Zan gestured for Shaw to look around the corner. The big fool hesitated but complied. Came back shaking his head no. He walked into the bedroom, flipped on the light. "Ain't nobody home," he said.

Zan scowled. Flipped off the light. Then, something else flipped. He nodded sideways.

Outside Zan pointed to the Chatty Kathys next door. They went down the porch, across the lawn, and paused at the white vinyl fence separating the two yards. There was a gate door—mostly closed, not latched. Taking a quick peek, he made out two figures sitting on a couch with a fire pit in front of them. Zan pulled the gun out of his waistband. Removed the suppressor from his back pocket and attached it to the 9mm. Body rigid, he mouthed, one-two-three. They burst through the door.

The pair on the couch startled. A young woman and an older white guy. The woman shrieked, while the man fluttered his hands next to his face.

"Who are you? What do you want?" asked the man.

The fire in the pit cast long shadows across the pair. Zan realized the woman was pregnant, giving him an idea of her identity. She looked scared but also pissed.

"Where's Drew Jones? He inside your house?"

The man looked at the woman.

"Pay attention to me, pops. I'm the one with the gun."

"No. No, he's not here. And you both need to leave right this instant."

"He can't be far. His van's here."

The woman shook her head. "He's not here. And I'm guessing you're Zan?"

"And you're Gaby."

The man interrupted. "I said, you both need to leave."

Zan shot Shaw a look. Shaw chuckled. Zan nudged him. Shaw walked over and stood next to the pair, his imposing size doing the job of shrinking them down, keeping them seated.

"Why do you want Drew?" Gaby asked.

"You're a smart girl. So, I bet you know why."

The older man was fidgeting, working on working up his courage, by the look of it.

Zan waved the gun at him for him to come over. The old man didn't budge. Shaw grabbed him by the arm and brought him over.

"What's your name?"

"Bernie."

"Nice place you got here, Bernie. I'm guessing Gaby and Drew are what, your tenants?"

Bernie hugged himself, nodded.

"Nice. Well, Bernie and Gaby. I'm going make this super easy on you both. Tell me where to find—" He paused. An excellent idea sprang to mind of how to wrap all this up for good. "On second thought. Gaby. Would you toss me one of those lovely pillows, please?"

Bernie shivered with his head tucked. He whispered something about Zan leaving Gaby alone. Gaby gave Zan a look, but did as he said. She had a great arm; the pillow sailed end over end right to him. He snatched it out of the air with ease, and handed the pillow to Bernie.

"Here. Hold this up, Bernie Boy."

Bernie took hold of the pillow by two corners.

"Higher. There you go. Yep, exactly like that." Zan raised the gun, pressed the barrel to the pillow in front of Bernie's chest, and squeezed the trigger twice. A tuft of feathers escaped and floated in front of Bernie's face, but no blood sprayed back onto Zan. Bernie dropped to the ground like a wet bag of sand.

"No! What did you do?" Gaby screamed.

Shaw grabbed her by the arm, pulled her in tight, and covered her mouth. She kicked and screamed, but his meaty paw muffled any further noise.

"Let's go," Zan said.

Chapter Thirty-Four

Officer Kelly Hanson hit Drew with charges of Disturbing the Peace, and Resisting an Officer. He didn't have to ask what both entailed as far as fines and such. She was all too gleeful to tell him on the drive to the San Diego Central Jail that he was looking at close to $5,500, so about $550 in bond to have his ass bailed out.

If only he'd kept his cool, he likely could have walked away with a mere $250 ticket for Disturbing the Peace. He would probably still have to foot the bill for the ambulance and any medical care the Dodgers fan needed, but at least Drew wouldn't be facing a night in jail.

Now, having languished in a musky interrogation room for who knew how many hours, still waiting to make his phone call to Gaby, his head absolutely pounding, he berated himself. What the hell had he done? How would he explain his actions to Gaby? Beating up someone? The last fight he'd been in was back in high school, and he didn't win. Of all the dumb things to do, he couldn't think how he could've fucked things up worse for himself if he tried. And he didn't get the chance either.

The door opened and Det. Billberry glided in with a huge smile.

Drew removed his elbows from the table. Leaned back in the chair. Watched Billberry step methodically across the room and take a seat across from him. The detective smoothed his mustache several times before speaking.

"Disturbing the Peace and Resisting an Officer, huh? What an eventful Friday night, and by the looks of your jersey, I'm guessing you also went to the Padres game earlier. Busy, busy."

Drew swallowed softly and continued staring at the detective without blinking.

"Now, I don't want you to think I've swung by on my night off just to rub your—" Billberry cleared his throat. "evening in your face. I've also come by to let you know I found out you and Jake are a little more than close friends."

Drew shifted in his seat.

"I can't say I'm surprised to find you two are former foster brothers."

"So what?"

The cop smirked. "I knew you were lying to me."

"Doesn't mean either of us did anything wrong."

"I need to remind you of how much trouble you'll be in if I find out your brother did do something wrong? Obstruction of justice, accessory to a shooting . . . You might want to get used to those handcuffs, Mr. Jones."

Drew would've been lying if he said the threats didn't rattle him. The old cop stared back intently, a grin tugging at the corner of his lips.

Billberry said, "You want to tell me which of those burner phones found in your possession goes straight to him, or should I keep trying them to find out?"

"They're for work."

"For work?" Billbery's tone was one of disbelief. "Now what could you possibly need burner phones for in your line of work?"

Drew sat up, leaned onto the table. "I've been waiting here forever to make my phone call. I'd like to make that call to my wife, let her know where I am, or else I'll be forced to ask you to call me a lawyer. Either way, I'm done talking."

Billberry leaned back, squinting his eyes. "You haven't made your call? Let's fix that injustice right now. Tell you what: You tell me where to find your brother, and I'll escort you to the phone personally."

"I can honestly tell you I have no idea," Drew said.

Billberry grumbled. Then stood. "To be continued." He walked out the door.

Drew took a deep breath. Placed a hand on his chest, felt his heart hammering away.

The door swung open and a uniformed male cop walked in. He helped Drew to his feet, and escorted him out of the room, and back down the long hall until they came to an office phone coated in ten layers of dust with all the buttons missing except the numbers.

"Dial nine, then the number," the cop said.

"Hey, what time is it anyway?"

"Eleven." Felt way later than that. Meant Drew waited in the interrogation room less than an hour. After getting his face bounced off the sidewalk, the paramedics cleaned him up and cleared him quickly. The last clock he saw was while being fingerprinted, and it had read 10:15.

Drew picked up the receiver, cradled it with his shoulder to his ear. The handcuffs jingled as he moved. He dialed Gaby's cell, thankful it was burned into his memory—probably the only one besides his own.

The call rang and rang. Went to voicemail.

"Shit." Her message played. "Hey, Gab. It's me. I'm in the Central Jail, downtown, and need you to come bail me out, please." He hung up, sighed. Looked at the cop.

"Give it a couple, and you can try again."

"Thanks."

Drew's palms were slick, his breathing punchy, like he'd ran a 10k. He'd never been arrested, so he'd never spent any time in jail. He felt ashamed, humiliated. How could this be happening?

"Try again," the cop said.

Drew dialed again. The phone rang. After the second ring, the call connected.

"Babe? Hey, it's me." The cop gave Drew space, but kept an eye on him over his shoulder. "I'm in—"

"Hey there, Drew." Zan.

Drew felt the blood drain from his face and his vision narrowed to pinholes.

"What the fu—"

"Yeah, it's me, buddy. I heard you got arrested. Sorry to hear it. I'm guessing you're calling from the jail phone. So watch what you say. Remember your rights. Just listen."

Drew's mind reeled. He felt like the ground under him was opening up and he'd be swallowed up at any minute. How did Zan find him? Was it because Billberry said he'd been trying his burners? Maybe he got through and Zan felt him out, or Billberry flat-out said Drew was in jail? But how the hell had Zan answered Gaby's phone? There was only one possible answer and it scared the living shit out of Drew. So, he kept quiet to listen.

"Don't worry. I'm bailing you out. Gaby's here, by the way, and says hi."

Drew clenched his teeth so he wouldn't yell or react in any way, while on the inside he screamed in horror.

"Don't say anything until you hear from me again, okay? I know Gaby feels the same. We're both pulling for you, Drew."

"Please . . . Tell her I love her, and I'll see her soon."

"You most definitely will," Zan said. "Now, hang tight. I'll get you out of there soon."

The call ended suddenly with a hollow dial tone left in Zan's absence.

Drew hung up the receiver. The pain from the back of his head wrapped around to his forehead. Blood pounded there and behind his eyes.

"All good?" said the cop.

"I wouldn't say that."

The cop raised an eyebrow.

Drew waved his hands, the handcuffs rattling. "It's fine," he lied.

Chapter Thirty-Five

Drew didn't make it back to the interrogation room or even spend a second in a jail cell. The cop who escorted him to the phone received a message through his shoulder mic that "Drew Jones has made bail." He escorted Drew directly to intake. His belongings were returned to him—three cell phones, wallet, keys. He signed paperwork, and was set free.

On the way out, Drew looked over his shoulder, expecting Det. Billberry to be there to re-arrest him and drag him back for more questioning, but he wasn't. Drew chalked it up to the old cop not having anything substantial on him. He wanted Jake anyway. Probably best to make sure Billberry didn't follow him so he couldn't intercept his brother.

A gentle rain fell outside. The sky pitch-black, while the parking lot glowed a sickly yellow from the multitude of sodium lamps dotting the area. While still huddled under a tiny awning, Drew checked the time on his phone. Eleven-thirty. He swiped through his apps, looking for a ride share provider, when a voice from the parking lot called his name.

Drew looked up. There sat a small silver or white sedan—hard to tell in the unnatural light. The driver's window rolled down. "You Drew?"

"Yeah, who are you?"

"Thomas. Your friend Zan ordered you a ride."

Friend. Shit. Drew took a shallow breath and approached the car.

Thomas rolled up the window.

Dropping his head, Drew got in the back, sat behind the driver's seat.

"Where we going?" the driver asked.

"Forty-eight fifty-four 34th Street. Quick as you can, please."

Thomas stepped on the gas, but not as hard as Drew would've preferred. He wiped the rain off his arms and face with the underside of his jersey. A violent itch crawled and spread beneath his skin. His head ached, and as he settled into his seat, his mind went to a dark place.

Zan had Gaby's phone. Which meant he was with Gaby. Or more precisely, Zan and Shaw were holding her hostage. Drew pictured her huddled on their couch while that beast Shaw hovered over her. Zan, with his sunken face and shark eyes watching her every move, her every breath. Needling her with questions she couldn't answer.

Maybe what scared Drew the most was Gaby's personality. Fierce. Strong. She didn't take shit from anyone, and that wouldn't bode well for her. Shaw loved to dole out gut punches like they were solicitor leaflets outside a Trader Joe's. What if Gaby mouthed off and Shaw punched her in the stomach? Could his concrete blows kill their baby?

"Can you speed up, please?"

"I'm going as fast as is safe in this weather," Thomas said. Typical Californian, scared of a little rain. The driver turned on music—a soft rock song from the 70s Drew couldn't identify. Like that would distract or soothe him.

Craning his neck, Drew peered out the windshield. They were finally on the 163.

Drew pulled all three phones out of his pockets. No missed calls on any of them. The battery on his cell down to twelve percent. He took Zan's burner and dialed. It rang and rang. When Zan didn't pick up, Drew ended the call. Should he call Gaby's number next to reach him? Why Drew even hesitated at the obvious exposed his true terror of the situation.

How could he live with himself for putting Gaby in peril? Zan had threatened her, too, and he was more focused on Jake and his own safety. He should've stayed with her, slept on the porch if he had to. If anything happened to her, he'd never be able to forgive himself.

He willed himself to change the focus of his mind, brought up a good memory of Gaby. Probably his favorite memory. The time he finally worked up the courage to ask her out after a volleyball match between their two teams. She was toweling sand off her arms when he came up from behind her and said hi. But she didn't respond, so he figured she hadn't heard him. He sidestepped to face her. She must have heard *something*, because she turned quickly and they bonked heads.

While both still rubbed their heads, Gaby asked what he had said.

"Hi," he said.

"Hi."

"No, that's what I said—hi."

"And I'm saying hi back." She smiled at him, and her cheeks flushed.

They were off and running from there. For their first date, they met at Swami's in Encinitas the next day and got in an early morning surf session, followed by breakfast tacos in town. Drove up Mt. Soledad and parked on their second, and ended up messing around instead of taking in the view as planned.

Gaby invited Drew over to her parents' house for dinner for their third date. She hadn't told him ahead of time she had two moms, not that it mattered to him. Parents were parents. Something he craved his entire life. Turned out, Vicky and Ester proved two of the warmest, nicest people he'd ever met. Totally put him at ease. They didn't pry into his childhood, and let him share what he wanted to share. In a way, he felt like her moms adopted him even while they were dating. It was Vicky who encouraged Drew to propose to her daughter, giving him that last nudge needed. He loved how Vicky so willingly wanted to include him in their family. Parent approval aside, Drew knew he'd won the lottery when Gaby married him.

She was the single best thing to ever happen to him—so hell fucking yes he was scared to death of what awaited him when Thomas the ride share driver slowed to a stop outside Bernie's house. Gaby's car was parked on the street, directly in front of them.

The car hadn't entirely stopped moving when Drew darted out. A steady rain pelted him. He was drenched when he made it to the porch. Darkness enveloped their house. He dug into his pockets for the keys. Gripped the storm door handle to insert the key, but the knob turned freely. The main door was unlocked as well. Panic shot through him; felt like his heart seized. He took a deep breath and couldn't be sure he exhaled.

Thrusting open the door, he shouted, "Gaby? Where are you?"

He flipped on the light. No one on the couch, or anywhere. Drew ran to the bedroom, flipped on the light, and found nothing there as well.

"Fuck." Sweat beaded on his forehead. The throbbing of his head intensified. "Where are you?" Asking the question to which he knew the answer. Zan had taken her. It was the sole explanation. Drew punched the bedroom door, then stormed out of the house.

On the porch, he pulled out his cell phone and scrolled until he got to Gaby's contact. His thumb trembled, hovering over her name. The wind increased, blowing rain into his face.

A banging sound distracted him.

He looked around, but it was dark as hell. The sound persisted. A steady banging. He turned on the flashlight on his phone and scanned the yard.

Bernie's vinyl gate door was swung completely open and knocking against the fence.

The sight gave Drew a glimmer of hope. Maybe Gaby was at Bernie's. Maybe she decided to stay with him in case Drew came back home. Made some sense. The two were close. And Bernie was much closer in proximity than her moms. No way she'd drive that far in the rain either, with the willing ear of Bernie right next door. But what about her phone?

Drew crossed the yard to the fence. Maybe Gaby left her phone inside their home and Zan came by looking for him and took her phone? A stretch, but Drew needed something positive to cling to right then.

He went to call for her but stopped. Between the wind and the rain and the banging gate, no way they'd hear him from inside Bernie's house.

Drew shined the light at the back door, which stood directly across from the open gate door. His flashlight reflected off the panes of inset glass in the door. Even still, he could tell the house was dark. They could be asleep. He stepped apprehensively into the small backyard patio. The gravel between the flagstone was slightly flooded and made a sickening wet crunch under his steps. Head up, focused on the back door, he tripped over something. He flailed his arms and was able to catch his balance to stay upright.

As he collected himself, a light flashed on. A motion-activated lamp affixed to the back of the house. White light flooded the tiny patio and that's when Drew saw a body.

Bernie. Lying in a heap on his side. Soaking wet. Not moving.

"No—Bernie! Bernie, are you okay?"

Drew dropped to his knees. Grabbed his landlord by the shoulder and rolled him onto his back. Shining the flashlight on him, the sight made Drew's entire body buck. He gagged.

Bernie's basic white t-shirt, the same kind he wore at the end of every day, was soaked in blood. His face was slack, with his eyes wide open, frozen, glaring off in the distance in shock.

Drew pitched to the side. Thought he was going to throw-up. But nothing came.

Gaby.

Jumping up, he rushed for Bernie's back door. It was unlocked. Inside, Drew stood in the kitchen and shouted Gaby's name into the darkness of the rest of the house.

"Are you in here, Gaby?"

He tore through the house, flipping on lights in room after room. Living room across to the breakfast solarium. On to the main bedroom, office, and guest bedroom. He even checked the bathrooms, pulling back the shower curtain in each to reveal empty bathtubs.

She wasn't in the house.

Zan had killed his neighbor and kidnapped his wife.

Standing in the living room, the edges around his vision frayed and narrowed. The pain of his head, face, and stomach didn't register. Only a sinking feeling bloating every cell of his body. He raised the phone for the time. The screen was black and wouldn't come on. Dead.

Drew trudged to the kitchen, found the charger cord Bernie kept plugged into an outlet by the sink, and connected the phone. He fell back against the oven. Rubbed his face. Water dripped off him, puddling on the floor. He stood there feeling empty, lost. Despair washing over him.

Whatever good he'd thought he'd been doing, trying to find Jake and save him from being murdered, had severely backfired. There was no doubt Zan meant what he said earlier in the evening about killing Jake and him if he didn't get his money back. Drew believed him then, except now it was a lock. Only question: would Zan kill *everyone* Drew cared about?

If he wanted to, it sure as hell felt like there was nothing Drew could do about it. His landlord's dead body outside proved as much. God, poor Bernie.

His phone's screen illuminated. It displayed a three percent charge. Drew reluctantly decided to let it get to five so he'd have enough juice to call Gaby's phone to plead for her life.

What else could he do?

He'd lost.

If only he'd grabbed Jake and ended this two days ago. Or Zan hadn't seen him at the game. Or he hadn't been arrested. None of it mattered now. Zan was in complete control. With only part of Zan's money in his possession, his brother not answering his phone and god knew where, what did he even have to barter for Gaby's life? The walls were closing in fast around him, and everything looked bleak as hell.

Without warning, Drew couldn't breathe past the knot in his throat. He slid down the front of the oven until his ass hit the floor. He hugged his knees and began to weep.

Chapter Thirty-Six

Seated in a heap on Bernie's kitchen floor, Drew forced himself to stop crying. Slowly, he took his hands away from his face. He sleeved tears from his cheeks. Raised his head. Bernie's body lay directly in his line of sight, through the open kitchen door. The rain continued to fall, but its soothing sound did little to settle the anxiety squatting in his chest.

What did Bernie do to deserve being killed? Nothing. Collateral damage in this stupid cat-and-mouse game Zan was playing with Drew to get to Jake. The sight of his landlord's dead body should have made him keep crying, but his tears were for Gaby and his fear of the fate which unjustly awaited her.

With a pitiful moan, he worked himself off the floor. He grabbed the phone off the counter. The charge read five percent. He unlocked the device, keeping it plugged into the charger cord. The phone began ringing, startling him. It was Gaby's contact. Blood drummed in his ears. He fumbled with the phone, but recovered and answered it.

"Hello?"

"Are you home yet, Drew?"

"Yes, you piece of shit. Where's my wife? I swear to fucking god, if you hurt her—"

"Whoa, whoa, whoa. Simmer down and shut the fuck up. You think I want to hurt a pregnant woman?"

Drew glanced at Bernie's soaking body, didn't reply.

"What kind of person do you think I am, Drew?"

"Relentless."

"Fucking A. You found out the hard way."

"What do you want, besides—"

"Same thing I've wanted this entire time. Ever since your dumbass brother robbed me. I want my money and Jake."

"Why'd you have to kidnap Gaby though? She has nothing to do with this. I told you I'd get you what you wanted."

Zan tsked him. "You failed though, didn't you? You said it yourself, Drew. You met up with your brother. Even saw my money. Why you didn't grab both and make this right by now is one-hundred percent on you, motherfucker. Gaby . . ." He sucked his cheek. "She's insurance. She's going to ensure your motives are as true as a dope set at Black's."

Drew unclenched his jaw. "I've done everything you asked and still had three days to get you what you wanted before you flipped out on me."

"Really? Arguing semantics while your wife sits here bound and gagged?"

"You fucking asshole. Let her go right now!"

Zan laughed hard. "Guess you had to try that. I mean, what if it worked? You're funny."

"Let me at least talk to her."

The other end of the line fell silent. A second or two later, he heard the muffled cries of his wife, and his whole body tensed.

"Gaby!"

"That's all you get," Zan said, coming back. "This is how it's going to go. Listen close."

Drew tensed, but paid attention. Zan continued.

"It's right at midnight. You're going to meet me at the OB Pier, on the beach, at 3 a.m. I'll bring Gaby, you bring Jake and my money. We'll trade, and that will be that. No one has to get hurt, besides your brother, and we all walk away with what we want. But, if you can't find Jake and get him there in three hours, well, things won't go well for Gaby." Zan paused, stretching the silence to an unbearable length. "I'll drown her ass, Drew. I won't even hesitate. You understand me?"

Teeth clenched, Drew growled, "Yes."

"I'm not fucking around."

"I believe you. I'll make it happen."

"Three hours, Drew. Don't fuck this up. Don't be stupid. Don't tell anyone or call the cops. I see anyone besides you or your brother, your wife dies. Just get Jake and my money there, and this all ends once and for all. We straight?"

"Yeah. We're straight."

Zan hung up.

Drew sunk back to the floor.

***

Drew wanted to stay down on the floor for hours, but he couldn't. He needed to get out of there. Mentally and physically.

But first, Bernie. Drew couldn't leave him out there like that even though time wasn't on his side. If he called the police, he'd get roped into hours of questioning he couldn't afford. He couldn't even drag Bernie out of the rain because he'd risk incriminating himself. Wait.

He had two burner phones. Jake's, he still needed, obviously. But Zan's. He pulled it out, dialed 9-1-1.

When the operator answered, Drew threw his voice, going with a gravelly, deep tone. "There's a dead guy in a backyard at forty-eight fifty 34th Street. Send an ambulance, or whatever."

"Sir, what is your—"

Drew ended the call. Broke the phone in half like he'd seen in movies, and pocketed the pieces. He'd dump them somewhere far away from here.

And Drew needed to do the same—get away from here.

One place sprung immediately to mind. A place he could hunker down. A place so close to the OB Pier he could use all his time focusing on getting Jake to meet him there.

The Surfview Cottages.

Before he could leave, Drew remembered to turn off all the lights and close up the house like he was never there. Back in the kitchen, he looked around. He had everything. And any fingerprints he left behind didn't matter since his and Gaby's were already all over Bernie's house anyway.

Drew dashed out the back door, shutting it behind him. Rain poured off the gutterless roof, drenching him again. Turning around, he looked down at his dead landlord.

"So sorry, Bern," he said before running out of the yard and to the Transit Connect.

***

By pushing the Transit Connect close to ninety all the way down the 8, Drew pulled into Ocean Beach ten minutes after leaving his house.

The neighborhood was desolate. As far from normal as it got on a Friday night. The rain the culprit. He drove through a green light at Newport Ave. and glanced right. Empty parking spots as far as he could see down the main drag. Multi-colored neon light reflecting in pools of rainwater left in the absence of vehicles. Normally, you couldn't find an open spot until everything closed at 2 a.m. Probably why Zan chose 3 a.m., Drew realized.

Less people out then. The middle of the three-hour—maximum—time window when the beach town slept. By 5 a.m., the water would be teeming again with surfers. Not tonight though. Not with the rain. Even the homeless would likely scatter from the pier. Taken to find dryer shelter under the awnings of businesses and in covered parking structures.

Zan knew what he was doing.

Drew hooked a right on Niagara and found an open spot to park. The cottages were several blocks away still, but he told himself a walk—even in the rain—would do him good. He was soaking wet already anyway.

When he got out of the van, the rain slowed to a heavy sprinkle. He went around to the side and threw open the sliding door. After pulling away the drop cloth hiding the gym bag full of cash, Drew paused. He removed Jake's burner, opened it, and dialed.

The phone rang and rang, same as earlier in the evening. Drew closed the phone with a grunt, grabbed the gym bag, and closed the van.

If Jake didn't answer the phone, Drew would be fucked.

He crossed the street, palms and other trees acting as a screen against some of the wind and rain. How had it come to this? Gaby's life at risk. Drew bit his lower lip and squeezed his fists so tight the skin on his knuckles felt like it would tear.

Zan was right, that monster. Drew should've grabbed Jake when they met at Fiesta Island. Even though there was that cop. He should've followed Jake then or not let him off the hook later when they talked. He should have forced the issue, convinced Jake to return the money to Zan. Threatened to call the cops. To disown him. Anything. He should've put his foot down and not let his brother do whatever he wanted.

Though, Jake wasn't the real issue.

Drew reached the cottages and took out his keys. He instinctually went to the unit he'd left off work at, the one containing some of his gear and work lights. Inside, he plugged in the halogen light fixture and switched it on. The small space filled with bright light. He slung the gym bag against one of the finished living room walls.

The real issue was Drew fucked all this up from the beginning. All his shitty decisions were to blame. Gaby was right. He chose to protect Jake from Zan and the police, without including her in any part of it. He should have called the cops when Zan and Shaw broke into their house and beat him up. Hell, he should've reported the Chinook stolen when Jake took off in it, like Gaby wanted. The cops probably would have found him a lot quicker than it took Drew, with all the hoops Jake made him jump through. Drew cringed at the thought of calling the police. On second thought, maybe not that. But he definitely would've made different choices knowing what he knew now.

Drew threw his back against the wall and slumped down until his ass met uncarpeted floor, the bag of cash to his left.

And how would he explain any of this to Gaby's parents? Ester would cry forever and Vicky would murder him if anything happened to Gaby. He wouldn't be able to look them in the eyes ever again. He'd rather die than tell her moms that their only daughter . . .

Drew shook his head, threw his gaze around the room to stop his mind from completing that horrible thought. Half the living room was sealed up with drywall; the other half exposed studs. Though, work was the furthest thing from his mind. He took the phones out of his pocket and set them next to the gym bag. He examined the two pieces of Zan's burner. Picked them up and turned them over in his hand. The device was lighter than his tape knife, but its weight had dragged him down ever since Zan forced it on him.

Pursing his lips, Drew squeezed the pieces. Cocked his arm and threw them as hard as he could, screaming. The two pieces struck an exposed beam in the wall opposite him and shattered into a dozen other pieces.

Drew pounded the floor with his fist. Fucking Zan. Gaby didn't deserve this. She didn't have one goddamn thing to do with any of it. It took a weak-ass man to kidnap a pregnant woman, use her as a pawn in a game he already held all the advantages. Coward. Piece of shit.

It was one thing when Zan threatened Jake and promised him a severe beating—Jake brought that on himself. And while Jake's actions burdened Drew, at least he understood Zan forcing him to bring in Jake and the money—Drew was with his brother when he stole it.

Kidnapping Gaby, though. Fucking low. He wished he could make Zan pay for that.

Drew's growing anger was suddenly interrupted by a shot of fear, like a bullet to the brain. Zan held the future of his family in his hands. Gaby and their unborn child. If she and their baby died, so did Drew's dream of a stable, normal life.

The fear of losing them both, of their lives being under threat, must have been the reason something clicked right then in Drew's mind.

In his heart. A realization he'd questioned for more than six months whether it would ever happen . . . He wanted to be a father.

He embraced the feeling now with unwavering confidence.

Like there had never been any other choice.

Drew wanted to be a father.

All the shit and heartache he'd experienced as a child—he would make sure his boy didn't go through the same. His son would have a father. A father to change his diapers, teach him to walk, to ride a bike, catch a baseball, shave, surf. Gone was his standing fear of fucking up his future child. Even the thought of it now made him shudder in disbelief, embarrassment. Jake was right. Mon was right. Gaby was right. Drew held a PhD in what not to do as a parent. For the first time in six-and-a-half months, he no longer felt a creeping dread in the pit of his stomach.

For the first time, he wanted this child, desperately wanted to be his father. Instead of fear, he felt excitement. Anticipation. Trips to the beach, to Padres games, the zoo, Balboa Park; hikes in the mountains, drives up and down the coast. They lived in an incredible city, and it was theirs to explore. San Diego was such a diverse area that you could spend the morning high in the mountains, and go surfing in the afternoon. He had a second chance to explore all the things he missed out on in his childhood, and view them through the eyes of a child. And not just any child. His son, his own blood.

Except . . .

Zan threatened to take it all away.

Drew shook his head.

Fuck. That.

Chapter Thirty-Seven

The first thing Drew knew he needed to figure out was how to separate Zan from Gaby.

Drew stood up.

He began pacing the small space, hands pressed to temples.

He could lure Zan into a fight. The thought of beating the shit out Zan for a change gave Drew a charge. First, he'd have to deal with Shaw, which wouldn't be easy either.

Drew's steps echoed off the unfinished floor. The work light cast his shadow four times his size against the opposite wall. As he continued to pace, a panic built inside him. His palms became sticky, his throat parched. He needed to solidify a plan and fast. Reaching into his pocket for his phone to check the time, he came up empty. Drew turned around, found the phone on the ground by the gym bag where he'd left it. He went over and grabbed it up, pressed the home button. The time read 12:47 a.m.

In his lower peripheral, Jake's burner lit up. He practically dove for the phone, snatching it with excitement. Three missed calls. Drew opened the phone, dialed Jake back. The line clicked after one ring. He felt relief, like a warm rush flowing under his skin.

"Drew? You there?"

"Jake! Holy hell. I've been trying to get a hold of you all night."

"Yeah, no shit. I was about to ditch the phone too since I decided to swing by your place to tell you in person."

"What are you talking about?" Drew asked.

"I'm taking off, and wanted to give you the Chinook back—"

"What? No, you can't."

"Bro, listen. I'm calling for another reason. I'm at your place, and it's absolutely fucking swarming with cops. What the hell is going on?"

"That's why I've been calling you. I got arrested earlier—"

"Seriously? For what?"

"Doesn't matter. While I was inside, Zan went to our house and killed our landlord and kidnapped Gaby."

Jake gasped.

"Holy fuck, dude. I'm so fucking sorry."

Drew had never heard his brother speak so quietly, and with such an edge of fear.

"Jake, I need you to bring me the rest of the money right fucking now." Drew paced the living room again, head down, spitting out his words as fast as possible before Jake could argue. "If you don't get over here before three a.m., Zan is going to kill Gaby."

"Bro. Enough said. I'll head there now. Where are you?"

"The Surfview Cottages . . . The place in OB where you slept in the van while I worked up a bid."

"By the pier, right?"

"That's it." As soon as Drew answered, he heard the Chinook's engine rev.

"I'll be there as fast as I can, little bro. Twenty minutes, tops."

"Don't drive stupid and get pulled over, Jake. I can't afford for you to get detained. By the way, did you spend any of the money?"

"No. Not much. A couple hundred."

Drew groaned. "Okay . . . Just get here safely and as quick as you can."

"We're gonna trade me and the cash for Gaby, right? That how this is working?" Jake's tone was innocent-sounding, childlike.

Drew swallowed, stopped still. That was Zan's plan, and Drew knew it wouldn't ensure Gaby's safety. He looked up and was blinded by his work light.

Jake continued. "'Cause I'm willing to do that—sacrifice myself for Gaby. I should have listened to you about this guy. I only worried about myself. I never thought it'd get this bad."

While Drew blinked away spots of colors from the blinding light, a plan came to him. "Jake. I'm glad you finally want to do what's right. But I just got an idea of how to save Gaby and also keep you alive. I gotta let you go so I can make another call."

"Okay, see ya soon."

Drew ended the call. Switched to his personal cell and dialed.

"Come on, answer . . ." The call rang four times before the person on the other line picked up. Drew pumped a fist.

"A groggy voice said, "Jones? Why're you calling me at one a.m.?"

"So sorry, Mon. But this is an emergency. I need your help."

"What's going on?"

"The psycho that was after my brother has kidnapped Gaby." Mon gasped. "I'm supposed to hand over Jake and the money he stole to get her back. We're meeting at 3 a.m. on the beach, below the OB Pier."

"Fuck me. What can I do?"

"I don't trust this guy, obviously. He's already killed my landlord earlier tonight, and there's no way he doesn't kill Gaby and Jake—"

"I'm guessing calling the cops is out?"

"Yeah. No cops. But I've got a plan and need you if I hope to pull it off."

"Where are you?" Mon asked.

"The Surfview. Look for the unit all lit up."

"I can be there in ten minutes."

"Thank you so much. One more thing, first."

"Anything."

"Bring four halogen work lights and all the heavy-duty extension cords and waterproof connection boxes you've got."

"Can do. Hold tight and I'll be there soon."

After ending the call with Mon, Drew checked the time. One a.m. on the nose. They had two hours to prep his plan.

This would work.

It had to work.

Chapter Thirty-Eight

Drew bolted from the unit to retrieve some things from his work van. The rain picked up again, and he now wished he hadn't parked so far away or would've at least had the opportunity to grab a jacket before leaving home.

Heading down the sidewalk, the ocean churned with violence behind him; so loud he could hear it over the rain. The forecasted Southern swell had clearly arrived. If the tide was too high, Drew wondered if Zan would move their meeting off the beach. Please let there be a beach, Drew prayed to no one in particular. His plan would only work if they stuck to meeting on the beach. Once he reached the Transit Connect, Drew threw his focus onto gathering the specific items he needed.

First, his work boots. Thankfully he kept a back-up pair in the van. You only get to a job site having forgotten work boots once. Next, he retrieved two portable phone chargers and a power cord from the glove box. He hoped they held enough juice to keep his phone charged enough to receive Zan's call and make other necessary calls after everything was over.

Finally, Drew gathered a couple tools, a roll of electrical tape, and a container of heavy-duty zip ties. Rain pattered on the van's roof. Drew steeled himself, then jumped out of the van and into the rain. Slid the side door closed and dashed across the street.

Headed back to the Surfview, he kept his eyes ahead. On the pier. He was tempted to keep going, to check out the beach conditions below, but he was more anxious about getting back to the room for when Mon and Jake arrived.

Back in the unit, Drew did his best to shake the rain off himself. If he had thought about it, he would've also grabbed a roll of contractor paper towels from the van. Didn't matter. More important prep work called, and time wasn't a luxury.

He sat down by the gym bag of cash and took off his sneakers. Next, he put the work boots on, loosely. He checked the gap between his right ankle and the boot. Just one finger fit, so he loosened the laces a bit more, and retied them. This time he was able to slide two fingers in the gap. Perfect. He'd add the last step right before they went down to meet Zan.

A knock at the door.

"Come in," Drew said.

The door creaked open. Mon barreled in wearing a yellow slicker, arms stacked with sets of black extension cords. Connection boxes hanging by her fingers.

"Hey, Jones. Lovely weather we're having."

"Right?" Drew got up and went to her.

"Anywhere?" she asked. Drew said yeah.

Mon dropped the supplies, and Drew immediately pulled her into a hug.

"Thank you so much, Mon."

"Of course. Anxious to hear this plan of yours."

"Jake's on his way. Let's grab the rest of your gear. I'll fill you both in when he shows."

"Sounds good." Mon turned around and walked out, Drew following right behind.

She'd double-parked right off the property. She opened the back of her work van, and Drew pulled out two of the work lights. Mon stacked two sets of extension cords on top of them for him. Drew headed back. He heard the van doors close, then nothing but ocean and rain.

Back inside, Mon carried in the other two work lights and three more bundles of extension cords. "I'll go grab the rest of the cords. Over two-thousand feet worth."

Drew laughed. "Fuck yeah. That's awesome. Keep an eye out for Jake, wouldya?"

Mon shot him with a finger gun and left. Drew gathered up the four work lights, placing them with his. He gave them a once-over and felt good about his plan. Even better when his brother stormed in.

"I'm so, so sorry." Water dripped off Jake as he stood in the entryway staring at Drew like a little boy who'd lost his dog.

Drew hesitated. The pull to instantly forgive his brother was a kneejerk reaction he realized was something he needed to work on. His wife and unborn child were in peril thanks to Jake. Drew fumed at the thought.

Jake inched closer.

"I know you are. Thank you for coming."

Jake launched himself at Drew and swallowed him into a hug.

Drew hugged him back, but not tightly. Their heads together, he went to say something into Jake's ear when he glimpsed Jake's old green backpack clutched in his hand.

"It's the rest of the money," Jake said, holding up the bag.

Drew nodded to the gym bag on the floor. "Add it to that one."

Jake went over, squatted down, and did exactly that.

Seconds later, Mon walked back in carrying more extension cords. "Hey," she said. "Good to see you again, Jake."

"Right on, same," he said. Jake jumped up and offered his hand. Arms still full, Mon awkwardly shook his hand. After tossing the extension cords down with the others, she folded her arms. Jake moved next to her, propping hands on his hips.

"So, little bro. What's the plan?"

"Okay." Drew took a breath. "Couple things you need to know first, so you can see where I'm coming from. First, Zan said to meet him on the beach, under the pier. On the beach. And the second thing was he said if I didn't bring Jake and the money, he would drown Gaby. Not just kill her—*drown* her."

Both Mon and Jake looked like they followed. "Okay," Mon said.

Drew continued. "I'm taking both those things to mean that when we get down there, Zan will have Gaby down by the water, threatening her safety. Pressing us to hand over the money."

"Didn't you say you think Zan will kill her anyway?" Mon asked.

"Exactly." Drew pointed at her. "Why say he'll drown her if he hasn't already decided that's what he'll do? I disregarded several of his threats in the past. I'm not doing that again."

"So, how are we going to stop him?" asked Jake.

"Knowing, or hopefully knowing, that Zan will be at the water, or even *in* it, we'll set up a counterattack ahead of time," Drew said. "Mon. We're going to connect all these work lights, and run extension cords from the cottages down to the beach. We'll set it up now. Then stash the lights in the bushes at the bottom of the cliff, out of view."

"And the connector boxes are to keep everything dry," she said.

"Right. When Jake and I go to meet Zan, you'll move the lights down onto the beach, and be ready for my signal. It will be dark, and also with the rain and his full attention on me and Jake, Zan won't see shit."

Jake rubbed his hands together. "I'm digging it so far."

"Here's the main idea." Drew held out his hands. "When I yell, Mon, you'll blast Zan with all those lights and blind his ass. That will give me a few seconds of opportunity to jump him and separate him from Gaby. I know he has a gun, so if we can get it away from him, we can end things even quicker."

"Bro, that sounds nuts . . . but maybe it could work."

"It has to work," Drew said. "We literally have no other choice other than to trust him, and I'm not risking Gaby's life on that."

"He'll never expect to be flashed with however many hundreds or thousands of watts of blinding light at three in the morning," Mon said. "It will work. One question, though. When am I doing this? Like right away?"

Drew took another breath. "No. So, I haven't mentioned it yet, but Zan will have his enforcer there too. Shaw. He's a huge dude, and he'll definitely frisk us. Does it every time I see him. He'll also get some shots in if either of us mouth off. Jake."

"Noted," Jake said.

"Knowing Shaw's going to pat us down, I have a plan to use him to try to get Zan to give up, take the money and leave. If Zan really wants a trade, he'll go for what I'm offering. But if he doesn't take the deal right away, that means he plans to kill us all like I think, and we blind his fucking ass and jump him."

"Fuck yeah," Jake said.

Drew took out his phone and checked the time. "It's one thirty-seven. Let's prep and get back here by no later than two-thirty so Zan doesn't spot us."

Mon and Jake nodded enthusiastically.

Jake held out his palm. "You got music on that?"

Drew checked the phone's charge—eleven percent—and reluctantly handed his brother the phone and charger. "It's low, so how about one song?"

Jake thumbed the screen, scrolling and tapping. "I know just the one for this moment." He pressed the volume up all the way.

The unmistakable sound of a guitar slide leading into the punch-in-the-mouth intro of Pearl Jam's "Even Flow."

In his youth, the song's energy gave him the desire to fight, but listening now, he focused on the lyrics and the way in which they were sung with a feral passion so urgent that they now carved deep into his chest, dug into his heart, made him acutely aware of every promise, every word of love he'd given Gaby and he wanted desperately in that moment to have the opportunity to provide her with his best for all the years they had remaining in this life.

Drew squeezed his eyes closed, thrust his face to the ceiling. Gaby's face appeared; her smile warm and reassuring. He wanted to yell for her to hang on, that he was coming. The words danced on the edge of his tongue but never did escape his lips. Still, he felt a confidence surge inside of him to the point where it bordered on unabashed.

The drums crescendoed with a flourish, bringing the song to a close. The trio fell slack. Mon and Jake gave Drew a look like, Are we really doing this? In turn, he reassured them with a commanding nod.

***

First thing they did was go down to the beach to get a lay of the land and measure.

As expected, no one was down there. Not one homeless individual—no one. Not even under the pier. Plain to see why: The rain drenched where it normally would've been dry. Meant no eyewitnesses. Check it as an advantage for Zan.

The beach, though. It was holding. Advantage Drew. The water churned for certain, but mainly farther out, keeping a reasonable-sized beach intact. Mon shined a flashlight at the pylons. The waves were breaking on the fifth set. Good news as long as it held. Plenty of space for Zan to set up, and enough beach for Drew to stage his plan.

"Mon, take the end of this tape," Drew said. "I want to measure how much length you'll need to move the lights."

Mon held the tape and stayed in position at the bottom of the cliff, where they'd discussed stashing the work lights. Drew walked the other end of the tape measure down, side-stepping over the seawall. That would be tricky while carrying the light stands. Once on the beach, his work boots sunk in the oversaturated sand. Mon would have to take deliberate steps not to fall, especially carrying the work lights. He doubled-back under the pier and stopped about where he thought Zan would be most impacted by a sudden blast of light while also not noticing Mon. The spot was on the right side of the pylons. The tape read fifty-one-feet.

Drew waved at her. Mon freed the tape. It zipped up to him quickly. Mon and Jake trudged down to him.

"It's fifty-one-feet to this spot, so we'll need to run at least that much in extension cord in addition to what we run from the cottage over the side of the cliff."

"And that much between light to light, or at least two sets, since I can only grab two lights at a time and I'll have to make two trips to get all four down here," Mon said.

"Good point."

"You gonna be able to do that twice without tripping in this soggy-ass sand and getting noticed?" Jake asked.

"That and the seawall will be tricky, which is why we're going to practice it," Drew said.

Mon nodded. "Anything else we need to check out while we're down here?"

It continued to pour, rain streaming off the bill of Jake's raggedy Padres hat, while Mon appeared almost comfortable in her slicker—the hood keeping her hair and face dry. Both of them looked at him with trust in their eyes, and it gave him some further needed confidence, counteracting the worry gurgling in his gut that he'd let Gaby and them down in the end.

Drew looked around. The ocean was choppy, yet the water level mimicked a low tide. Even still, it made Drew nervous knowing the swell could raise the surf at any time and swallow up the beach. He pushed down that worry and checked off the parts of his plan. The lights seemed good. He and Jake would distract Zan. He would catch Shaw off-guard, use him as leverage. And besides setting up the lights and running through Mon getting them down to the beach, the rest would be play-it-by-ear. Felt like leaving too much to chance, but what else could they do?

"That's it," he finally said. "Let's go prep the lights and get them down here."

The three went back the way they'd come: Up the stairs to the pier; opening the closed but thankfully not locked gate, and hustling back to the cottages.

Inside, they wasted no time, working quickly.

Jake uncoiled the extension cords. Laid them out as much as possible for Mon, who connected each light stand to another with 100-feet of cord between each. As she completed each connection,

Drew took the electrical tape and wrapped each connection with a generous amount. Next, he secured each connection inside its own waterproof connector box.

They had the lights prepped and ready in ten minutes.

"I'm not a construction guy, so sorry in advance if this is a dumb question," Jake said. "The cords will be waterproof, but what about the actual bulbs?"

Drew bulged his eyes at Mon. She grimaced, then looked more certain.

Mon said, "As long as we keep the bulbs facing out, and not up so the rain can't hit them, I think we'll be okay."

"I'll go with that. She's the boss," Drew said. "And even if they do blow eventually, we only need a few seconds."

"Hell, maybe it won't be raining by then," Jake said.

"I hope it still is. We could use the distraction. Okay, Mon. If we're ready, I want to get these down there and run through this."

She nodded.

Jake said, "Okay if I stay here, keep dry?"

"Long as you don't take off again," Drew said.

***

Down on the beach, Mon and Drew readied the work lights after running an extension cord from the cottages down the face of the cliff. Mon set each light to the on position so all she'd have to do when it came time to blast all four on at once was plug in the main extension connected to the four work lights. She held both cord ends, prepared to test it. Drew said good. Mon plugged in the two ends and all the lights fired up, blasting the pier's pylons and the beach with a band of enough light to simulate day.

"Okay, unplug it." Drew said, impatient. Mon did so. "Thanks. Jake got in my head about blowing the bulbs."

"No worries. What time is it?"

"Two-oh-eight. Want to run through this?"

"Yep," Mon said.

"Getting over the seawall's gonna be the trickiest part, so take your time. Be deliberate."

"Got it."

Drew counted down from three with his fingers, then tapped start on his stopwatch app and said go. She squeezed a light stand in each hand and began walking. The wet sand made a sucking sound with every step. Drew shadowed alongside her, watching for anything that might improve her process.

"I know it's dark but try to stay aware of where the cord is so you don't trip."

"I got it, Jones," Mon said, grunting. She made it to the predetermined spot and set the lights down. Drew clocked one-minute and forty seconds. He kept the stopwatch running.

Mon slunk back up the beach. Drew stayed in position. He lost sight of her before she even crossed under the pylons. Perfect. It was dark enough, and the pylons created cover as he'd hoped. A minute later, he caught a glimpse of her carrying down the second set of lights.

When she parked them next to the first set, Drew hit stop.

"Four minutes and eight seconds," he said. "We can work with that. Great job."

Mon looked at her boot as she pulled one foot out of the sand. "Shit is tough to walk in. But I think I got it. Glad we practiced."

"Yeah, you're good to go." Drew picked up two of the light stands. Mon grabbed the other two, and they walked them back to the bottom of the cliff.

"It's two twenty-three. Better get inside in case Zan shows early to stake it out like us."

"Good thinking," Mon said.

Once on top of the pier, Mon made a reluctant-sounding noise.

"Something up?" Drew asked. They reached the fenced gate with OCEAN BEACH stamped into the top of the metal. He lifted the bar out of the concrete to release the gate, and swung it open.

She walked through. "I'm sorry . . . you know. About Gaby."

"It's not your fault." He pushed the gate closed and reinserted the bar.

"I know, it's all so crazy. I've been wondering if I should have pushed you harder to call the cops when you told me everything about your brother."

"Nothing you could have said would have changed anything. This is all my fault. I should have told Gaby about Zan from the beginning. I was so afraid of losing Jake, so scared of Zan, I wasn't thinking straight." Drew snorted. "No, no. That's not right. I was dumb and selfish. If I would have told Gaby what was going on . . . and now it's her life on the line."

Mon didn't reply right away. The rain smacked against the asphalt, filling the gaps of silence. Drew turned and looked at the pier, at the black ocean all around. He let out an anguished sigh.

"It's gonna work out, Jones," said Mon in a subdued tone.

He faced her, gestured for them to keep going to the unit. "I really hope you're right." Which reminds me. As soon as you hit those lights, call the cops."

Chapter Thirty-Nine

Inside, Jake was sitting on the floor, where Drew sat earlier.

Mon walked to the kitchen and fell back against the sink. Flopped her hood down.

Drew went over to Jake, got on one knee, pushed the gym bag of money out of the way, and sat down next to his brother. He took out his cell phone and set it on his leg. Jake smiled at him but didn't say anything. He'd taken off his hat and his greasy hair hung in his face.

"Hand me those tools to your right?" Drew asked.

Jake leaned over and collected them. Gave them to Drew. "What are those for?"

Drew removed a metal file from the small leather case he'd transported the tools and tape in from the van. "Needed something to keep me occupied while we wait. It's going to feel like an eternity until he calls."

"Nah. That phone's gonna ring before you know it. Then we'll be off to save Gaby."

Drew slowly nodded; lips sucked in. He slapped the file against his palm a couple times.

"It's gonna work," Jake said.

Into his chest, Drew said, "Yeah."

They sat there for a few minutes in silence. The only sounds were the clinking and grinding of Drew messing with his tools and the constant patter of rain.

"Hey, can I tell you something that's been on my mind?" Jake said.

Drew looked up. His brother appeared serious, solemn even. Furrowed forehead over eyes that held a wounded look he rarely ever saw on his brother's face.

"Sure."

"Driving over, I had some time to think. When you told me Gaby had been kidnapped, it hit me hard. Really made me think about the way I've acted." A long pause, then a stutter. "A-and I want to apologize for how I've treated you. Not only about all the shit I put you through with the liquor store and the cash I stole. Our whole lives."

"What are you talking about?"

"I've left you holding the bag for me over the years more times than I can count. Ever since we were kids when I left home. I shoulda been there when Joe and Rose got arrested. Been there for *you*. I've never been there for you. The fucking opposite, if I'm being honest. You've always taken care of *me*. Given me money, a place to crash. I've always done what I wanted to do. And when I stole that money, I did it because I'd convinced myself I was finally doing something to help you and Gaby out to return the favor. Really though, I did it for me."

Drew stared at the floor between his legs. He opened his mouth to respond, but Jake rested a hand on his shoulder and continued.

"I don't want to be a selfish mooch anymore. I want to be your brother and not an inconvenience. I'm truly sorry for everything, Drew."

Drew cleared his throat. "Thanks for that, but you're not an inconvenience. A pain in the ass, definitely."

Jake chuckled. "I'm both but I don't want to be. I know you've always looked up to me and I've taken advantage of that. I had you chasin' after me, pulled you away from the family that needs you more than anything—and that's before Gaby got kidnapped. If I would've done what you said—brought the money back to Zan, Gaby would be safe at home right now."

"And you'd probably be dead," Drew said.

"You didn't know any better." A long pause. "Guess I need you to know that if we pull this off, I'm gonna be a better brother. You can count on it."

Drew clapped Jake's back. "Does this mean you're going to settle down, get off the road?

Jake let out a long whining sound, and said, "I don't know about that. We'll see. I do have a nephew on the way that I'd love to hang out with. Uncle Jake. Has a fun ring to it."

"Speaking of," said Drew, feeling his face flush. "I'm not afraid of having our kid anymore. I honestly can't wait to be a dad now."

"See? What'd I tell you? You're going to be a great dad."

Drew snorted. "Yeah, well. You weren't the only family member being a dumbass."

"Who said anything about me being a dumbass?"

Mon walked into the living room with her hand raised. "Right here."

The brothers laughed. Jake pulled Drew into a headlock. They tussled a bit before Jake let him go. "Okay, okay. Truth. I was being a huge dumbass, but I'll make up for it down there."

"Thanks, man." Drew gave his brother a one-arm hug.

"It's five till three," Mon said.

All eyes fell on Drew. He picked up his cell phone.

"Call, motherfucker," he said. He looked up at Mon. "Thanks again." Then to Jake. "I couldn't have done this without either of you."

"We got this, bro," Jake said. Mon nodded.

Then the phone rang.

Chapter Forty

Z an got right to the point.

"Have Jake and my money?"

"Yes," Drew said.

"Did you call the cops or anyone else?"

Drew shot a look to Mon. "No."

"Good." A pause. The sounds of crashing waves and rain crackled in the receiver. "Come to the beach. Shaw will meet you and Jake. He'll check you both and the money."

"Put Gaby on—"

The call ended. Drew looked at the phone. Then closed and pocketed it. "He said to go down to the beach. Shaw's gonna pat us down like I thought, and check the cash."

Jake and Mon both nodded. She took off her slicker. Must have seen the look Drew gave her, and said, "Yellow's not the most stealth color. We ready?"

"Yeah. Let's do this," Drew said.

They were standing in a loose circle by this point. Drew bent down and grabbed the gym bag by the handles. When he stood, Mon pawed his shoulder and pulled him in. Drew did the same to Jake. They stayed there for a moment, hugging each other.

Drew said, "No matter what happens down there, I can't thank you both enough for this."

"Let's get Gaby back from that fucking psycho," Jake said.

"Hell yeah," Mon said.

They fist-bumped as one, broke like from a football huddle, and marched outside.

Rain still fell, the sky one huge smudge of black ink.

Drew and Jake took lead, with Mon falling back. She'd make her way into position as the brothers went to meet Zan and Shaw. When they reached the pier, Drew swung open the gate. Jake walked through. Drew followed. He forced himself not to look back to check on Mon. He couldn't give her away with those types of trip-ups once down below.

Drew descended the stairs to the beach first; each step feeling like his boots were gradually filling with concrete. His heart thumped furiously in his chest and a solid rock wedged itself in the base of his throat.

"It's gonna be okay," Jake whispered behind him.

"Is it that obvious?"

"Breathing a little heavy's all. It's normal. You got this, little bro."

When they reached the bottom and he took the first step, Drew's legs buckled under him like they were made of rubber.

Jake cupped Drew's arms, keeping him from falling. "I got you."

"Thanks . . ." He cleared his throat and shook his arms to rid himself of his nerves. "I'm good." He took a deep breath. Continued. Once he turned the corner, he climbed over the seawall. He led them out from under the pier to the main part of the beach. Slowed down and poked along. Having no clue where Shaw would appear from, he didn't want to get too far away from where Mon would set up.

It was dark and the rain didn't feel like it was close to letting up. The surf had climbed, based on the water now lapping up twice as much beach than it had a mere thirty minutes earlier. Still enough room for Mon to work, even if the level rose more. They'd waterproofed the connections, so if she needed to put the light stands down in the water, so be it.

"See anyone yet?" Jake asked.

"No."

A beam of light struck the left side of Drew's face and shined in his eye. Jake shouted, "Hey," a second later.

Shaw barked, "Stop right there."

Drew froze. The light stayed on his face and its brightness increased as Shaw approached, apparently from the water. He appeared in Drew's periphery. Shaw bodied up to him, burned the light directly into his eyes. Next, into Jake's.

"This your bitch-ass brother, huh? You bring the money too?"

Drew held up the gym bag. "Where's Zan and Gaby?"

Shaw whipped his small flashlight out to the ocean. Scanned the water left until the beam illuminated pier pylons way out in the water. Next, he made a production of dragging the light in, shining it closer and closer until it hit the third set of pylons closest to the beach—the second set in the water. There, knee-deep in the surf, stood Zan. He practically lounged in front of the right concrete pylon. A gun in one hand and a flashlight in the other.

"Glad you both could make it," he said. He was close enough his voice carried over the waves. Probably no more than ten, fifteen yards from Drew, Jake, and Shaw on the beach. "Got something to show you . . ." Zan moved dramatically to his right. Then slowly swept his flashlight back to where he'd been standing. The beam of light moved up from the water until it finally revealed . . . Gaby. Gagged and strapped to the pylon.

"You son of a bitch." Drew yelled, rushing past Shaw. "We're here. Let her go." Shaw grabbed him by his collar before he could make it to the water, and pulled him back to Jake. He punched Drew in the stomach. It hurt, but the pain nowhere near diluted his anger.

"Let's do this. I've got your money. C'mon."

Zan barked a loud laugh. He shined the flashlight on Gaby's face.

Though Drew's night vision already adjusted to the darkness, he still couldn't make out the details of his wife's face. Just the stark white beam of light giving her a ghostly appearance. It was probably best he couldn't see Gaby's beautiful eyes and the likely horror they held. Motherfucking Zan really strapped her to a fucking pylon? Rage burned inside of Drew like an out-of-control bonfire.

Zan said, "Water's rising, Drew. It's cold too. Gaby can't stay out here all night. You know the drill by now, so shut the fuck up and we'll go from there."

"Go from there? You mean you'll let her go, right?"

Zan clicked off his flashlight in response.

Jake nudged Drew with a quick elbow. Flicked his chin at Shaw. "Hey, big guy." Jake held out his arms. "I'm ready. Let's get this show on the road."

Shaw stuck the end of his flashlight in his mouth and shoved Jake's chest with both hands. Snapped a look back at Drew. His words came out garbled, but clear enough: "Hands up, Jones. Stay where I can see you."

Drew complied even though he wanted to tear off into the water after Zan. But knew he would only get himself shot and ruin their chances of saving Gaby. *Stay calm. Stick to the plan.* The thought tempted him to flash a look over his shoulder, but he didn't. Hopefully

Mon was getting the lights into position and Zan was too focused on Jake and Drew to notice.

Shaw kicked Jake's feet apart, sloshing sand. The big fool patted Drew down in the same way as the two previous times. He gave Drew a side-eye every few seconds. He stopped on Jake's pockets, dug into his right one. His meaty paw came out clutching a set of keys. The Chinook keys. He chucked them toward the sea wall. If they hit concrete, it couldn't be heard over the rain.

"C'mon, man," Jake protested.

Shaw sucker-punched him in the stomach. Jake doubled over, coughed.

"C'mon, man," Shaw mocked. He straightened Jake up and finished searching his legs, down and around his shins, and finally his ankles. Shaw took the flashlight out of his mouth. "Okay, Jones. You're next." Back to Jake. "Same for you. Hands up. Stay where I can see you."

"Shaw," Zan shouted. "Hurry up and check my cash."

"I'm handling this," Shaw growled in response.

Jake raised his hands while Shaw moved to pat down Drew.

Those meaty hands crashed down on Drew's shoulders, slowly swept out. Shaw smacked the undersides of Drew's arms with the backs of his hands, slid them into his armpits. *Get on with it.* Patted his chest next. When he moved to his stomach, Shaw bent over slightly. Drew stole a look over his shoulder out to the pylon. The waves were getting choppier by the second. Pounding the pylons—pounding Gaby. He strained his eyes, but couldn't be sure of the water level. It had to be rising though. Shaw felt around Drew's waist. Next, squeezed the cell phone in his left pocket and keys in his right, but didn't remove either. Drew rolled his right ankle slightly and the ace in his boot poked him. *Good.* It was still there. As long as Shaw didn't dig into Drew's boots, Drew would retain the leverage he'd created. Shaw had never searched *in* his shoes before, so when Drew changed into his backup work boots earlier, he'd done so for a precise reason.

Shaw's hands felt around Drew's quads and hamstrings; his knees, and his calves. In one quick motion, he brushed down Drew's shins and ended with a lackluster sweep of his ankles.

"You're both good, Shaw said. "Now, give me the money."

Jake shot Drew a look. Drew bent over and picked up the gym bag. Held it out to Shaw.

Shaw snatched the handles with one hand and shoved Drew in the back with his other. "Move." He pushed Jake next, and positioned himself behind them.

It was clear he wanted them to approach the water. The brothers began walking, side-by-side. Shaw jabbed them in their backs every few steps. The rain and the waves hammered in Drew's ears, like he'd had the audio turned all the way down while being frisked. His eyesight had fully adjusted though, and he could now make out some details in the darkness. The surf was erratic—breaking uneven and in multiple points. Drew recognized the beach had shrunk with the water rising significantly. He wanted to look to confirm Mon was where she should be but knew he couldn't risk it. Instead, he glanced out at the pylon. His stomach dropped when he saw the water level made it up to the middle of Gaby's stomach. To Zan's waist. He still waded there to her right, blinking his flashlight at them like communicating in morse code.

They reached the water's edge, and a wave crashed onto the beach, splashing their legs up to their knees. Shaw poked them, wanting them to continue south, presumably to get in line with Zan. Fine by Drew. The closer they got, the less ground to cover if they needed to use the lights. All the better.

Drew peeked at Jake. He was biting his lower lip. Probably to keep himself from mouthing off to Shaw about him jabbing them in the back so much.

"Hold up," Shaw said.

They stopped several paces from the pier, giving them a clear view of Zan and Gaby at an angle past the second set of pylons. They were so close it hurt Drew to remain still. Shaw gave them both one final shove in their backs.

Drew waved. "Hang on, Gaby. This will all be over soon—"

Shouting over him, Zan said, "You check the cash yet?"

"Not yet," Shaw said with attitude. "Look like I had a chance?"

The nerve in Drew's left eye began to spasm.

"Check it," Zan said firmly.

Drew lowered his head to glance behind him. Saw Shaw transfer the handles to his left hand so he could unzip the bag. Drew squeezed his hands into fists. Gave it a second or two . . . Shaw's head dipped, and Drew simultaneously raised his right boot up to his hand. Shaw thumbed the cash. *Go time.*

Drew slipped his thumb and index finger into the side of his boot and secured the handle of his tape knife. Pulled it out swiftly and gripped it tight. He swung around and jumped Shaw, wrapping his left arm around his huge neck.

Shaw shouted and dropped the bag of cash. Jake grabbed onto Shaw's left arm. Shaw punched the side of Drew's face. Zan was shouting something Drew couldn't make out in the commotion. Felt like he was riding a wild bull for a second before he set the edge of the tape knife to Shaw's throat.

Shaw instantly stiffened and stopped fighting.

Jake darted around in front and punched him in the stomach. Shaw exhaled sharply but didn't seem affected otherwise.

"What the fuck are you doing?" Shaw said in a low growl.

Zan said the exact same thing, but louder.

Jake did a quick pat down, said, "No weapons."

Drew kicked the back of one of Shaw's knees and the big mountain buckled and dropped. Once on his knees, Drew told him to place his hands on his head. Edge of the tape knife still pressed below his jugular, Shaw scowled at Drew, but obeyed.

Drew moved off to Shaw's right shoulder, shielding himself partly while maintaining pressure on the knife.

"I said, what the fuck are you doing, Jones?" Zan shined his flashlight on the two brothers and Shaw.

"You got this, Drew," Jake said.

"You know what you're doing?" Shaw asked.

"Everyone shut up." Drew looked at Zan. "Zan. I've got a tape knife to your boy's throat, and what you need to know about me in this moment is I'm a fucking artist with this tool. I can remove a single grain of rice out of the sloppiest California burrito you've ever seen with a flick of my wrist. So, imagine how easily I can sever this asshole's carotid." He moved the knife to the side of Shaw's neck.

"Shit, man." Legit fear clung to Shaw's words.

Zan walked forward, leaving Gaby's side. Raised his arms over his head to keep the surf from overwhelming him while moving closer. Drew allowed him to get about halfway between Gaby and them before shouting, "Stop. Don't move, or I'll do it."

Zan stopped. "What do you want, Drew?"

"Take your fucking money, let Gaby go, and call us even. Leave all of us alone."

Waves splashed around Zan. Behind him, Gaby thrashed her head side-to-side. The water now rose above her belly. Drew could tell she was bound to the pier just below her shoulders and across her arms, the water splashing the restraints.

Zan stared dead-eyed at Drew. "No. That wasn't our deal. My money *and* your brother."

Jake stood his ground on Shaw's left and remained quiet.

"Yeah, well that was before you kidnapped my wife and tied her to the fucking OB Pier!" Drew felt Shaw tense, so he tightened his grip and poked his neck with the edge of the knife.

"Ow, fool."

"Shut up."

"Nah, nah, nah," Zan said. "You think you got one over on me—" He gestured with his gun at them. "But really, you're doing me a favor."

"Zan, man. What're you talkin' about?" Shaw said.

Drew flashed a curious look at Jake, who did the same. Both looked back to Zan.

"Shoulda stayed in your lane, Shaw."

"Wait—"

Zan raised the gun.

The muzzle exhaled fire. Two soft pops more like puffs of air sounded.

Shaw's body jerked out of Drew's hold. He folded backward onto his bent legs in slow motion. Awkwardly stuck there for the rain to smack against his sky-turned face. A second later, he slouched and flopped onto the wet sand.

Chapter Forty-One

Time slowed to a near complete halt after Zan fired those bullets.

Vision tunneled, and the sounds of ocean and rain gone static, Drew stood slack-jawed and disoriented. Logically, his brain screamed for him to run or fight, but his arms remained anchored to his sides. He hadn't seen that coming. Not by a mile. Zan shot Shaw twice in the chest, ripping the enormous man from Drew's grasp like he was a single sheet of paper taken by a gust of wind.

Somehow through the fog of senses, he heard his brother yelling his name.

Drew shook his head. Clarity took hold with Zan coming into view. Pressing forward, gun still raised. A sick smile spread across his sunken face.

"Drew," Jake said. "Watch out!"

Drew kept his eyes locked on Zan, and shouted for Mon. "Now, Mon. Now!"

The lights burst on.

The whole beach went stark white.

Zan startled.

Mon got the angle correct: the center mass of the lights blanketed Zan and the surrounding water.

"The fuck?" Zan shouted, raising his arm to shield his eyes. The gun lowered to his side. He took a few curious steps toward the lights.

Jake smacked Drew's arm. "Go!" he screamed.

Drew nodded.

The brothers bolted.

The saturated sand wasn't easy to run in but they closed ground on Zan fast all the same.

He'd waded through the surf and made it onto the beach.

The lights shined hot.

Jake and Drew bore down on an oblivious Zan. Drew had a bead on his back. He couldn't wait to drive Zan's face into the sand. Knock the gun away or maybe even beat him with his own weapon. But only a few steps from making that happen, Jake shouldered Drew hard, knocking him off course.

Both came to a stop when their bodies collided.

Drew shot Jake a dirty look. Jake shouted, "Gaby," and took off again. Two seconds later, he launched himself at Zan, wrapped him up, and tackled him into the water.

A sense of relief washed over Drew as he watched their bodies roll around in sand and water, fighting. His brother took on Zan to allow him to rescue Gaby.

He turned to find a churning ocean. Drew took off, high-stepping through the water, desperate to reach her. The water was cold and coming at him in all directions. It felt like running through thick mud—he wasn't making enough progress.

A wave rolled in and towered over him. Slow to set his body, Drew got pounded and driven under. He popped up, spit and hocked saltwater. Wiped his eyes.

Growling, he powered forward.

He was able to reach the surf line before another set formed.

The next wave, one frothy and wild, came barreling at him. This time, he set his body, intent on putting a shoulder into the wave. But this one ran right through him anyway—toppling him, burying him underwater.

Drew sprung up and flung the hair out of his eyes, determined to clear the line.

The next set charged in. Drew anchored his feet to the ocean floor, leaned forward, setting his body. He eyed the wave, trying to get his timing right. The wave approached, and at the last second Drew dove under the wave. The world went oddly quiet as he felt the wave's energy and power overhead. When it passed, he emerged out the other side unmolested.

His feet found purchase on the sandy bottom, but he decided to go prone. He beat his arms and legs through the water. It had to be quicker to swim to Gaby than wading out in this swell. While he swam, he thought he heard another puff of air. Another gunshot? He couldn't be certain with the deluge of noise surrounding him.

Drew kicked hard and drove his arms through the water with all his strength. He could hear Gaby whimpering in the close distance. He pushed forward and soon found himself fighting a cross-section of rogue waves. They spun him off course, wiping him out. Drew smacked the surface and cursed. But didn't let the frustration linger. He took off again, working to regain his position and momentum.

"I'm coming, Gaby," he shouted.

She cried back with a muffled wail. Hearing her sent a surge of determination through him. Drew looked up and saw her a few armlengths away. He dropped his head and beat, beat, beat the water with his arms. Saltwater splashed in his eyes. Stung like hell, but he kept going.

Finally, he made it to the pylon and chopped at the water, working himself upright. Standing, the water made it up to his chest. Up around Gaby's throat.

"I'm here, baby. I'm here." Drew loosened her gag, a bandana tied around her face.

"Drew. Are you okay?"

He snorted. Gave her several quick kisses on the lips. "Fine. How are *you*?"

"Better now."

"Did he hurt you?"

"I mean . . ."

"I'm going to free you."

Drew moved frantically around the pylon, searching for how to free her from the restraints—thick nylon straps wrapped five or six times around her and the pylon.

"Drew?"

He heard her, but was so focused he didn't answer.

"DREW!"

"Sorry, what?" He didn't look at her—still searching for the tied-off end, or a release latch, or something, but the straps were obscured, underwater now.

"In your hand."

Drew glanced down and saw his tape knife still clutched in his right hand. "Fuck me. Hang on."

"Love you, Drew."

"I love you so much, and I'm so, so sorry." Drew moved behind her. Yes, the straps were underwater, which wasn't ideal. But being pressed against the concrete pylon would give him a guide and make his work easier and potentially quicker. At least he hoped. Sets of waves were coming in now one after the other. The ocean pounding them. Drew worked through the churning water to locate the top of the straps with his left hand. He gripped the tape knife tight, set the edge against the pylon and sliced down through the straps. The tool cut through two of the straps with ease right away.

Another wave crashed into Drew's back, and wrapped around the pylon.

Gaby was coughing and spitting. "Hurry," she said.

Drew swallowed a mouthful of water as well and coughed too. His eyes stung and the water burned his throat. He let out one more huge cough, then readied his hand. He dragged the edge of the knife down the pylon and through the straps again. Two more broke. Gaby thrashed and was able to loosen the rest considerably, but not enough to free herself.

"I'm almost there. Hang on, babe."

Drew went to hacking at the remaining straps with zero finesse, his arm chopping through the water, hoping to make contact. He couldn't tell if it was working, and about the time he told himself to stop and locate the straps and do it the correct way, all the tension released.

Gaby fell forward into the water. Free.

Drew hollered her name and swam around the pylon. When he reached her, she was bobbing there, her beautiful round face the only part of her above water; eyes staring up at the pier's planked underside.

"Hold on to me," he said. She flung an arm around his neck, and he hugged her to him. "Hang on tight."

She moaned but didn't say anything.

Another pop went off—a gunshot. No doubt about that one—the lights on the beach went out right after. Darkness reigned once more.

Drew paddled with his left arm and held Gaby firmly to his right side. A million thoughts ran through his mind, but the one he chose to zero in on: Gaby was alive. He'd never take her for granted again, always trust her with every fiber of his being. Let them make it to the beach safely and escape, he prayed.

"How're you doing?" he asked.

"Cold."

"I know, baby. Stay with me."

She hugged him tight, and it encouraged him.

They weren't making much progress until the next set came in and pushed them forward a good stretch. Felt like surfing, but without a board. Gave Drew an idea.

"Hold on, baby. We're gonna ride these waves in," Drew said.

"Okay . . ." Gaby said. "Here comes a big one."

Drew glanced back, and she was right. A wall of water approached fast.

"I'm gonna start kicking, so hang on." She did. He leaned toward the beach and kicked with everything he had. Soon, he felt the wave's energy build behind them, and he pumped his legs harder. The wave hit them in perfect stride. It lifted them off the ocean floor and propelled them forward.

They rode the wave all the way in.

Drew and Gaby tumbled onto the beach without a shred of grace. He was able to grab her and roll her on top of himself. She stared down at him, breathing heavy, but with a smile on her face. Soggy sand never felt so good.

"Come here," he said. Drew worked his way out from under her, while helping her to her feet at the same time. Then, scooped her up in his arms. Bounced her once to secure her, and walked up the beach. She kissed his cheek.

"Was that Jake who went after Zan?" she asked.

"Yeah. Do you see them?"

Gaby whipped her head around. "No . . . It's too dark to see . . . I can't tell."

"K."

"Who turned on the lights?" Her voice quivered.

"Mon."

"I thought I heard you shout her name."

"Yeah, she was all in."

Drew made it to the seawall and sat Gaby down on it. She immediately hugged herself tightly. Her entire body shook. He tried to fling the water off his hands and arms, but it was pointless, so he began rubbing her arms briskly.

"We've got to get you dry before you get sick."

"It's . . . probably too late . . . for that," she said, shivering.

Drew dug out his cell, tapped buttons, but nothing happened. "Fuck, it's dead." He looked around, feeling helpless.

Suddenly, a figure emerged from out of the shadows behind Gaby. Drew jumped.

"Who's there?"

"Jones. It's me. Mon."

"Mon!"

Gaby scooted around. "Hi, Mon."

"Hey there, Momma. So glad you're safe."

"Where's Jake and Zan?" Drew asked.

Mon looked up. "Still down on the beach, last I saw. Zan shot out one of the lights, and they all blew. I lost track of them after that. I was going to go down to help, but I got distracted watching you swim out to Gaby, I wanted to keep an eye on you in case you needed help. Guess I didn't know what to do. We only talked about the lights."

"You did great, Mon," Drew said.

"Oh, and I called 9-1-1. They're sending cops and an ambulance."

"Perfect."

"Did you hear that?" Gaby said.

Drew looked at her, rubbed her arms some more. "No, what?"

"Sounded like little zips through the air."

Drew spun around.

"Like the noise Zan's gun made when he shot Bernie."

"Shit."

"Go," Gaby said.

He turned to her.

"I'm okay," she said. "Go help Jake."

Drew gave Mon a look.

She sat down next to Gaby. "I'll take care of her. She's safe with me."

Drew bent down and hugged Gaby. Into her ear, whispered, "I love you. I'm going to make this all up to you."

"You sure will. Now go." she said.

Another pop sounded—this time all three heard it. Their heads swung to the beach.

Drew kissed Gaby on the lips. Then he stood, turned, and stumbled forward.

***

Darkness. It's all he saw. Dark beach. Black ocean. Overcast sky blanketed by black clouds. Drew looked back once to see Gaby and Mon huddled together, faces illuminated by Mon's cell phone, before he staggered to the water's edge and pushed south.

His feet felt encased in concrete. Body soaked, frozen, and rigid, every step proved challenging. Fighting the ocean damn near wiped him out.

Slowly, the dull pier came into view ahead of him like a ghost emerging from a cursed forest. He tucked his chin and aimed himself toward it. Two thoughts kept him moving forward.

The first: Gaby was alive and safe. Not a single better feeling. And the other: His brother ran *at* his problem, not away from it, for maybe the first time Drew could recall. Not only had he ran at his problem, but he faced Zan head-on, knowing full well he had a loaded gun. And to allow Drew to rescue Gaby. Pride pushed on the walls of Drew's chest.

His toe then slammed against something solid and he went down hard. He was able to throw his hands out at the last second to keep from face-planting in the sand. And thankfully, he repositioned the tape knife in his hand as he went down to avoid cutting or stabbing himself. Sucking his cheeks in discomfort, he worked himself onto his elbows, then to his knees. Drew slipped the tape knife into his back pocket.

When he stood and turned around, he found what tripped him. Shaw's body lay there on its side, water lapping over his legs and torso. Drew cringed when he realized he'd kicked Shaw's head.

"Fuck you," he said before pressing on.

When he made it to the pier, he looked left. The lights stood there, darkened.

Walking under the pier, the leviathan creaked and groaned. He could also hear rain smacking the wood and concrete.

Still no sign of Jake or Zan. And the water level was rising fast. Drew gradually moved up the beach as he walked to stay out of the water. He thought about calling Jake's name, but didn't want to give Zan any kind of advantage.

Then, he tripped again, but this time managed to remain upright.

Drew spun around and found Jake lying motionless on his back at the edge of the water, his feet in the ocean. Water lapped onto his legs.

"Jake!" His eyes were closed, and Drew couldn't tell if he was breathing or not. Drew grabbed his brother by the wrist with two hands and pulled. Jake didn't react, but Drew didn't have time to stop to worry about it. He only focused on dragging him all the way to the seawall.

When he reached it, he propped Jake up into a sitting position.

"Jake! Jake!" Drew smacked his cheeks but nothing happened. He began to panic. It then occurred to him maybe his brother had swallowed water, so he laid him back down on the sand. Drew interlaced his hands and pumped Jake's chest. Told him to breathe.

"Come on, man. Breathe."

After a half-dozen compressions, Jake suddenly spit up saltwater and coughed violently.

Drew dove at him, hugged his neck. "You okay?"

Jake sat up. Eyes barely open into slits. "Yeah," he croaked.

Drew helped him sit up, and moved him back against the seawall.

Jake grabbed his left leg with both hands, grimacing.

"You hurt?"

"Shot."

Drew pushed Jake's hands away. He didn't see anything definitive in the darkness, and since his body was soaked, the entire area felt wet. "Above your knee? Here?"

Jake bit his lower lip, nodded.

Drew didn't take his eyes off the spot as he tore the left sleeve off his jersey with three violent tugs. Then ripped the sleeve apart. "Lift your knee." Jake did. Drew wrapped the sleeve around his leg, covering the wound. He tightened it as tight as he could, knotting the sleeve off.

"You good?" Drew asked, squeezing Jake's shoulder.

"Yeah," Jake said.

"Where's Zan?"

"Still down there, I guess. Think he's dead." Jake coughed some more. "We wrestled with his gun. He shot me, and I shot him. Then I must have passed out."

"Mon called an ambulance. Think you can hang here while I go check?"

Jake looked up, hesitated, but nodded.

"Keep pressure on that." Drew patted his shoulder and left him.

He bounded back down to the water. It wasn't that he didn't believe Jake. He just couldn't trust Zan to not come after them if he was still alive.

Making it to the water, Drew hunched to get a closer look as he searched. Zan couldn't be too far away, alive or dead.

He tried to listen past the roar of the ocean, lapping of waves.

Sure enough, he heard moaning. *Zan.* Drew picked up his pace.

The moaning got louder, or he was getting closer.

Seconds later, like the heavens parting, Zan appeared before him. Crawling on all fours away from him, through the sand, getting splashed by incoming waves. He was moaning and sweeping his arms side-to-side, searching for something. Drew didn't care what for.

He launched himself onto Zan's back. Zan let out a frightened wail. Drew slammed the heel of his palm into the back of his head.

"Fucker!" Zan cried. He wriggled and rolled until he spun around onto his back.

Drew let him.

As soon as his smug face appeared, Drew jabbed him in the nose. Zan barely reacted. Instead, he reached out and grabbed Drew around the neck with both his hands—drove Drew backwards, flipping their positions. Ocean and rain pounded Drew while Zan squeezed his neck.

"You little bitch," Zan spat. "You couldn't listen? Now my money's gone, washed out to sea or lost on this fucking beach. I should have killed all of you from the beginning."

The edges of Drew's vision went fuzzy. Sounds waned. Innately, he knew he was losing consciousness—he couldn't let that happen. What would it mean for Gaby if he died here? For their baby to grow up without a father? Same as Drew had.

Zan lowered his reddened face. Pressed his nose to Drew's, growled. Zan's squeeze on Drew's neck got tighter.

Everything went white.

Drew summoned all his strength and lurched as hard as he could, slamming the crown of his head into Zan's forehead.

"Fuck." Zan lost hold of Drew's throat as he fell backward.

Drew gasped for air.

Zan rolled onto his shoulder. Cursed and collapsed onto the beach.

Drew jumped up and dove onto Zan, who bucked and rolled Drew onto his back. Drew returned the favor, and they began rolling around, each gaining the advantage, to only instantly lose it to the other.

They rolled dangerously close to the surf. Then again . . . If Drew could gain the upper hand, he could do to Zan what he'd threatened to do to Gaby: drown him. Water and sand flew everywhere.

Zan rolled Drew onto his back for what felt like the tenth time. Something hard jabbed Drew in the middle of his back. He stopped and let out a yelp. Zan's eyes lit up with lightening.

"Move." Zan pushed Drew and dug his hands under Drew's body.

"Fuck you." Drew shoved him back. Zan flew off, landing a short distance away.

Both men stood. Drew rested his forearms on his knees, in need of a breather. That's when he saw what Zan had been going after—the gun.

Zan lunged for it. Drew dove on him. He had no idea if the gun had any bullets or if it would still fire having been in the water, but no way in hell did he want to find out.

Writhing around under him like an earthworm after getting cut in two, Zan fought to work himself face-up. Drew smothered him with his body best he could while reaching into his back pocket.

Zan bucked with his hips and used the leverage to flip over . . . right as Drew brought the tape knife from around his back.

Drew saw the long pistol in Zan's hand and didn't hesitate.

Drew plunged the edge of the tape knife into Zan's throat, right below his Adam's apple.

Zan's eyes went impossibly wide.

He exhaled a frothy gasp.

Blood gurgled out of the wound and pooled in Zan's sternum and over Drew's hands.

Drew pressed his weight down onto the knife's handle, driving the metal deeper.

The gun went limp in Zan's hand and fell to the sand. His arms slackened and dropped to his sides. His sunken, wide eyes stayed fixed on Drew.

Drew stared back, unflinching.

One final breath escaped Zan's mouth along with a spittle of blood.

Drew held his position, straddling Zan's waist. Didn't blink, didn't move. He needed to make sure Zan was really dead.

The wound slowed its flow of blood. Drew's hands were covered and sticky with it.

A wave washed onto them, and completely flooded Zan. He didn't react or blink.

The wave receded, washing away the blood into the surf.

Zan still didn't move.

He was dead.

Drew emptied his lungs with a sputtering exhale.

Removing his hands from the tape knife, he sat up.

The rain stopped.

Drew slowly worked himself off Zan and walked away.

***

With Jake's left arm slung around Drew's neck, the brothers made slow progress down the boardwalk. For every step Drew took, Jake hopped on his good leg.

Lots of cringing and muffled cursing.

"Almost there," said Drew. "See the emergency lights? Must be in the parking lot."

Jake raised his head. "Good."

"Doing okay otherwise?"

His brother didn't respond right away. Drew looked at him to check on him.

"Yeah," Jake said finally. "Let me ask you something."

"Shoot."

"Fuck you, bro."

"Oh, shit. Sorry."

Jake chuckled, and Drew broke as well. They shared a punch-drunk laugh. Felt good.

"What I was gonna ask . . . What'd ya think would've happened if I didn't call you back?"

Drew thought on it before letting out a deep sigh. "God. I don't want to think about it."

"Right? I hope Gaby's all right."

"Me, too."

They shuffled a few more steps before Drew cleared his throat.

"Uh-oh," Jake said.

"Shut up. You don't even know what I'm going to say."

"Little brother sermon, incoming."

Drew looked at Jake. "Hardly. Just listen. You really came through tonight. The past week hasn't been the best between us, but when it mattered most, you showed up. You were the caring, unselfish brother you talked about wanting to be earlier." Drew paused, heard Gaby in his head say he forgives Jake too quickly. She was right, and he was doing it again. He knew he needed to work on that. "Gaby's alive because of you"

"And you," Jake said.

"And Mon."

"Thanks, little bro. That means a lot."

Drew smiled.

A few seconds later, Jake said, "You didn't find the gym bag while you were down there, did you?"

"You kidding? Even if I did, I would've chucked it so far into the Pacific, even that swell wouldn't bring it back."

"Yeah, right."

"Dead serious."

"I'm not sure I believe you. But anyway." Jake's words trailed off. "Probably gonna be one super-stoked surfer in Tijuana later today."

A beam from a flashlight shined in their eyes. Up ahead, two paramedics, one holding the flashlight, and the other rolling a gurney, were coming right for them.

The brothers stopped.

When the paramedics reached them, the one with the flashlight wrapped a blanket around Jake's shoulders, then Drew's.

"What's your injury, sir?" he asked of Jake.

"Shot in the leg."

"Hey, is my wife—Gaby Jones—okay?"

The gurney paramedic said, "Yes, sir. She's receiving warmed saline right now. They're about to transport her to Scripps Mercy."

Drew waved at Jake, who was being helped onto the gurney, and took off running.

When he reached the parking lot, he slowed to a stop when he saw her.

Gaby sat upright in the back of a well-lit ambulance. She wore a gray blanket wrapped around her snugly and a red knit hat on her head. A paramedic was treating her.

She looked up and saw him. "Drew!" She waved, but her face gave nothing away.

Drew waved back. His heart pounded in his chest as he jogged over to her.

Chapter Forty-Two

Drew handed the officer the paper sack and thanked him. The officer asked for a second time if Drew was sure he didn't want to go in and give the meal to Mr. Dwyer himself.

Drew declined.

Three doors down the hallway, Drew carefully opened the door and slipped in the room.

Inside, Gaby slowly rolled her head to the side, one eye peeking, nose wrinkling. "What you got there?"

"Thought you and the baby could use a few thousand calories of heaven after the night you both had." Drew sat in the visitor chair already at the bedside.

Gaby didn't respond but raised the bed and scooched up.

After swinging the tray in front of her, Drew removed the Hodad's burger and onion rings from the bag and set them on the tray.

"Don't mistake my moaning for forgiveness," Gaby said, unwrapping the burger.

She looked comfy in the sweats they'd dressed her in as part of the precautionary warm treatment she and the baby had received. Thank everything good, both were fine. Gaby had some light contusions from the straps and the pounding surf, but no broken bones, no internal injuries. And when the care team had checked an hour ago, the baby's heart rate registered strong and consistent—the two words Drew hoped would describe him as a father.

Gaby wrangled the burger with two hands and took a big bite. The aroma of grilled beef, melted cheese, and golden-fried food enveloped the room.

"I'm so sorry, babe," Drew said. She flicked a look at him. "For everything. For lying to you, for dragging you into this mess, getting you kidnapped and nearly killed. I would've thrown Jake out on his ass if I knew any of this was going to happen."

Gaby set the burger down, the wrapper crinkling. Wiped her mouth with a napkin. "That's a start."

Drew sat back in his chair, content to watch Gaby enjoy the rest of her meal.

His mind drifted to the long interview he'd had overnight with Billberry in one of the hospital meeting rooms. Drew explained everything that went down on the beach. How Zan killed Bernie and kidnapped Gaby, and that Drew killed Zan in self-defense. Billberry confirmed they'd found Zan's gun, so Drew hoped that would back up his account.

Gaby had finished her Hodad's and both were dozing when a throat cleared behind Drew, startling them both.

"Glad you're both here so we can clear up a few things," said Det. Billberry, appearing like Drew's thoughts summoned him.

"Hi, Detective," Drew said.

Gaby waved.

Billberry walked to the end of the bed but stared at Drew. "I'm going to get right to the point. I don't believe you or Mr. Dwyer told me everything that occurred in Hoppy Time Liquor that day . . ." Long pause. "That said, both your stories seem to check out. For now."

Drew stayed silent.

"We followed up on this Zan West. Searched his two homes, and among many interesting finds, we discovered the liquor store clerk, Ahmed Mohammed. Dead, in a garage."

"Shit," Drew said. Gaby gasped.

"And with the gentleman who Mr. Dwyer said Ahmed shot during the liquor store incident having died a few days ago, I have no other living witness to tell me differently. Mr. Jones, everything we've found on the beach so far points to self-defense as you indicated. But if I find anything says different, you better believe you'll hear from me."

The room fell silent. Billberry scrunched his face and spoke again.

"I'm still trying to piece together how you and Mr. Dwyer fit into all this besides being at the liquor store—and why Zan West killed Ahmed, killed your landlord, and kidnapped you, Mrs. Jones. There are some big holes. I'm going to get to the bottom of this. Count on it."

"I hope you do, Detective," said Drew. "I'd love to know why that psycho was after my brother, killed those people, and what my wife had to do with any of it. I'm just glad she and our baby are unharmed."

Billberry sucked a cheek, stroked his mustache. "We'll be handing your brother off to Phoenix PD as soon as the doctor clears him. Piece of shit robbed a rash of box stores there. Not one, not three. He's also wanted in Spokane for robbing a weed dispensary at gunpoint right before he came to San Diego.

Drew didn't know how to respond. His inside voice screamed, "What the fuck, Jake?" but he kept a straight face. "Okay."

Billberry walked to the door. Turned around. "Don't leave town for a while, Mr. Jones. I'll have more questions for you."

After Billberry left, Gaby said she thought for sure Drew would have asked how much time Jake would serve.

Drew leaned forward, took her hands in his and squeezed. "I'm not worried about him. He'll get what he deserves. I'm concerned with you—with us." He jutted his head at her stomach. "All this reinforced how much you mean to me and how much I want to spend my life with you and be a good father to our child. I've made my choice and it's not Jake. I'm here with you, not him. Until the day I die, it's you and our baby, Gaby. I'm never going to take you for granted again. If I have to spend the rest of my life showing you how sorry I am and how much you mean to me, I'm going to do it. I love you that much. I just beg you not to give up on me."

A tear rolled down her cheek. "The rest of your life sounds good to me. And I love you, too, Drew."

Epilogue

Four months later

Two minutes after texting Gaby to let her know he was around the corner, Drew backed the Chinook into his in-laws' driveway. The rear tires struck the lip of the concrete, bucking him in his seat. On instinct, Drew checked the side mirror. Gaby filled the reflection, standing next to the front shrubs, bouncing baby Lucas Bernard Jones in her arms. She took one of his arms and made him wave to his Daddy.

After guiding the RV into the driveway, Drew killed the engine, left the keys in the ignition, and hopped out.

"Who's that?" Gaby said in baby talk. "Es tu Padre."

"Si, aquí estoy." Drew pinched his son's socked feet and wiggled his chubby legs. Kissed his forehead, then kissed Gaby on the lips.

"Everything go okay?" she asked. "They get it fixed?"

"Yep. Blows cold as ice."

"Excelente," said Ester. She and Vicky appeared on the front porch, four matching floral-print suitcases surrounding them.

"Thank you so much for getting the air conditioning repaired, Drew," said Vicky.

Drew walked over to them. "Of course. It's the least I could do. And let me grab those for you both." He took the two large suitcases, and Ester followed him with the two smaller ones.

"Joshua Tree in August with no air? That wouldn't end well," Gaby said.

Drew loaded the four suitcases into the Chinook. He looked around the interior one last time. Smiled. When he climbed down, Vicky and Ester were cooing and kissing on Lucas.

"We can't thank you again for everything," Drew said, gesturing with both arms at the house. Two months after everything went down, Gaby's moms presented them with a proposal that took Drew and Gaby by complete surprise. Fresh off retirement, they wanted to travel the country, see all the National Parks. They offered to sell their house to Drew and Gaby for twice what they originally paid for it, but one-third its value—$500,000. Shocked and extremely grateful, Drew extended the Chinook as a down payment. The moms accepted, and in return, gave Ester's low-mileage Honda Accord to Gaby so she could have a reliable vehicle.

Ester smiled at Drew. "It's our pleasure."

"We raised our family in this house, and now you two can do the same," Vicky said.

"Moms. I'm going to miss you both so much."

Ester and Vicky hugged their daughter, making sure to not squish Lucas. "We'll be back in a month," Vicky said. "We have to pop in to see our precious Lucas."

"Don't forget," Ester said. "Clases de Español todos los Martes."

"As long as you can get Wi-Fi or phone reception, we'll be there," Drew said.

Ester hugged him. Then Vicky did as well.

"Take good care of my daughter and grandson," Vicky said.

"I promise."

The moms walked over to the RV. Vicky climbed behind the wheel and Ester in the passenger seat. The Chinook started up smoother than ever.

Drew wrapped an arm around Gaby and squeezed her and their baby. She wiped away a tear that wet her eye. The RV puttered out of the driveway. Drew and Gaby waved goodbye until the Chinook disappeared over the crest of the street.

Gaby looked up at Drew. "How did we get here? It all feels like a dream."

The first two months following everything had been the worst for Gaby. Night terrors. Random crying in the middle of the day. Not wanting to be touched. How she hadn't divorced him, he still questioned. All the trauma he'd caused her. All the trust he needed to rebuild. He didn't balk at going to therapy, and to his surprise it helped him as much as her. Gaby was resilient, a fighter, and more forgiving than he deserved. And Bernie. Drew wasn't sure if the guilt would ever subside, but he'd gladly carry it since Gaby experienced the horror firsthand and had no choice but to live with it forever. "A dream," he said. "It really does."

"Want to go to Daddy, Lucas?" Gaby handed him to Drew.

"Come here, son. Aw, look at your little Padres onesie."

"So cute, right?"

"I love it. Perfect timing too, 'cause the game's coming on."

"Oh, I know," Gaby said.

Drew raised an eyebrow.

"I set everything up on the back deck for you two to watch it. I even made popcorn."

"Oh yeah?" He gently bounced Lucas on his left arm, kissed Gaby. "You're the best."

"Come on. I hear the Padres are about to go on a tear."

"You mock, but they're totally making a playoff run this year."

Gaby snickered, waved for Drew to follow her to the back through the side gate. He followed. She looked over her shoulder at him, smiled. His head filled with needles. He thought he might lose it and cry. This woman. She now knew every flaw, vulnerability, and insecurity in him and she still chose to stay. To love him, to work through all the pain he'd caused her.

Lucas grabbed Drew's index finger and squeezed. Right then, something enormous bloomed in Drew's chest—the same way it did when he laid eyes on their baby and held him for the first time in the delivery room.

"Come on, son. Let's watch the Padres take down the Dodgers."

ACKNOWLEDGEMENTS:

This novel and I traveled a long road to reach this point to where you are holding it in your hands. I wrote the first draft in 2022 and finished editing it in early 2023. In the years from then until now, I experienced many highs and lows. I didn't experience any of it alone, however, thanks to supportive friends who helped me along the way. I appreciate each of them, from those who read early drafts of this novel to those who offered encouragement, referred me, commiserated with me, gave me opportunities, or were simply a good friend through good times and bad. I want to give a big thank you to the following people who fall into one or more of those categories: Holly West, Hector Acosta, Chad Williamson, Rob D. Smith, Paul Garth, Lina Chern, Marco Carocari, Shawn Cosby, Steve Weddle, Aaron Philip Clark, Puja Guha, C.W. Blackwell, Tim Hennessey, Chuck Cox, Jim Ruland, Carl Vonderau, John Coppenhaver, Heather Levy, Scott Von Doviak, Tod Goldberg, David Olsen, Craig Clevenger, James Queally, Lawrence Allen, Dave White, Alex Segura, KC Grifant, my always first reader Sharon Ippolito, my siblings—AJ, Eric, and Alisha—and family, and everyone in the Cord. And a very special thank you to my dear friend Bernie, who allowed me to put him in this novel and show what a big heart he has.

I also want to thank the authors who provided kind words about this novel. Gary Phillips, Matt Coyle, S.A. Cosby, and Lee Matthew Goldberg. Their work is amazing, and you should read their books.

And a huge thank you to the team at **Rock and a Hard Place Press** for making all of this possible. I couldn't have asked for a better home for this novel. Thank you to Roger, Jay, and the entire editorial team. An additional thank you to Paul Garth for his dedication in helping me make this the best novel it could be, and to Heather Garth for the beautiful cover art she created.

Finally, I want to thank you for reading this novel. Reading is an act of resistance these days, so thank you. I hope you enjoyed it and recommend it to a friend.

ABOUT THE AUTHOR:

Photo Credit: Carol Sonstein

CURTIS IPPOLITO (IG: @curtis_sd) is an Anthony Award- and Derringer Award-winning writer. He is the author of *Waves of Burden*, and *Burying the Newspaper Man*. Additionally, his short stories have appeared in numerous prominent publications, as well as being featured in several anthologies. He lives in San Diego and is a member of Sisters in Crime, Mystery Writers of America, and serves as vice-president of the San Diego chapter of Sisters in Crime.

ALSO BY CURTIS IPPOLITO

*from **ROCK AND A HARD PLACE PRESS:***
On Fire and Under Water: A Climate Change Crime Fiction
Anthology (Guest Editor)

OTHERS:
Burying the Newspaper Man